"Are you cold?" he asked

The shore breeze was chilly, but Lucia's skin burned wherever Malcolm touched it. "I don't know," she answered honestly.

"We could go to my room."

She rested her head on his shoulder and tried to clear her mind. This was awfully quick, awfully sudden. Yet she'd known things might happen quickly and suddenly between them. She'd known it from the moment their eyes had met across the Baccarat Room.

She wanted him as much as he wanted her, but to go to his room with him would be to take an enormous chance. Malcolm hadn't mentioned anything about wanting to see her again after tonight. He hadn't so much as implied that he was looking for a relationship with her.

But Lucia wanted to trust him. She could chance it. She had the Midas touch. Maybe this gamble, too, would pay off.

ABOUT THE AUTHOR

Like Lucia, the heroine of *Jackpot*, Judith
Arnold has been to Atlantic City only once, on
a junket. She and her husband wound up
spending their rolls of silver dollars on a floor
show at one of the cabarets, though, instead
of the slot machines. If Judith did hit the
jackpot, she claims she'd give most of the
money to charity, though anticipating the cost
of tuition, she'd set some money aside for her
small son's college education.

Books by Judith Arnold

HARLEQUIN AMERICAN ROMANCE
104—COME HOME TO LOVE
120—A MODERN MAN
130—FLOWING TO THE SKY
139—JACKPOT

These books may be available at your local bookseller.

Don't miss any of our special offers. Write to us at the
following address for information on our newest releases.

Harlequin Reader Service
P.O. Box 52040, Phoenix, AZ 85072-2040
Canadian address: P.O. Box 2800, Postal Station A,
5170 Yonge St., Willowdale, Ont M2N 6J3

Jackpot
JUDITH ARNOLD

Harlequin Books

TORONTO • NEW YORK • LONDON
AMSTERDAM • PARIS • SYDNEY • HAMBURG
STOCKHOLM • ATHENS • TOKYO • MILAN

Published February 1986

First printing December 1985

ISBN 0-373-16139-5

Chapter One

For some reason, he reminded Lucia of James Bond.

It wasn't that he looked like a spy, or that he even remotely resembled any of the actors who had portrayed James Bond on the screen. It wasn't simply that he was wearing a tuxedo; a number of the men in the Baccarat Room wore tuxedos. But the man Lucia had her eye on looked . . . well, at home in his tux. He looked appropriate. She couldn't actually put her finger on what it was about him, but he knew how to wear formal clothing.

She leaned against the gilded railing that marked off the Baccarat Room and watched the man as he studied his cards. His physique—what she could see of it, since the table hid his legs from her view—had a lean power that seemed perfectly suited to the tailored black jacket, the pleated white shirt, the narrow bow tie. His face was also lean, composed of hard, definitive lines. His eyebrows cut two dark lines above his deep-set hazel eyes; his nose shaped a long, patrician line; his lips occasionally spread to reveal a nearly straight line of glistening white teeth above the sharp, angular lines of his chin. His hair was dark brown, practically black, and parted in a neat line above one ear. A single lock fell rakishly onto his forehead, almost demolishing the polished effect of his grooming. Almost, but not quite. Somehow, even the errant lock of hair seemed right on him.

Another line appeared on his face, creasing his high forehead as he examined his cards. A waitress in a skimpy outfit circled the table to his chair. He didn't look at her as she bent over and whispered into his ear: he simply nodded. The waitress moved away, and the man ran his tapered fingers over the edges of his cards and then folded them into a tidy stack. His eyes flickered towards Lucia, and he smiled.

She turned away, abashed at having been caught staring at him. Behind her, the sprawling casino was a cacophony of bells ringing, slot machines grinding, coins chinking together, and people, thousands of people, babbling, cheering, groaning, cursing. The Baccarat Room was as sedate and subdued as the rest of the casino was raucous. A broad-arched doorway connected it to the rest of the casino, but the railing and the two carpeted steps leading down into the cozy room created an invisible barrier, clearly denoting that the rowdy behavior tolerated in the casino would not be acceptable in the Baccarat Room.

Nor would ordinary clothing, Lucia surmised, digging her hands into the pockets of her denim skirt and fidgeting with her silver dollars. In the casino proper, Lucia's casual skirt, short-sleeved pink jersey and canvas espadrilles didn't stand out. Everyone was dressed equally informally, with the exception of the croupiers in their black tuxedos and ruffled shirts. Unlike the man in the Baccarat Room, the croupiers all looked like high school students on their way to the senior prom.

The Baccarat Room evidently required fancy apparel of its patrons. Its decor seemed to demand it. Thick midnight-blue carpeting covered not just the floor but the walls and ceiling. Three elliptic teak tables were arranged in the dimly lit space, two of them currently in use; the male players were in tuxes or elegant suits and the women in gowns or cocktail dresses. Above each table hung an elaborate crystal chandelier. Lucia wondered whether the chandeliers were constructed of Baccarat crystal, whether that was why the room was called the Baccarat Room.

"Hey, high roller," Evvie's voice chirped into her ear, shattering her concentration.

Lucia turned from the railing to acknowledge her friend. Evvie's round face was aglow with excitement. She held a large paper cup containing a hefty handful of chips. "How's it going?" Lucia asked.

"Fantastic," Evvie said with a giggle. She shoved her cup of chips in front of Lucia's face. "I finally won at roulette. *Rouge et noir*. This place is a scream, Lucia. I love it."

"That makes one of us," Lucia muttered.

It had been Evvie's idea to visit the Shangri-La Hotel and Casino, the newest and—it touted itself—most exciting casino on Atlantic City's boardwalk. The package deal she'd seen advertised in the newspaper included bus transportation to and from Atlantic City, a roll of ten silver dollars and a free five-dollar supper—all for eighteen dollars. "It's like they're paying us to go," Evvie had explained over lunch the week before in the company dining room. "How can we not go? We practically make a profit just by paying eighteen bucks."

Evvie's cockeyed logic had amused Lucia. She often found herself wondering how Evvie could manage to be such a competent patent attorney when she was afflicted with such ridiculous notions as her current one: that dishing out eighteen dollars to go to Atlantic City was a profitable venture. Lucia hadn't bothered to set Evvie straight, however. All she'd said was that casinos didn't interest her.

Evvie had managed to talk her into accompanying her on the gambling junket, anyway. The bus left the parking lot of a neighborhood shopping center at five o'clock—Evvie and Lucia had to take off from work a half hour early in order to make the bus—and deposited them at the underground garage entrance to the Shangri-la at seven. They ate their free five-dollar supper— cold sandwiches and soft drinks, which, Lucia decided, couldn't have been worth more than a buck-fifty—and had a few hours to spend in the casino before the bus would be heading north again at 11:00 P.M. As Evvie had rationalized, the late departure time wasn't a problem; they'd be able to sleep during the drive home, so they'd be fresh and alert for work the following morning.

Evvie had chattered during much of the trip south to the gambling mecca by the sea, gossiping about how Rick Lansing, Parker Chemicals' most celebrated roué, had made passes at three of the patent department's secretaries in one week—quite possibly a record, Evvie had maintained—and about how two of the three secretaries had actually responded positively to his advances—quite possibly another record. "He always goes for the secretaries," Evvie had observed. "Good-looking man, but he just doesn't have the guts to face up to a woman who's on a par with him professionally."

Lucia had nodded absently, only half her attention on Evvie. The other half was on their destination. A casino. Gambling. She *hated* gambling! Why in the world had she allowed Evvie to talk her into taking this stupid trip to Atlantic City?

She knew why. She'd never seen a casino before, except on television or in the movies—specifically, in an old James Bond movie. She'd never actually been inside a casino, surrounded by avaricious, half-crazed gamblers. She felt an almost perverse curiosity about viewing such a place firsthand, surrounding herself with a virtual epidemic of gambling. She wanted to see what it was that made gamblers tick, what it was that made them so sure that they'd be lucky just this once, that they, of all the hundreds of thousands of people throwing their money away in Atlantic City, would be the chosen ones, the winners. She wanted to see the fever of greed and money hunger that fueled a place like this.

While Evvie had pranced about the opulent casino, wide-eyed and astonished, Lucia had studied the gamblers around her with scientific detachment. Evvie obviously wasn't an obsessive gambler like the glassy-eyed women Lucia saw pumping quarter after quarter, dollar after dollar, into the slot machines, or like the surly, uncommunicative blackjack players who were unable even to spare a smile for the waitresses who kept them supplied with liquor. Evvie wasn't like the dazed young man who, time after time, set a hundred-dollar stack of chips on the double-zero square of a roulette table and watched emotionlessly as the silver marble settled into some other number and the croupier swept the chips away.

No, Evvie wasn't a gambler. She was just an exuberant tourist. "I think this is an absolute riot, don't you?" she enthused as they watched a frenetic group of people flinging dice and screaming around a craps table. Lucia couldn't begin to figure out what that game was about. It reminded her of televised news clips she'd seen of commodities brokers bidding up the price of pork-belly futures on Wall Street.

"Well, I've got these ten silver dollars burning a hole in my pocket," Evvie announced after she and Lucia had circled the sprawling casino three times. "I'm going to go for it."

"What about the so-called profit you're supposed to make on this trip?" Lucia teased.

Evvie shrugged. "I'm here. I may as well play. The worst that'll happen is, I'll lose." She strolled to one of the change booths to cash in her money for chips. "Are you going to play?"

"Not on your life," Lucia declared. "I'll just take another walk and study the zombies."

And so Lucia walked, pausing to listen to a mediocre trio singing country-and-Western tunes in a cocktail lounge off the casino, pausing again to watch an obese woman go into near convulsions when she won two hundred dollars on the wheel of fortune, pausing once more at the entrance to the Baccarat Room. Pausing to watch an attractive, debonair, dark-haired man in a tuxedo play cards.

"What is baccarat, anyway?" she now asked Evvie.

Evvie shrugged and tucked a curl of her dirty-blond hair behind her ear. "I'm not sure," she said. "But it's expensive, whatever it is. I think those tables have a one-hundred-dollar-minimum bet."

"Why are the players dressed in formal clothing?" Lucia asked.

Evvie shrugged again. "I guess to prove that they can afford the minimum bet. Beats me, Loosh. They sure *look* rich, don't they?"

Lucia's eyes flitted to the man again. She was surprised to see his attention on her instead of on his cards. The dealer murmured something to him, and he reluctantly turned back to the game.

Why had he been staring at her? Lucia wondered. She wasn't that eye-catching. She was slightly taller than average, on the thin side, with ordinary brown hair that hung unstylishly down her back and a prominent nose that might have looked pleasant on someone else's face but didn't look terribly good on hers, or so she believed. Her cheeks were nicely defined, with delicately arching bones and faint hollows below, and her eyes, large and thickly lashed, the color of dark chocolate, were probably her best feature. But compared to the chic women in their glamorous dresses seated at the baccarat table, Lucia didn't think she herself was much to look at.

Maybe the man had been staring at her because she'd been staring at him. She turned back to Evvie and tried to ignore him altogether. "How much longer till our bus leaves?" she asked abruptly.

Evvie glanced at her wristwatch. "An hour," she announced. "Have you gambled any of your money yet?"

"No. I thought the whole idea was to get a profit out of this trip."

Evvie rolled her eyes. "Oh, don't be such a drip, Loosh. You've got to play something."

"Here." Lucia dug into her pocket and pulled out five silver dollars, which she dropped into Evvie's cup of chips. "Play them for me. I'm willing to invest in you."

"What if I lose it all?" Evvie asked.

"Then you'll be like ninety-nine point nine percent of all the other nuts in this room. A loser. That's what Atlantic City is all about." She stifled herself before her grim lecture could douse her friend's excitement, and offered a smile. "Go ahead, Evvie. My treat. Enjoy yourself."

Evvie eyed the coins in her cup. "If you insist. I'll try to win for you." She vanished among the throngs of people swarming through the casino.

A gong chimed near Lucia's shoulder, and she located its source: a slot machine spilling coins out onto the floor, where two elderly women were squatted, gathering every last quarter and cackling with glee. Shaking her head and grinning, Lucia turned away. A waitress balancing a tray of drinks was entering the Baccarat Room, and Lucia's gaze followed the woman as she distributed the drinks to the players. She handed the dark-haired man his drink, and he lifted it toward Lucia in a silent toast before sipping.

She ought to leave the railing, she reproached herself. The man was obviously flirting with her, and if she didn't move away from the Baccarat Room, he'd continue. She hadn't come to a boisterous casino two hours from home to flirt wordlessly with a stranger, no matter how dashing he looked.

Besides, even if she *were* interested in flirting, somebody who played a game of chance with a minimum bet of one hundred dollars was certainly the last man Lucia would want to meet. She didn't know much about casino gambling, but she knew more than enough about gambling in general, the addictive gambling that led people to bankrupt themselves and their families in their mindless search for easy money, for the big kill, for the good luck that seemed, by its very nature, to elude gamblers all their lives.

Mildly depressed by the thought, she cast the handsome man one final look before moving away from the Baccarat Room. She lost herself in a forest of slot machines and took a moment to adjust the tortoiseshell combs that were holding her hair back from her face. She wandered as far as a blackjack table, but the sullen players there depressed her even further.

She found Evvie at a slot machine, her supply of coins noticeably depleted. "So much for making a profit," Lucia commented.

Evvie smiled and stuffed another quarter into the machine. "I think it has to do with how you flick your wrist," she explained as she yanked on the chrome lever. "That lady two machines down told me."

Lucia eyed the woman, whose collection of coins seemed no greater than Evvie's. "Here, wrist-flicker," Lucia said, tossing the rest of her silver dollars into Evvie's cup. "Have fun."

"You don't have to give me all your money," Evvie protested. "I brought some spare cash with me, just in case."

"Just in case what? Just in case you want to increase your losings?" Lucia clicked her tongue. "I'd rather you use up my silver dollars than to start gambling with real money. We'll chalk this up to an interesting experience that cost eighteen bucks, no profit, period."

Evvie stared at Lucia, then at her cup, then at the slot machine's window, which displayed a lemon, a cherry and a bell. She fished from the cup the silver dollars Lucia had dropped into it and pressed them into Lucia's hand. "You do something with these," she insisted. "Save one, at least. For a souvenir."

"I'm not sure I want a souvenir of this place," Lucia argued.

"Well, then, go gamble," Evvie ordered her. "I don't want to think I gambled away your last dollar. That's a privilege you deserve for yourself."

"Gee, thanks," Lucia said, chuckling. She watched Evvie stick another coin, and then another, into the slot machine, and her laughter waned. Who in the world could possibly think this sort of nonsense was fun?

"You're bringing me bad luck," Evvie complained, clasping her cup and walking to another machine. "Go away, go watch the baccarat game some more. I was doing really well when you were watching baccarat."

Sighing, Lucia ambled away from Evvie. She didn't want to go back to the Baccarat Room, yet her legs carried her in that direction. She immediately spotted the man, leaning back in his chair and stretching his lanky body. His gaze alighted on her, and he sat up and smiled.

Lucia felt herself momentarily being drawn in by his eyes. Their unique color was formed by concentric rings of gray, green and gold, each hue dissolving into the next. Why in the world did he have to be a high-stakes gambler, she wondered, unjustifiably peeved. If only he weren't a gambler, if only he weren't so obviously rich and polished...

The dealer said something to him, and he shook his head and rose from his chair. Lucia didn't know whether he was planning to approach her, but she thought it best to move along before he got any ideas. She strode briskly past several craps tables, ducking to avoid being struck by the flailing arm of a flamboyant dicer, and then past a series of blackjack tables. She wound up face to face with an oversize slot machine decorated with flashing colored lights. A sign above the machine read: Super Jackpot—A Quarter of a Million Dollars Plus!

The mere thought of a quarter of a million dollars made Lucia queasy. The Shangri-la Hotel and Casino made her queasy. Atlantic City made her queasy. The remaining silver dollars in her pocket made her queasy, and she impulsively stuffed them into the slot machine, eager to rid herself of them. She heard the coins click into the machine, then yanked the arm down. Releasing it, she started toward the regular slot machines in search of Evvie.

A strident whooping noise stunned her, rendering her immobile. It sounded like an air-raid siren, a loud, rhythmic honking. The oversize slot machine erupted in a blinding display of lights, and a valve at the bottom of the machine opened, disgorging silver dollars into a tray that quickly overflowed.

Lucia gaped numbly at the coins the machine was spitting at her feet. Then she lifted her eyes to the machine again. The Super Jackpot sign was flashing on and off. Dumbstruck, she stared at the three black bars arranged in a neat row in the machine's window.

"Lucia!" Evvie's clear soprano cut through the excited drone of voices surrounding Lucia. "Loosh! What in the world?" Evvie elbowed her way to Lucia's side, gawked at the machine and grabbed Lucia's arm. "Oh, my God," she whispered. "You won! You won! I don't believe it!"

Lucia didn't believe it, either. But the Super Jackpot sign was still flashing, and her feet were nearly buried in silver dollars. Three uniformed casino guards suddenly materialized to cordon off the machine and hold back the surging crowd. Lucia entertained the vague idea of gathering up the money on the floor, but she couldn't seem to move. She was paralyzed by shock.

"Lucia," Evvie murmured. "You're rich."

Lucia opened her mouth and then shut it. If she'd felt queasy before, she felt far queasier now. She struggled to lift one foot, and several silver dollars slipped inside her shoe. She laughed helplessly.

"Excuse me, miss." An energetic man in a tuxedo worked his way through the crowd to Lucia, and when the guards permitted him to reach her, she assumed he must be safe. He seemed safe, anyway—an inch shorter than she, prematurely balding, with a cloying grin plastered across his face. "Excuse me, miss," he repeated, extending his hand. "I'm Paul Devane, and I'm the general manager of the Shangri-la Hotel and Casino. May I be the first to congratulate you on winning the Super Jackpot?" He took her hand and pumped it up and down, then angled her toward the crowd of onlookers and pumped her hand again. Several flashbulbs flickered as people took Lucia's photograph. "I'm sure you're very excited," Paul Devane continued, still holding Lucia's hand. She was too stupefied to ask him to let go of her. "Mack, Danny—gather up the lady's coins, would you?" he ordered the guards. He turned back to Lucia. "I've got a check for the balance I'd like to present to you."

"The balance?" she echoed hazily.

"A quarter of a million dollars, plus whatever's in the machine. Congratulations, young lady!" He shook her hand again, and more flashbulbs popped. Lucia was temporarily blinded by a dozen purple afterimages. "What's your name?" the manager asked.

"My name?" she mumbled.

Evvie sidled up next to her. "Her name is Lucia Bowen. I'm her friend, Evelyn Hooper. This is our first time in Atlantic City."

"Your first time?" Paul Devane reiterated loudly. "Well, well, I bet you'll be back again soon, won't you?"

Another man, dressed in a nondescript suit, worked his way through the crowd. "Miss Bowen, is it?" he said crisply, pulling out a pad and pen. "I'm Leo Ruckel, from the IRS. I'm going to need some information from you." Before Lucia could speak, one of the guards shoved his hat toward her. It was heaped full of silver dollars.

Lucia shook her head in disbelief. One of her combs slipped through her hair to dangle by her ear. She fumbled with it, taking heart in its familiar shape, its curved teeth and smooth spine. Her combs she knew. A super jackpot, a quarter of a million dollars plus, a man from the IRS and a hatful of money—these were things she didn't know, and they frightened her. She began to shiver. She'd never fainted in her life, but now seemed like a suitable occasion for her first swoon.

"Evvie," she muttered shakily. "I think I'm going to do something embarrassing, like throw up or keel over or something. Can we . . . can we get out of here?"

The manager evidently overheard her. His hand tightened on hers. "Of course, of course, honey. We can go to my office if you'd like, and you can sit down and give yourself a chance to let it sink in. And then, of course, we'll want to take some official publicity photos, and Mr. Ruckel here will want to get some information from you."

"Cool it, Devane." A low, husky voice penetrated Lucia's befogged consciousness. She peered past the manager to see the dark-haired man from the Baccarat Room break through the crowd. He was taller than Lucia had imagined, extremely long-legged. He discreetly removed Paul Devane's hand from Lucia and smiled gently at her. "The lady needs a drink and a chance to recover."

"Yes, yes, of course," Devane conceded. "You're right, Mr. Royce."

"Let's retire to my suite, and you can take her picture later—if she decides it's all right with her."

"Yes, Mr. Royce."

The man peered down at Lucia, his eyes sparkling with glimmers of green and gold. Then he took the hat of coins from the guard and nodded courteously at Evvie. "Ladies? Please follow me."

Evvie shot Lucia an intrigued look. Lucia gritted her teeth and said nothing. She didn't want to tell her friend about the man's silent flirtation earlier that evening, or about how she'd been trying to elude him when she happened upon the Super Jackpot slot machine and tossed in her last dollar. Instead, she tried to analyze the deferential attitude the hotel manager exhibited toward the baccarat player. If Paul Devane was the manager of the Shangri-la, then was Mr. Royce the owner?

What on earth would the owner of a casino be doing playing cards in his own casino? Talk about busman's holidays, she mused as she followed him into an elevator. Evvie, Paul Devane, the man from the IRS and a guard all wedged themselves into the car, and Lucia was unwittingly pressed up against Mr. Royce.

Her head reached his shoulder, and her cheek rubbed against the twilled silk of his jacket. He had a warm, subtly spicy scent. When he loosened his bow tie, his fingers ran along the bare skin of her arm, leaving in their wake a strange tingling sensation that made Lucia more uncomfortable than she already was. She stiffened slightly, and he glanced down at her, his eyes transfixing her with their steadiness as he undid the bow tie and unfastened the button at his collar. His neck was a sun-drenched tan color, in contrast with the stark-white shirt.

When the elevator coasted to a stop, Lucia was relieved. She didn't know what his enigmatic gaze was trying to communicate to her, but she knew that the man from the Baccarat Room made her feel uneasy. He was much too handsome, for one thing, and much too suave.

Much too in control of things. If he did own the casino, he was definitely not in a line of work Lucia had much respect for.

The group was moving en masse down the luxuriously decorated hallway to the man's room, and Lucia didn't have much choice but to follow. He unlocked a door at the end of the corridor and pushed it open.

Lucia and her entourage entered a sitting room furnished with two modern velour sofas, several chrome-and-glass occasional tables, a leather recliner chair, a wide-screen television set and a sleek desk and chair in a corner. A wall of windows overlooked the boardwalk and beyond it the Atlantic Ocean, but Lucia imagined that if she crossed the room to inspect the view, she'd probably suffer an acrophobia attack. Instead, she collapsed onto one of the sofas and rested her head in her hands.

Evvie took a seat beside her. "You don't seem very happy," she noted softly.

"I'm not sure I am," Lucia confessed.

"You're just in shock, honey," Paul Devane cheered her. "Once you have a chance to think about what a quarter of a million dollars is going to mean to you—"

"Let's not forget that that's her gross winnings," the man from the IRS interjected. "Now, Miss Bowen, if I could just get some information from you—"

"Leave her alone; she's not going anywhere," the dark-haired man broke in. He shrugged off his jacket, tossed it onto the desk, and lifted the receiver of the telephone. "Room service," he spoke into it, "this is Malcolm Royce, Suite 1515." He covered the mouthpiece with his hand and eyed Lucia. "What would you like?"

"Some aspirin," Lucia answered.

He smiled. She hadn't noticed before, but he had enchanting dimples. "A glass of ice water and some aspirin," he said into the phone, then turned to Evvie. "And you, Ms...Cooper, was it?"

Evvie glanced at Lucia, then grinned. "Hooper," she corrected him. "I'll have a glass of wine, thank you. It seems to me that somebody here ought to get drunk."

Malcolm Royce apparently agreed. "Send up a bottle of Piper-Heidsieck and a few glasses." He hung up the phone, then glided across the plush beige carpet to the couch, facing Lucia. "Perhaps after you've had your aspirin, you'll join us in some champagne," he suggested as he sat.

She nodded vaguely, then concentrated on trying to unfurl her fisted hands. She wished she could feel as festive as the others. She wished Evvie had won the jackpot instead of her. Evvie liked money; Evvie would know how to handle this sort of event. Lucia didn't. To keep her nausea at bay, she focused on her fingers, straightening each one out in turn, then pressing her palms together to keep from fisting her hands again.

"Uh, if you don't mind," the IRS man mumbled, "I'd just like to get your social security number and your address, Miss Bowen."

"It's Dr. Bowen," she told him.

She noticed Malcolm Royce's eyebrows arching slightly at this revelation. "Dr. Bowen?" the IRS man repeated.

"That's right. Dr. Lucia—that's L-u-c-i-a—Bowen, B-o-w-e-n." She recited her address, her phone number, her Social Security number, her age.

"You understand," Leo Ruckel said apologetically as he took down the information, "we have to keep tabs on big winners like you. Gambling winnings are taxable, after all."

"I have no intention of cheating on my taxes," Lucia remarked dryly, feeling strangely weary. A knock on the door alerted her that her aspirin had arrived, and as soon as a room-service waiter wheeled the cart containing a bottle of champagne in an ice bucket and several tulip-shaped glasses toward the couches, her spirits lifted slightly. He presented the aspirin and water to her, and she gratefully swallowed two tablets.

Malcolm Royce proceeded to open and pour the champagne. He extended a glass to Lucia, who refused it with a shake of her head. He studied her for a long moment, then smiled tentatively and handed the glass to Evvie.

Paul Devane helped himself to a glass, raised it and toasted, "To Miss Bowen, our first Super-Jackpot winner!"

"Dr. Bowen," Malcolm reminded him, shooting an unreadable glance Lucia's way.

"Yes, of course. Dr. Bowen." He chuckled coyly. "I imagine some people will consider it the height of injustice that a doctor should be the beneficiary of such huge winnings, but what the heck. It's all just a matter of luck—and you, little lady, are one hell of a lucky gambler tonight. Well," he said after downing his champagne in one long swig, "I'd better head downstairs and get the photographer. You understand, Miss Bowen, that we want to milk as much publicity from this as we can. For a quarter of a million dollars, I think we deserve a little bit of positive press, am I right? Come on, Ruckel," he said, beckoning the IRS agent to join him at the door. "You've got her number—she's not going to rip you off. Leave her alone so she can fix herself up for the pictures." The two men left, and Malcolm gestured for the guard to leave as well.

The room seemed oddly peaceful without the over-bearing hotel manager and the pushy tax man in it. Malcolm drifted to his desk, tactfully giving Lucia and Evvie a modicum of privacy in the spacious room. Lucia leaned back into the soft sofa cushions and groaned. "We're going to miss our bus," she commented.

Evvie checked her wristwatch and grimaced. "You're right." Then she laughed. "We can always take a cab home, Loosh. You're rich."

"Once Uncle Sam gets through with me, I won't be," Lucia noted, though the possibility of handing over her entire winnings to the government had a certain appeal to her. What in the world would she do with all that money? How many cab rides would a quarter of a million dollars buy?

"I'll take you home," Malcolm offered.

Lucia turned to him. As soon as her eyes met his, she felt something hot and powerful grip her, a vague but undeniable sensation of being imprisoned by his stare. His eyes were truly awesome, she decided, dazzling in their multitude of colors, in their shimmering splinters of light.

"It's a two-hour drive," Evvie pointed out. Her words short-circuited the current coursing between Lucia and Malcolm, and Lucia was grateful to be released from his peculiar power.

"No problem," he assured her, striding to the phone. "What bus did you take here? We should contact the driver and tell him not to wait for you."

Evvie named the bus line and number, and Malcolm dialed the front desk and requested that they inform the bus driver that Lucia and Evvie would not be making the return trip. After hanging up, he strolled back to the room-service cart and refilled his champagne glass.

Wonderful, Lucia thought, trying to contain her edginess. This strange man with his unnerving eyes was going to tank up on champagne and then drive them home. Lucia might wind up the casualty of a drunk driver before she had a chance to make her first payment to the IRS. "Do you own this place?" she asked him.

He gazed at her. His eyes sparkled mysteriously for an instant before vanishing into slits as he laughed. "I hope not," he answered cryptically.

"What's that supposed to mean?" Lucia challenged him, her undeniable response to him dismaying her.

"It means no, I don't own this place," he clarified. "Are you sure you won't have some champagne, Dr. Bowen?"

She sighed, then shrugged. He took that as a yes and filled a glass for her.

"What's your specialty?" he asked as he handed her the glass.

"My what?"

"Your medical specialty."

Evvie laughed, and Lucia managed a wan smile. "I'm not a medical doctor," she explained. "I'm a research chemist. I just told those guys I was Dr. Bowen because they were getting on my nerves."

"She *is* a doctor," Evvie hastened to add. "A Ph.D."

Malcolm turned to Evvie. "Are you a doctor, too?" he asked courteously.

"No, I'm a lawyer," Evvie answered. "I work in the patent department at Parker Chemicals. Lucia's in Research."

Lucia resented Evvie's blabbing to this stranger about where they worked and what they did. But she was also thankful that Evvie was acting cheerful and courteous enough for both of them. Lucia couldn't seem to overcome her discomfort at her predicament. She wasn't certain whether she was more uncomfortable about her windfall wealth or about the attractive man seated just a couple of feet from her. Deciding that it wasn't worth delving into the ultimate reason for her tension, she sipped her champagne. The bubbles tickled her tongue, and with a weak chuckle she countered the urge to sneeze.

"You've finally decided to laugh about this, huh?" Evvie playfully chided her.

"If I don't laugh, I'll cry," Lucia admitted. "What on earth am I going to do with all that money?"

"Quit work," Evvie suggested. "Take a world cruise. Buy a house. Eat caviar omelets for breakfast."

"I wish you'd won it instead of me," Lucia said. "You've got so many good ideas about how to spend money. I don't."

"I just gave you four good ideas," Evvie reminded her.

"Caviar?" Lucia hooted, curling her lip. "Fish eggs? Forget it."

A knock on the door alerted them to the arrival of Paul Devane and a photographer lugging a professional-looking camera. "Hello, honey, I'm back," said the manager, waving an envelope toward her. "Do you know what's in here?"

"A dunning notice from the IRS," Lucia deadpanned.

"What a sense of humor!" Paul Devane guffawed, overreacting to what Lucia considered a rather limp joke. "Well, Miss Bowen, what we'd like is for Joe here to take a picture of me handing over the check. You'll see it's actually for two hundred fifty-two thousand, three hundred thirty-five dollars—we've added in the sum of what came out of the machine. All right?"

Lucia's hands fluttered to the combs in her hair. She turned to Evvie, who groped in her purse for a pocket mirror and handed it to Lucia. She inspected her reflection and shuddered. Her hair was neat enough, but her expression was obviously drawn, her eyes oddly teary and her mouth strained. She didn't look joyful or grateful, or for that matter, pretty. "Do we really have to do this?" she asked.

Paul Devane arranged his mouth into a patient smile. "Understand, Miss Bowen, when we give away a quarter of a million dollars, we don't do it for our health. We do it to get maximum publicity, to encourage other people to visit the casino. Now, all I'm asking of you is a few photos. For a quarter of a million dollars, don't you think you can do that for us?"

Pressing her lips together, Lucia mulled over his words. It wasn't only that she didn't want her face peering out from hundreds of newspapers above the caption: "Woman Gets Rich at Shangri-la." It was that she didn't like Paul Devane's unctuous attitude. She recalled what Malcolm Royce had said in the casino downstairs, something about how Lucia would pose for pictures *if she wanted to*. He might not own the Shangri-la, but he certainly had some clout at the hotel. She turned to him for help.

He appeared sympathetic. "Dr. Bowen," he said softly. "I think you ought to know that the Shangri-la is already in possession of videotapes of you winning the jackpot."

"What?" she blurted out. "How can that be? I didn't see any television cameras down there."

"You didn't see them because they're hidden behind one-way mirrors in the ceiling of the casino," Malcolm explained. "All casinos maintain constant video surveillance to reduce cheating. I'm sure that Devane here has plenty of blurry, unflattering tapes of you gawking at the slot machine and looking very pale and flabbergasted. If you pose for a few pictures now, you'll look better in them.''

She twisted back to Paul Devane, who nodded in confirmation. ''All right,'' she acquiesced. ''Evvie, do something with me.''

Evvie spent a few minutes brushing Lucia's hair and adjusting the combs. She lent Lucia her powdered blusher and lip gloss, and Lucia did her best to bring some color to her pallid cheeks. Resigned to the fact that she wasn't going to look ravishing, she obediently stood and held several stiff poses while the manager presented her with the envelope, shook her hand and smiled.

''Well,'' he said as the photographer wound his film. ''Enjoy the money in good health, Miss Bowen.''

''Thank you,'' she said listlessly. She suddenly felt exhausted, both physically and emotionally. She wasn't used to being out after eleven on weeknights. And she definitely wasn't used to being rich. Winning a jackpot in Atlantic City, she was learning, could be an unbelievably draining experience.

Paul Devane and the photographer left the suite, and Evvie packed her cosmetics back into her purse. ''Were you serious about taking us home, Mr. Royce?'' she asked Malcolm.

''Absolutely.'' He tugged his bow tie completely off, pulled his room key from the pocket of his jacket, and moved to the door.

''Mr. Royce.'' Lucia approached the door, then hesitated. ''Look, I don't know who you are, or what you have to do with all this, but really, you don't have to drive us home. We can take a cab.''

His eyes settled on her upturned face, perusing it thoughtfully. "You don't have to be afraid of me," he assured her, accurately discerning her anxiety. "What I have to do with all this is that the Shangri-la owes my company a number of loans, and I'm staying at the hotel to work out refinancing. Don't worry. I'm legitimate."

"Maybe you are, but..." Lucia shifted edgily beneath his penetrating gaze. She simply didn't know whether she could stand being cooped up in a car with him for two hours. Of course, Evvie would be present, but even so... She didn't like the way the man looked at her, the way his warm, male scent aroused her, the way her nerves prickled with erotic heat whenever their eyes met. "It's an awfully long drive, Mr. Royce."

"Malcolm," he murmured. "Call me Malcolm."

She took a deep breath. His eyes hadn't moved from her. She felt another wave of heat ripple down her spine, and she groped for any defense she could think of to ward him off. "You've been drinking champagne. Do you really think you're in any condition to drive?"

He chuckled—a deep, husky sound. "Don't worry about my condition," he said enigmatically. "You'll be perfectly safe with me. Ladies?"

Evvie preceded Lucia through the open door, then glanced over her shoulder and arched her eyebrows, obviously confused but intrigued by the overtones of Lucia's exchange with the man.

Lucia didn't answer the unspoken question in Evvie's eyes. She couldn't. Malcolm had cupped his hand about her elbow, and even his gentle, chivalrous touch sent Lucia's nervous system into turmoil.

Whoever this man was, however legitimate, whatever his condition, he exerted a force over Lucia that astonished her. She lost her consciousness of her unexpected wealth, of the check Paul Devane had pressed into her hand, of everything that had occurred during this long, bizarre night in Atlantic City. The only thing Lucia could think about was Malcolm's hand on her arm, both comforting and unintentionally disturbing, and his potent eyes peering down at her.

Instinctively, Lucia knew that one thing a quarter of a million dollars couldn't buy was immunity from a man like Malcolm Royce.

Chapter Two

When they reached the underground garage, Malcolm abandoned Lucia and Evvie outside the attendants' glass-enclosed office and entered alone. He conferred with the man on duty, who nodded and spoke into his telephone. The attendant hung up, and Malcolm joined the women and ushered them to the driveway.

Within a minute an elongated black limousine coasted to a halt in front of them. A uniformed chauffeur emerged and strode briskly around the car to open the passenger door.

Lucia's eyebrows shot up, and she turned to Malcolm. "Is this your car?" she blurted out.

He chuckled. "No, it belongs to the hotel. Hop in."

Scowling slightly, she entered the car and slid down along the plush velvet seat. Evvie climbed in behind her, and Lucia experienced a rush of relief at the realization that Malcolm wouldn't be sitting next to her. She was having enough difficulty trying to regain her equilibrium without having him cuddled up next to her for a long drive.

But he undermined her expectations by closing the door behind Evvie and loping around the car to Lucia's side. Cringing, she shifted as close to Evvie as she could, leaving Malcolm more than enough room on the broad seat. "How about this car?" Evvie gushed as Malcolm and the chauffeur chatted in the driveway.

"I'm glad he isn't driving, after all he's had to drink," Lucia muttered grimly.

"What? A little bit of champagne?"

Lucia shook her head. "He was putting it away in the casino," she informed her friend.

Evvie appeared quizzical, but before she could question Lucia about how she happened to know what Malcolm had been consuming in the casino, he climbed into the car and settled himself beside Lucia. Evidently he'd overheard her remark. "Putting what away?" he asked.

She sighed. "Booze," she said. "When you were playing cards. I figure you're in no condition to drive."

He issued a soft chuckle. "I was drinking straight tonic water," he asserted, not at all offended by her suspiciousness. The driver resumed his seat behind the wheel, and after Evvie directed him to drive to Edison, the central New Jersey town where she and Lucia lived, he shut the glass partition separating the front and back seats. He cruised up the ramp to the street and headed west toward the causeway leading to the mainland.

"So, this car belongs to the hotel, huh?" Evvie said as she surveyed the posh interior with its paneled walls, thick carpeting and miniature television screen attached to a small ledge abutting the front seat. "What a scream. Just think, Lucia, you can afford a vehicle like this now."

"Hm," Lucia grunted. She couldn't deny being impressed by the spacious interior, or by the smooth silence of the limousine as it glided down the street. A mild late-spring drizzle soaked the night, causing the road to glisten and reflect the streetlights and the headlights of other cars, but the limo sealed its passengers in their own cozy, hermetic world.

Malcolm lounged in his seat, extending his legs. Lucia wondered whether a man with such long legs could possibly be comfortable in any car smaller than a limo. She pushed away the thought with an irritated shake of her head. She didn't want to contemplate the length of Malcolm's legs, or the masculine contours of his chest, hinted at by the soft draping of his shirt, or the nearness of his arm to hers. Her edginess made her defensive, and she grumbled, "The hotel must be into you for a lot of money if they'd let you use a car like this."

Her obvious uneasiness seemed to amuse him. "They're running scared," he confirmed. "They've made it clear to me that I should make use of every convenience while I'm in Atlantic City. Their financial situation is iffy, to say the least."

"Gee whiz," Lucia commented wryly, fingering the envelope containing her jackpot winnings. "Maybe this check is going to bounce."

Malcolm chuckled again. "A quarter of a million dollars is spare change to a place like the Shangri-la. It's written into their advertising budget. Good for publicity. That's why Devane was so eager for photos. He'd gladly part with a few hundred thousand dollars if it'll attract millions of gamblers to his casino. I don't mean to burst your balloon, Lucia, but—"

"What balloon?" Lucia cut him off, then laughed softly and patted the envelope with her hand. "This lead balloon? By all means, burst it."

"So the Shangri-la is in financial trouble?" Evvie questioned him. "They just opened a year ago."

"Which, I hope, means it isn't too late to straighten them out," Malcolm commented.

"But a casino! I can't believe a casino could be losing money, given how much they take in. The odds are in favor of the house, aren't they?" At Malcolm's nod, Evvie giggled. "Maybe they're losing money because they've got to pay off the gangsters."

Lucia winced. The newspapers frequently ran stories about mob infiltration of the lucrative casino business in Atlantic City, but Evvie's remark struck her as indiscreet. After all, what did she and Evvie know about Malcolm Royce, besides the fact that the hotel owed him money? Couldn't he himself be a mobster? Someone as cool and complacent as he was, duded up in his elegant apparel and traveling around in a limousine, having Paul Devane fawn all over him as if the hotel manager owed Malcolm his life...As Lucia added up the evidence, a new kind of fear seized her. Malcolm Royce could be the most bloodthirsty gangster ever to hit southern New Jersey.

But he seemed totally unruffled by Evvie's supposition. "That thought occurred to me, too," he said. "I've only just begun to go through their records. I don't suppose I'll find any expenditures in the files labeled as payment for services rendered to John 'Bone Crusher' Jones and Bob 'The Silencer' Smith." He considered, then grinned. "I'm hoping it's just a matter of mismanagement, something that can be rectified without too much overhauling. I certainly don't want to find myself wearing concrete shoes at the bottom of the Hudson River."

Still not convinced of his trustworthiness, Lucia asked him, "Why did you loan money to a casino, if you're afraid of dealing with thugs?"

"I didn't," he told her. "My company did. I work for an investment firm in Manhattan, and this is our first casino venture. It wasn't my decision. Which is why I got volunteered to come down here and straighten out the mess."

"Hey, for a swanky suite like yours and the use of a set of wheels like this," Evvie said, "I'd volunteer, too. Being rich ain't half-bad." She eyed Lucia impishly. "So tell me, rich lady, what are you going to do with all your loot?"

Lucia gazed at the envelope in her lap and sighed. "I don't know. Give it away, maybe."

"Make sure you put me on your list," Evvie teased, then grew serious. "Why don't you want to spend it on yourself?"

"What do I need that I haven't already got?" Lucia asked. It was true; she had everything she needed. A comfortable apartment, decent clothing, three squares a day, a dependable car. Her salary as a senior research chemist at Parker Chemicals was more than adequate, and she got her paycheck reliably, once a month, on time. She wanted financial security, and she had it. More than that she didn't need. She examined the envelope thoughtfully, then shrugged. "Maybe I could set up a trust fund for my sister's kids."

"Loosh, if anyone doesn't need money, it's your nephews," Evvie reminded her.

Lucia nodded. Her sister's husband was quite wealthy, and her two nephews had been born with the proverbial silver spoons in their mouths. They probably wouldn't even notice an extra hundred thousand dollars. "I can give it to charity, then," she decided.

"Oh, God, how disgustingly noble," Evvie scoffed. "Why don't you give it to the Lucia Bowen charity? Buy yourself some designer ensembles and pop off to Acapulco for a month."

"Acapulco?" Lucia protested. "I thought you were pushing for a world cruise."

Evvie grinned slyly. "I suppose that depends on whether you'd like to meet distinguished gray-haired widowers or sensual Latin lovers."

"Neither, thank you," Lucia retorted tartly.

"Loosh, old girl, you're a rich bachelorette," Evvie pointed out. "You're going to be meeting men whether you want to or not."

Lucia gnawed at her lip to keep herself from muttering that she didn't want Evvie to discuss her romantic prospects in front of Malcolm. She wasn't certain why that should be; she and Evvie often kidded each other about their respective social lives. But not in front of Malcolm. Not in front of this virile man, with his long legs and his enticing scent and his jewellike eyes. "I think I'll just give it away," she resolved, putting an end to the conversation. "I just want to get rid of it and return to normal."

"You could invest it," Malcolm recommended. His voice was subdued, as if he wasn't sure he had the right to offer Lucia advice.

She glanced at him. His face was fleetingly illuminated by the headlights of a passing car, a flash of white catching the distinctive angles of his features. Then he vanished in shadow again, and Lucia's eyes strained to adjust to the darkness. "Why should I invest it?" she asked.

"Why shouldn't you?" he countered sensibly.

"Because," she insisted. "Because I don't want the money. If I invest it, it'll just increase in value. I'd rather give it away."

"If you invest it wisely, you could give away the interest while retaining the principal. That way you could be charitable without diminishing your capital."

She considered his words, then shook her head. "I'd just as soon give the principal to someone else and let them invest it." She lowered her eyes to her lap and scowled at the envelope. Then she jammed it into her pocket so that she wouldn't have to look at it. "I really don't want the money," she whispered.

"Why not?" he asked. He reached out and pulled a strand of her hair back from her cheek. His personal gesture nearly made her flinch, as did the unexpected heat that spread through her when his fingertips brushed her throat. "Don't you like money?"

She opened her mouth, but her voice cracked when she tried to shape a reply. She pressed her lips together and shook her head.

The truth was that she despised money. She had seen money—or rather the lack of it, and the lust for it—ruin her father and her family. While her father had never even played nickel-ante poker, he was, in his own way, a compulsive gambler, forever staking the family's security on ridiculous schemes that he was convinced would garner him huge profits. There had been the mail-order business he'd run out of the living room in Des Moines, and the shoe-restyling venture some fool had convinced him to invest the family's meager savings in in Tucson, and the talent agency he'd established in Indianapolis. There had been the moves Lucia's family had made, time after time, in the dark of night, so that the neighbors wouldn't see them and shame them, and the emergency jobs her mother had taken here and there to cover the month's rent when her father trudged home with his pockets empty and his bank passbook stamped "Canceled.'' There had been the day Lucia's mother had finally declared that she was tired of moving, that the Bowens were going to remain in Indianapolis no matter what, and her father had been forced to throw himself at the mercy of the bankruptcy courts. Lucia remembered the constant fights, the constant fears, the constant pipe dreams her father would chase. *This* time, he'd swear, everything was going to work, *this* time he'd score big, *this* time he'd be so rich he'd be able to give his daughters anything their hearts desired. And instead, he'd given them the humiliation of having their classmates point at them and ridicule them and whisper about how their family was bankrupt.

Lucia hated money because her father's mindless quest for it had deprived her of a normal life. She hated money because that was the only thing her father cared about—having it, getting it, making it. ''This time, princess,'' he used to promise her. ''You'll see, Lucia, my princess, this time our ship will come in. People don't like to throw out their favorite, most comfortable shoes just because they've gone out of style. You'll see. This time I'm onto something big.''

Her sister had reacted to their precarious childhood by marrying the wealthiest man she could find. Celia had confessed to Lucia on more than one occasion that she didn't really love Arthur, but that love wasn't important. ''I want to spend the rest of my life knowing where my next meal is coming from,'' she'd grittily defended her choice. ''I want my children to know that our house belongs to us, and that if we sell it, it'll be our choice, and if we move, it'll be in broad daylight. Love isn't as important as that, Loosh. Arthur's a decent man and we've got a life together. I'm not going to apologize for being the first pragmatist in our family.''

Lucia didn't blame Celia, but she couldn't emulate her. Maybe it was because she was younger, more open-minded, the "princess" of their far-from-royal family. But her practicality took her in a different direction. She decided that she'd get a good education, forge a solid career, and depend on herself for security. She'd develop some aptitude in a profession that featured a regular salary and adequate benefits.

She had always enjoyed science, and she'd excelled in the subject at the three different high schools she attended during her unstable adolescence. Because her family was, as usual, broke when she went to college, she qualified for scholarship aid, and a series of fellowship grants saw her through graduate school. And then she found the job she was looking for at Parker Chemicals. She could do interesting research there, and more important, she'd be paid a steady salary. Lucia wouldn't have to depend on a man, as her mother had been forced to depend on her undependable husband, or as Celia had to depend on a man she honestly didn't love. Lucia would depend on herself.

She was content with her life now. She felt safe. Even if, by some disaster, Parker Chemicals went out of business, Lucia knew she had marketable skills. She'd find another job with another chemical company, and once again she'd earn her monthly paycheck. She'd have her home, her car, her three squares a day. That was enough to satisfy her. Anything more, anything beyond the money she needed to support herself, threatened the precious balance she'd fought so hard to attain in her life. Anything more reminded her of her father and his compulsive, self-destructive hunger for money. She simply didn't want it.

The limousine veered off the parkway, and Lucia glanced out the window. The rain had increased, giving the empty roads a surreal sheen. Lucia hadn't realized how long she'd been lost in thought. She glanced at Evvie, who was sound asleep, her head nestled into the lush upholstery of the seat.

Turning, she discovered Malcolm studying her intently. His lips were curved in a bemused smile, denting his cheeks with dimples. He really didn't look like a mobster, she mused. He looked inexplicably gentle, almost safe. "This is an awfully long drive for you," she mentioned softly.

"I don't mind," he reassured her.

"You've still got the return trip ahead of you."

"I don't mind," he repeated. He examined her face. "How are you feeling?"

"All right, I guess," she murmured shyly. A charged silence filled the air, and she broke it by asking, "How did you do at baccarat?"

He laughed softly. "I wasn't playing for money," he told her. "The casino gave me a bunch of chips and told me to entertain myself for the evening. They're bending over backward to make me think kindly of them."

"You're not a gambler, then?" she asked.

He reflected for a moment, then laughed again. "As someone who organizes investment portfolios for a living, I'm probably a bigger gambler than your average Atlantic City customer." He hesitated, then ventured, "I know it's none of my business what you do with your money, Lucia, but you ought to consider putting it to work for you. You have nothing to gain by throwing it away."

She was tempted to dispute him. What she had to gain by "throwing it away," as he disdainfully described it, was an escape from the burden of too easily gotten gains. But she didn't know how to tell him that without explaining her background, the childhood that had shaped her negative view of money, and she didn't want to tell him about her past. Someone like Malcolm, with his overwhelming confidence, would never understand.

"What sort of research do you do?" he asked.

It seemed like an innocent enough question. "Fungicides," she replied.

"Fungicides?"

"Chemicals that kill fungus."

He nodded. "You mean, like mushrooms?"

Lucia stifled her laughter at his unsophisticated comprehension of chemistry. "That's one kind of fungus," she granted. "I'm working on athlete's foot."

"Athlete's foot? Is that related to mushrooms?" he asked incredulously.

"Sort of," she informed him. Before she could elaborate, the chauffeur opened the glass divider and requested directions to Evvie's house. The car was stopped at a familiar intersection, and Lucia told him to turn right. Her attention remained on directing the driver to the condominium development where Evvie lived. As soon as the car traveled through its entry gate, she nudged her friend awake.

"Huh?" Evvie mumbled groggily. She rubbed her eyes and squinted. "Are we home?"

"Just about," Lucia told her.

"Oh." Evvie yawned. "What time is it?"

Malcolm checked an expensive-looking wristwatch half hidden by the cuff of his shirt. "Nearly one-thirty," he answered.

"Oh." Evvie yawned again. "I must've conked out," she deduced. "Sorry."

"Don't be sorry," Lucia argued. "At least you'll be awake at work tomorrow. I won't be."

"Take the day off," Evvie advised. "You can afford it, pal. That's my place," she called to the driver, pointing out the shingled town house at the end of a row of condos. "Seriously," she insisted, twisting back to Lucia, "take some time off. Go on a spree or something."

"Me? Go on a spree?" Lucia laughed at the absurdity of Evvie's suggestion, and Evvie laughed as well.

The car rolled to a stop, and the chauffeur left the wheel to open Evvie's door for her. "Too bad it's so late," Evvie complained. "I wish some of my neighbors were awake to see me arriving home in style for once in my life." The door swung open, and she patted Lucia's shoulder. "This has been one unforgettable night, Loosh. If I don't see you at work tomorrow, I'll give you a call."

"You'll see me at work," Lucia promised.

Evvie rolled her eyes, then smiled at Malcolm. "Thanks for arranging this transportation. It sure beats that crowded bus."

He brushed off her thanks. "No problem."

"Well, good night," Evvie said, allowing the chauffeur to take her hand as she climbed out of the car. He watched until she was safely inside her home, then got back into the car and asked Lucia where she lived.

"Drive out of the complex and take a right," she directed him. She realized that she could put more distance between herself and Malcolm on the seat, now that Evvie was gone, but she chose not to. There was nothing flirtatious about him now, nothing particularly dangerous. He didn't even remind her of James Bond anymore. Maybe it was because he wasn't wearing his bow tie or jacket, or bossing around the manager of the casino. Maybe it was because he was gazing at her with a vaguely detached curiosity. "Athlete's foot," he remarked.

She chuckled. "My research really isn't that interesting."

"I'm interested. Are you trying to invent a drug for it or something?"

Lucia relaxed in the seat, warming to her subject. "Actually, what I'm trying to do is find a way to bond the fungicidal agent to a polymer—"

"Whoa!" he cut her off. "Speak English."

She chuckled again. "Okay," she explained. "My company produces a medication which destroys the fungus that causes athlete's foot. The project I'm involved with is aimed at finding a way to bond the medication to a substance—a fiber, say—that can be woven into socks. Someone who suffers chronically from athlete's foot could wear these socks and prevent recurrences of the ailment."

"No kidding?" He seemed impressed. "Like gym socks?"

Lucia nodded. "Gym socks, sweat socks—actually, any sock at all. The fungus is usually activated by moisture. If a chronic sufferer knows it's going to be a damp day, he might want to wear the socks just to ward off an attack."

"Antiathlete's foot socks," Malcolm mused. "Fascinating."

"Do you get athlete's foot?" Lucia asked.

He shook his head. "Do you?"

"No. I understand it's pretty uncomfortable, though. And once you've got it, it comes back again and again. Many fungi are like that. The fungus that causes dandruff, for instance—"

"Dandruff?" he exclaimed. "You mean dandruff is caused by mushrooms?"

Lucia burst into laughter. Talking about her research made her feel as confident and comfortable as Malcolm seemed to be in formal attire. "It isn't mushrooms," she corrected him. "Mushrooms are fungi, but not all fungi are mushrooms."

"I see," Malcolm said uncertainly. "As you've probably guessed, the natural sciences aren't my forte." He pondered what Lucia had told him. "Do you enjoy the research?"

"Definitely," she claimed. "I'm a regular test-tube jock. As we chemists like to joke, put me in a lab and I'm in my element."

He smiled tentatively. "It all seems mystical to me. The last time I was in a chemistry lab, back in my high school days, my lab partner's hair caught fire in one of the Bunsen burners. I think I was more traumatized by that than she was."

"We don't use Bunsen burners anymore," Lucia informed him. "Was she seriously hurt?"

"No," Malcolm told her. "The next day she showed up in lab with a new hairstyle."

"Well, there are plenty of dangers in a lab if you aren't careful," Lucia commented. "Parker's got a pretty good safety record. Even though we don't have Bunsen burners, I always wear my hair pinned back for work. And I wear latex gloves, lab glasses and a baggy white coat. I look like a creature from the primordial soup lagoon."

"Primordial soup?" he asked.

"That's a theoretical brew of compounds that...Never mind," she said, grinning at his perplexed frown. Her attention was caught by a neighborhood supermarket and she gasped. "Uh-oh, we went too far. Excuse me," she called to the driver.

"Keep driving," Malcolm overrode her. "I'm learning everything I'd ever want to know about athlete's foot."

Lucia experienced a mild twinge of anxiety at the knowledge that she was trapped in a moving car with Malcolm, journeying farther and farther from her apartment. "I really do have to get home," she scolded him, though his whimsical smile eased her tension. "I've got a group meeting at work first thing tomorrow morning."

"Your friend is right," Malcolm argued. "You ought to take the day off and celebrate."

Her tension returned, this time a result of Malcolm's reminder that she had an unwanted check for an enormous sum of money in her pocket. "I don't feel like celebrating," she muttered. "I'd just as soon have my life return to normal."

"Coming into money doesn't mean your life has to be abnormal," Malcolm asserted quietly. "Why aren't you thrilled about it, Lucia?"

"Because I—" She sighed, unwilling to dwell on what money represented to her. "Call me disgustingly noble," she said, citing Evvie's epithet. "I'd rather give it away and forget about it."

"You can keep it *and* give it away," Malcolm maintained. "If you invest it carefully."

"I'd rather not," she said laconically. "I don't want it."

He measured her apparent distress, clearly puzzled by it. "If you want to do noble things with your winnings," he said slowly, "I think that's very praiseworthy. But you don't have to be deliberately stupid about it. There are ways you can shelter the money so you won't have to pay out an inordinate sum to the IRS. That would leave you with more to give to worthwhile causes. Think about it, Lucia. If you want to do good, by all means, do good. But plan ahead, and you can do even more good."

She lapsed into thought. Her desire to rid herself of the money was a reflex—understandable, given her background, but a mindless reflex all the same. She considered money something evil, something corrupting and destructive. But maybe Malcolm had a point. She did want to do good things with her windfall. Forking over half of her winnings to the IRS wasn't all that noble. She'd rather donate as much as she could to some respectable charity. "What do you mean, shelter it?" she asked cautiously. "You mean I should bury it in some disreputable oil-leasing boondoggle or something?"

Malcolm smiled tolerantly. "I'm not thinking of anything disreputable," he answered. "You could consider a profitable real-estate purchase, perhaps, or some municipal bonds that would give you tax-free interest. There are plenty of possibilities." His grin expanded. "This happens to be my specialty, Lucia—creative investment. That's what my company does."

"Maybe I should invest in an Atlantic City casino," she remarked dryly. "That way I can wake up one morning at the bottom of the Hudson River with my feet encased in concrete."

Malcolm chuckled. When he laughed, Lucia noticed, his eyes seemed to laugh as well, glittering with brilliant light. "As I said, our investment in the Shangri-la was our first—and probably last—venture with a casino. Mostly, we're involved with mutual funds, the money market, stock portfolios, bonds. Maybe you ought to look over some of our literature."

She eyed him skeptically. "Do you get a commission for selling me on this?" she asked, wondering if the only reason he'd accompanied her home from Atlantic City was to pitch her on his company's services.

"No," he declared. "I'm not generally involved in the consumer end of things. But Advent is a successful firm. We do quite well for our investors."

"Advent?"

"Look us up in the financial pages," he suggested. "We're listed under money markets and mutual funds."

She groaned softly. The concept of getting herself involved in the sort of business activity that would require her to read the financial pages of a newspaper weighed heavily on her. It seemed much too complicated. If Malcolm thought chemistry was mystical, well, Lucia thought stocks and bonds and mutual funds were mystical.

If she hadn't won the jackpot, she wouldn't feel such a responsibility pressing down on her now. She knew Malcolm was right: she mustn't let her mild neurosis concerning money color her decision about what to do with it. She ought to be rational, to keep her impulses in check until she'd considered all her options. "You have some literature, huh?" she asked dubiously.

"Back in my hotel room," he answered. "I always carry a few brochures around, just in case I run into a rich, beautiful woman like you."

His compliment jolted Lucia. Suddenly he seemed much too close to her—even if she jammed herself against the opposite door, he'd be too close to her. She didn't like flirtatious men, and certainly not men who lied to her. She wasn't beautiful, and she didn't want to think of herself as rich. "I'd like to go home," she said tautly.

Malcolm measured her abrupt change in mood. His eyes darkened slightly and a crease etched itself across his brow. However, he didn't comment on her withdrawal from him. He only turned to the driver and said, "She'd like to go home."

"Yes, Mr. Royce," the driver responded. "I need directions."

Lucia provided them, forcing her voice past the knot of tension in her throat. The driver steered around the block and then retraced his route, heading back toward town. Other than Lucia's crisp warnings to turn right or to take the left-hand fork, the car was silent.

Eventually they reached her neighborhood of modest but well-maintained garden apartments. She indicated her building to the chauffeur, and he parked and left the car to open the door. Before he reached it, she groped for the door handle, anxious to let herself out.

Malcolm stayed her hand with his own, curving his long fingers around hers. She detested the river of warmth that rose up her arm at the contact. Although he wasn't holding her forcefully, she couldn't seem to find the strength to pull away. "I have to go," she whispered.

He ignored her statement. "Did I say something wrong?" he probed.

She fixed her eyes on her lap and pressed her lips together. Malcolm slipped his other hand beneath her chin and lifted her face to his. He searched her eyes, wide and glistening with discomfort, her rigid mouth, her flared nostrils. His smile was tenuous.

Something about the mysterious luminescence of his eyes compelled the truth from her. "A rich and beautiful woman," she muttered. "That's a corny line, if ever I heard one."

"It wasn't a line," he replied. "What you've got in your pocket makes you rich. And what you've got in your soul makes you beautiful."

Now, that's a corny line, she thought, though she couldn't deny that she liked the sound of it. The second part of it, anyway. Malcolm couldn't possibly know much about her soul, other than that she wanted to give her money to charity. But even that decision wasn't born out of altruism as much as out of a desire to dispose of the money as quickly and efficiently as she could.

He continued to scrutinize her, and she managed a nervous laugh. "What I've got in my soul may or may not make me beautiful," she allowed. "But what I've got in my face makes me a pretty ordinary woman with a big nose. Please don't flirt with me, Malcolm. I don't like it."

Her bluntness took him by surprise. As soon as he recovered, he smiled appreciatively. "Be forewarned, Lucia," he alerted her. "A lot of men are going to think you're beautiful as soon as they hear you're rich."

"Which is one more good reason to give the money away," she declared.

His smile expanded. "A lot of men are going to think that, but I'm not one of them. I think you're smart—which has nothing to do with being rich but has something to do with being beautiful. It also has something to do with how you manage your newfound wealth. I also think . . ." He drifted off, his gaze softening as he ran his thumb along the fragile line of her jaw. "I also think your nose is lovely." He let his hand drop from her face and nodded at the chauffeur, who was standing just outside the door. He swung it open for Lucia. "Good night," Malcolm murmured, releasing her other hand.

She didn't move for an instant. She felt as if she ought to say something more to him, something about resenting his forwardness. Yet, she couldn't. Maybe he wasn't being overly forward. Maybe he was simply reacting to the undeniable current that continued to pass back and forth between them, to wrap around them like an invisible cord. She felt it. Maybe he felt it, too, and he was simply honest enough to put the feeling into words.

The damp night air entered the car to caress her bare arm, and its rainy fragrance cleared her mind. She attempted a smile and stepped out of the car. "Good night, Malcolm," she said quietly. Then she turned and hastened up the walk to her building, not daring to cast him a parting look.

MALCOLM LOUNGED in the backseat, stretching his legs diagonally across the floor, and closed his eyes. He knew he ought to get some sleep during the long drive back to Atlantic City. He had a great deal of work facing him the next day—and every day that week if he was to get the Shangri-la's finances settled by Friday. He didn't want to have to spend longer than a week at the hotel-casino if he could help it.

He ought to rest. But he was unable to. Thoughts of Lucia ran through his mind, stimulating him in an unfamiliar and delightful way.

Her friend was arguably prettier, he contemplated—Cooper, or Hooper, or whatever her name was. With her loose, blondish curls and her little pug nose, her effervescent smile and her giddy laugh, she was, if he compared the two women objectively, the darling of the pair.

But Malcolm had felt nothing when he looked at her. When he looked at Lucia, he felt...alive. More alive than he'd felt in years.

What a paradox she seemed to him. Quiet, inexplicably troubled about what anyone else would have considered the thrill of a lifetime, guarded, reserved and yet . . . and yet he hadn't been imagining things when he spotted her just outside the Baccarat Room, staring at him. She'd been more than staring, he knew. She'd been ogling him. Admiring him. The way her eyes had fastened onto him, the way they'd expressed her obvious sentiments, was anything but guarded.

She had gorgeous eyes, he mused—such a rich, dark color, and fringed with extravagantly long, dense lashes. Whenever his eyes met hers, he felt . . . yes, very, very alive.

He wasn't averse to a little entertainment on the side while he was in Atlantic City. But Lucia wasn't the sort of woman he could think of as "a little entertainment." There was something serious about her, something basic and pure, something he hadn't sensed in a woman in quite some time.

He should have been wary about a woman making eyes at him the way Lucia had. He knew better than to trust a woman who stared at him coquettishly. Polly had approached him tht way, and he'd been foolish enough to respond, to be flattered, to become infatuated. What man wouldn't be taken by a beautiful woman with a definite come-hither look?

Experience had taught him that what Polly had wanted to come hither wasn't Malcolm, but his money. She'd had dreams of glamour, hopes of being supported in the manner to which she'd wanted to become accustomed. And, still, she was costing him, in more than money.

But Lucia wasn't like Polly, or like so many of the women Malcolm had met in the past two years. Lucia apparently loathed money. That alone made her worthy of Malcolm's interest.

She was a doctor, too. A chemist, researching athlete's foot. A quiet smile touched his lips as he reflected on their conversation in the car earlier. Antiathlete's foot socks . . . the mere idea of such a thing tickled him.

He really ought to put thoughts of her aside. He didn't have the time to be dwelling on the fascinating woman with the soulful brown eyes and the poignant smile, the woman with enough decency to become ill at the notion of her slot-machine winnings. He didn't have the time right now to relive in his mind the astonishing attraction he'd felt for her. Or she for him. It was more than just that she'd ogled him; it was the visceral jolt he'd felt whenever their bodies came in contact, whenever he even accidentally touched her. He hadn't imagined that, either. Something had flared between them, an almost palpable desire, leaping like a wind-borne flame from his body to hers, from hers to his. He hadn't imagined it. It existed.

For the first time since he'd been chosen by his colleagues to put the Shangri-la's books in order, Malcolm was glad to be stuck with the assignment. He'd resisted it all the way, arguing that any other senior partner at Advent would surely relish a week-long junket in Atlantic City more than he would. He'd had his fill of glitter in his marriage, and he considered casinos ridiculous. Shouldn't someone else take the project, someone who might appreciate the resort more than he ever would?

"You've got to go," Logan had refuted him. "You were the sole voice of reason when Cunningham proposed this investment in the first place. You were the one with the twenty-twenty vision; you were the voice of doom. To the victor go the spoils."

"Spoils is right," Malcolm had complained. "Just because I've got good eyesight doesn't mean I should spoil my week dealing with those turkeys at Shangri-la.

And anyway, I wasn't the sole voice of reason. Sheingold vetoed the investment, too."

Sandra Sheingold had chuckled, but refused the assignment. "Far be it from me to want to express sexist sentiments," she'd contended from across the conference table. "But, Royce, we're discussing Atlantic City here. We're discussing sleazy men who think that a half-naked chorus girl who can wiggle her hips in time to music is the ultimate in entertainment. The cash-flow problem at Shangri-la may not be something you're going to find neatly entered into the ledger books, and you know it. You may have to spend your evenings drinking with Devane and his cronies and nudging their ribs and swapping dirty jokes. They just aren't going to open to a woman the way they would to you."

"Besides," Logan had added, "you engineered those excellent investments in development projects out West. Our portfolio did beautifully on those. You know more about this kind of capitalization than Sheingold does. She's a commodities specialist, not a cash-flow expert."

Outvoted by his partners, Malcolm had reluctantly taken on the task of conferring with the other banks and financial institutions that had put together the package of loans the Shangri-la required a year ago. Even though Malcolm had opposed the investment from the start, he'd conceded at the time that most casinos evolved into profitable entities.

That belief hadn't been undermined during the first day he'd spent reviewing the Shangri-la's operating expenses. He knew the hotel could pay off its loans if only its managers exercised a bit more caution and foresight. He could probably straighten things out by Friday if he kept his mind on his purpose and devoted his energies to the business at hand.

But ever since his eyes had met Lucia's over the Baccarat Room's railing, Malcolm couldn't help but wonder whether he'd be able to keep his mind and his energies focused.

Because, right now, as the limousine carried him silently along the rain-soaked roads back to Atlantic City, Malcolm's mind, his energies, his soul, were entirely focused on the sweet, puzzling woman luck had thrown into his life.

Chapter Three

After her sleepless night, Lucia gave serious consideration to skipping work. Raising her head from the pillow, she stared disconsolately at her alarm clock and groaned. *Why not take a day off,* she pondered. *Why not call in sick today?* It wouldn't exactly be dishonest. She did need to recover.

To recover from her insomnia, she wondered. Or to recover from the shock of winning a jackpot?

Or to recover from Malcolm's eyes, the haunting hazel eyes that had imposed themselves on her dreams every time she succeeded in drifting off? They were at least as responsible for her restlessness as the check the casino's manager had handed her last night. Compared to the disturbing effect Malcolm's eyes had on her, thinking about her sudden wealth was almost comforting.

Groaning again, she heaved herself out of bed. She *had* to go to work. She wanted to continue functioning as normally as possible. If she took off a day today, it might be easier to take off a day tomorrow and the next day, and eventually she'd turn into a dissolute bum.

She knew she was exaggerating about the corrupting influence her money might have on her. She wasn't susceptible to the petty pleasures of affluence. However, she did want to hang on to her typical routines. That would help to keep her thoughts in perspective.

Her shower didn't do much to revive her, and when she returned to her bedroom to get dressed, another glance at her alarm clock informed her that she was running late. She slipped on a cotton shirtwaist dress, buttoning it on her way to the kitchen, and forced down a cup of black coffee, scalding her tongue because she didn't have time to let it cool off. She stuffed her check into her briefcase, figuring she'd use her lunch hour to go to the bank and deposit it, and hurried out the door, pausing only to toss the copy of the Newark *Star-Ledger* waiting for her on her doormat onto the coffee table. Then she stumbled down the stairs and outside the building.

She'd probably have to open several savings accounts, she calculated as she drove on automatic pilot to Parker Chemicals' research and corporate center across town. Savings accounts were insured only up to one hundred thousand dollars. She could open two new accounts and dump the remainder of her winnings into her existing account. Thinking logically about how she'd handle her money helped to calm her.

When she arrived at the locked front door of the sprawling building, she flashed her identification card at the guard. He gaped at it for a moment, then opened his mouth to speak. But he changed his mind after assessing her weary expression, and wordlessly released the door's electronic lock to admit her.

She checked her watch as she marched down the hall to the elevator. She was five minutes late. The elevator took its time answering her summons, but she was too tired to use the stairs.

She stopped in her office-laboratory long enough to drop off her briefcase, shrug on her white lab coat, and scoop up the notebook in which she kept a daily log of her research. Then she hurried down the hall, pausing in the lounge to fill a cup with coffee before she had to face her colleagues at their research group meeting.

"Sorry I'm late," she mumbled as she swept into the conference room at the end of the corridor. A fellow chemist was busy setting up a slide projector, and Lucia cursed silently at the thought of having to start her day off by staring at a series of boring slides. She didn't think her bleary eyes could endure such torture; the mere thought of it caused them to smart.

Josh, her research group's leader, stood at the head of the rectangular table, and the other two chemists and three lab technicians involved in the project all turned to her. Their round-eyed gawking disconcerted her, and she slumped into a chair and tossed her notebook onto the table in front of her. "Sorry I'm late," she repeated, assuming that that was why her associates were staring so strangely at her.

Josh lifted a folded edition of the morning newspaper from the pile of papers before him and shoved it down the table to her. "After reading this, I'm surprised you're here at all," he remarked, his mouth hinting at a smile. "Front page, sweetheart."

An undefined dread gripped Lucia as she unfolded the newspaper. The lower right-hand corner of the page was taken up by a huge photograph of her standing beside the Super Jackpot slot machine, with Paul Devane clutching her hand. Evvie was partially visible behind him. Lucia looked ghastly in the picture, her mouth twisted in a terrified grimace, her eyes wide and fearful, her hair disheveled and a tortoiseshell comb dangling by her ear. The caption below the photo stated, in bold print: "Central Jersey Woman Wins Record Shangri-la Jackpot.'' A sidebar accompanying the picture provided Lucia's name and address, as well as the sum she'd won and a few comments from Paul Devane. ''This was Bowen's first visit to Atlantic City,'' the brief article concluded.

She lifted her gaze at the sound of cheers and applause. Her colleagues all rose from their seats to give her a standing ovation, and the technician next to her slammed his hand against her spine in such a hearty congratulatory backslap that she coughed. ''Well?'' Josh roared mirthfully. ''What have you got to say for yourself?''

She focused on the newspaper again. ''This is the wrong photo,'' she muttered. ''They took a bunch of photos in—in an upstairs suite,'' she stammered, not wishing to provoke her co-workers' curiosity by mentioning Malcolm. ''Evvy fixed my hair for those shots. I don't know why they used this one. I guess the paper bought it from one of the onlookers. Everyone was taking pictures of me. I look like hell.''

''You do look a bit startled,'' Josh observed, circling the table to study the photograph over her shoulder. ''Perhaps they just wanted to capture you in your moment of glory.''

''My moment of glory?'' she snorted, thinking she looked not glorious but about to vomit. ''And they included my address,'' she added miserably as she reread the article. ''I can't believe they published that. My apartment's going to be ransacked by the time I get home.''

Josh patted her head. ''Don't worry about it,'' he comforted her. ''Anyone who reads this is going to realize that you couldn't possibly have run out and stocked your home with VCR's and mink coats overnight.''

"VCR's and mink coats?" she scoffed. "I think my first purchase is going to be a new dead-bolt lock for the door."

"Seriously, Loosh," one of the others called to her, "what are you going to do with all that money?"

"I don't know," she answered frankly. "All I know is that I'm going to go to the bank at lunchtime and deposit it. Beyond that, I haven't decided."

"My kid needs braces, if you're looking for suggestions," he commented helpfully.

"The hell with your kid," a technician overrode him. "*My* kid needs tuition money for Rutgers."

"Let him pay his own way," Josh declared. "My car's on the fritz, Loosh. And don't forget, sweetheart, I'm your boss."

She clapped her hands over her ears. "Enough!" she silenced them with a laugh. "If you all want to write grant applications in triplicate, be my guest. But the money's going into the bank for now. Can we start this meeting already? I'm absolutely dying to see Stan's slides."

The group reluctantly settled down, and Stan switched off the room's lights and commenced with a lecture on his current research, illustrating his procedures with his slides. One colorful diagram blurred into the next in Lucia's mind, and she let her thoughts wander to the newspaper item about her. That the photograph was arguably the least flattering picture she'd ever had taken in her life didn't bother her as much as the fact that her address had appeared on the newspaper's front page. She'd never before had to worry about the possibility of theft. Being wealthy might be more trouble than it was worth.

As soon as the slide presentation was over, her colleagues continued to badger her about their children's braces, their dilapidated cars, the pitiful disrepair of their roofs, their mortgage payments. She smiled wanly and promised to give their bids serious contemplation, then hurried from the conference room.

She spotted a figure hovering in her lab's open doorway, and as she approached, she recognized that it was Rick Lansing, the resident Romeo of Parker Chemicals. The company's chief safety officer, Rick was a notably handsome man with thick, wheat-colored hair and heavy-lidded blue eyes. Lucia had little to do with him; in general, he visited her lab only to spot-check on safety violations. As soon as she reached the door, she said, "I know, I haven't got on my lab glasses. They're right on my desk." She slipped past him into the lab and donned the bulky plastic goggles that were regulation gear in the laboratories.

Rick lounged in the doorway, his hands shoved into the pockets of his khaki trousers, and his smile cocky. "I didn't come here on business," he told her. "I came here on pleasure."

"Heaven help me," she muttered under her breath.

He awaited an invitation to join her in the lab, and when none was forthcoming, he entered anyway. "Take them off," he requested, gesturing toward her goggles. "I want to see your eyes, Lucia. I never before noticed what lovely eyes you have."

"Oh, please," she protested good-naturedly. "You didn't come up here to make a pass at me, did you, Rick? I thought you specialized in secretaries."

"Secretaries are fun," he murmured suggestively. "But when it's time to get serious, I prefer an intelligent professional. I've had my eye on you for a year, Lucia. Why don't we get to know each other?"

"Not interested," she flippantly discouraged him.

He plucked the lab glasses from her nose and flung them onto her desk. "You do have lovely eyes," he commented throatily. "Are you free for lunch today?"

"As a matter of fact, no," she informed him. "I've got to go to the bank."

"The bank?" he asked. His attempt at sounding surprised was so transparent that Lucia immediately comprehended why Rick was coming on to her. "We could go together," he offered, "and then visit Le Salon for lunch. Have you ever eaten there? It's got a dynamite atmosphere."

"Atmospheres that include dynamite do nothing for me," she said in a clipped voice. "I've got a lot of work to do this morning, Rick, so if you'll excuse me..."

He appraised her thoughtfully, then scanned her tiny lab. "You've got too many things plugged in here," he noted, pointing to a socket in her lab bench.

She dutifully unplugged one of her instruments and presented him with a saccharine smile. "Satisfied?"

"Hardly," he said, lapsing back into his seductive attitude. "How about dinner tonight?"

"I'm probably going to have to spend the evening cleaning up after the burglars who are certain to break into my apartment today," she said wryly.

"You could hire someone to clean your apartment," he suggested. "Surely you can afford that, Lucia. And we can have dinner at Le Salon."

She laughed at his persistence. "Nice try," she praised him. "But no. Go back to the secretaries in Legal. I understand you've been having decent luck there lately."

He smiled wistfully. "I'll go for now," he conceded. "But I'll be back, beautiful lady." He blew her a kiss, then sauntered from her office.

She sank onto her swivel chair and sighed. What had Malcolm said last night? Something about how a lot of men were going to consider her beautiful, once they found out she was rich. The last thing she wanted was to have scoundrels like Rick Lansing calling her beautiful. After all, what did he know about her soul?

For that matter, what did Malcolm know about her soul? Rick hadn't been the first man to call her beautiful since she'd won the jackpot. Malcolm had. Why did Rick's flattery antagonize her, when Malcolm's flattery had touched her?

Malcolm. Closing her eyes, she pictured him seated beside her in the midnight-darkened limousine, his lanky legs extended gracefully toward the front seat, his eyes luminous, his cheeks dimpled, his thick, dark hair flopping boyishly onto his forehead. Why had she felt such powerful stirrings in his presence? In all likelihood he was just another man calling her beautiful because she suddenly happened to be rich.

But he might well be rich himself. He seemed so suave, so sure, so natural in his tuxedo, in the limousine, in the elegant hotel suite, sipping champagne and speaking in his low, well-modulated voice. The man reeked of wealth. He had no reason to chase after a skinny lady with a big nose and a couple of hundred grand to her name.

Unless, of course, he wasn't actually wealthy. He could have just mastered the motions, perfected the impression. The fact that he worked for an investment firm didn't make him affluent. He'd been sent to Atlantic City on a rescue mission that apparently didn't thrill him. If he was so rich and powerful, wouldn't he have been able to arrange for some underling to take the assignment?

She sighed again and shook her head clear. She didn't have all day to sit around meditating about the stranger who'd accompanied her home from the casino last night. She had work to do, and the group meeting had already consumed much of her morning.

Her lunchtime visit to the bank wound up consuming much of her afternoon. The paperwork involved in opening two new accounts was tedious enough, but Lucia was also delayed by the excited tellers and clients who clustered around her, giggling and shrieking and shaking her hand. Two people even asked for her autograph—to say nothing of the bank officer who made her sign an endless stream of documents. Celebrity, Lucia decided as she drove back to the research center at two-thirty, was not her idea of a good time.

She couldn't get much work accomplished when she returned to her lab, either. She was constantly interrupted by colleagues who dropped by to talk to her. Their visits followed a predictable pattern: a casual greeting, an enthusiastic expression of congratulations on Lucia's good fortune, and then a rambling dissertation on the dire condition of their current finances. Bill's daughter needed a computer in order to face the academic rigors of third grade. Mary Frances's mother required cataract surgery. Tom's lawn mower was kaput. Josephine's marriage was in jeopardy, and if she and her husband didn't spend a week at the Masters and Johnson sex-therapy clinic very soon, all might be lost. By the time Evvie tapped on Lucia's door at four-thirty, Lucia didn't even bother to turn from her desk. "Take a number and wait your turn," she announced as she finished jotting some ideas into her lab notebook.

"Wait my turn for what?" Evvie asked ingenuously.

"Oh—Evvie!" Lucia dropped her pen and stood to welcome her friend. "I'm sorry," she said as she removed her lab glasses and rubbed the tender red dents they left in the bridge of her nose. "It's been a zoo here all afternoon. You'd never guess how many indigent people work for Parker Chemicals."

"Indigent?" Evvie echoed. "Parker pays well."

"Not well enough to spend a week at the Masters and Johnson clinic," Lucia remarked. "Did you know that Josephine Taggart is suffering from sexual dysfunction with her husband?"

Evvie curled her lip. "In all honesty, I wouldn't even want to know that."

"Neither would I," Lucia concurred with a doleful sigh. "But when you win a jackpot in Atlantic City a funny thing happens. Everyone wants to tell you their sad story. They all think I'm Santa Claus."

"You're the one who said you wanted to give it away," Evvie reminded her.

"To a charity," Lucia stressed. "Not to Josephine Taggart."

"Well," Evvie said with a blithe shrug, "it comes with the territory. Weird write-up about you in the newspaper, wasn't it?"

"And a lousy picture, too. Why did they have to include my address?" she moaned. "Somebody's going to rob me."

"Ah, the trials and tribulations of the chosen," Evvie emoted. "Don't cry to me, Loosh. I didn't tell you to put your money into that machine."

"You told me to gamble it," Lucia complained. "Believe me, it's the last time I'll ever listen to you."

Evvie brushed off Lucia's criticism. "Wanna have dinner with me this evening?"

Lucia shook her head. "I've got to go home and get some sleep. You know, you're not the first person to invite me out for dinner tonight. Rick Lansing's already put in a bid."

"Rick Lansing?" Evvie exclaimed. "Rick 'Casanova' Lansing? Uh-oh, Lucia. This situation is getting dangerous."

"Don't worry," Lucia assured her. "I gave him an emphatic no."

"You told him to take a number and stand in line?"

"I told him to go pester the secretaries in Legal." She yawned and rubbed her eyes. "I'm going home. I've had it with this place."

"I don't blame you," Evvie commiserated. "Having to listen to the woes of Josephine Taggart's sex life is grounds for resignation. I'll see you tomorrow, Loosh— unless you decide to wise up and lie low for a few days."

Grinning feebly, Lucia packed up her briefcase, tucking her new bank passbooks carefully into an inside pocket, and slung her lab coat over the hook on the back of her door. She locked her office, rode the elevator downstairs with Evvie, and then departed with a wave.

Thieves might not have ransacked her apartment in her absence, but her privacy had definitely been violated, she discovered when she opened her mailbox. It contained a couple of bills and three printed telegrams. She waited until she was inside her home, her door securely locked behind her, before she opened them. They were each from a different charity, requesting donations.

Grimacing, Lucia tossed them onto her kitchen table and started to her bedroom to change from her dress into something more comfortable. As soon as she reached the closet, her telephone began to ring. Answering it, she was hailed by a representative from a local civic group, who wished to describe its current fund-raising campaign to

Lucia. She made some limp response about having just arrived home from work and hung up the phone.

She wanted to call her parents and tell them about her winnings, but she didn't have a chance. Throughout the evening her telephone rang continuously. A couple of calls were from friends who had read about her in the newspaper, but the vast majority of the calls came from institutions looking for money: the chairwoman of the Friends of the Library, the financial aid officer of Lucia's alma mater, the head of docents at a neighborhood museum, a man who identified himself as the president of We Adore Snaildarters Today and Evermore—otherwise known as WASTE—seeking a contribution to save this endangered species of fish.

And finally, as Lucia was turning back the covers on her bed, a call came from her parents. "We read about you in the paper," her father declared. "Princess, this stuff about Atlantic City—is it true?"

"I'm afraid so," Lucia said as she sprawled out on the mattress. "It's also true that last night was the first time I've ever been to a casino. And the last time, too."

"Don't say that, honey," her father argued. "You've obviously got the Midas touch."

Evidently some things weren't hereditary, Lucia thought sourly. "Look, Dad, I'm absolutely wiped out. I hardly got any sleep last night, and—"

"Okay, I won't keep you," he said, his tone implying that he had every intention of keeping her. He cleared his throat. "Lucia, princess, I don't want to pressure you or anything. I mean, the money is yours, and yours alone. But I just wanted to let you know that if you're looking for a good investment, I've got a sure winner for you."

"What?" she asked apprehensively.

"Juggling skunks. Listen to me, Lucia—I've seen the act. It's great. You wouldn't believe what these animals can do with their tails."

"One thing they can do is spray butyl mercaptan at anyone who messes with them," she responded. "Although recent studies dispute—"

"These are de-scented skunks," her father interrupted her. "Let me tell you something, princess. You take the stink out of the skunk and you've got a lovable critter. I met this fellow who's trained his skunks to juggle Ping-Pong balls. As soon as they can master bowling pins, we're going into business together. We're talking television, Lucia, *The Tonight Show*. This is the big time, Lucia. This time I know what I'm doing."

"No, Dad," she declared firmly. "No, not juggling skunks. The money's in the bank, and that's where it's going to stay for the time being." She exhaled. "Is Mom there? I'd like to talk to her."

"Of course, princess. Of course. But think about the skunks, honey, okay? Just think about it."

"I will," she relented. "Put Mom on, okay?"

She listened to the phone changing hands, and then her mother came on the line. "Lucia, honey, we're very happy for you," she said.

"Mom, what's this garbage about juggling skunks? What the hell is he up to now?"

Her mother paused before replying. "Everything's fine, dear," she said, exercising tact. "I've got a nice job doing inventory at Hastings department store. We aren't going under."

"Mom, I'd be delighted to give you some money if you need it," Lucia said earnestly. "But I'm not going to give you money if Dad's going to pour it into some ludicrous juggling-skunk business."

"I understand," her mother murmured. "You just keep the money for yourself. It's yours to do with as you wish. It's just that your father's very excited about this new enterprise, and, well, you know."

"I know," Lucia commented sadly. "Take care, Mom, and hold on to that inventory job. You're going to need it."

"Okay, sweetheart. I'd better get off. We don't want to run up a big phone bill."

"I'll call you soon," Lucia promised. "I love you both." She hung up and moaned. Juggling skunks? She ought to put her father in touch with the man from WASTE. She was certain they'd hit it off.

She slept soundly that night, which was fortunate, because she needed every ounce of strength in her body to survive the following day. She barely had a moment to herself at work. Even when she went to the bathroom, Joyce Dailey from Personnel tracked her down and shouted through the locked stall door that she was so glad Lucia had won the Shangri-la Super Jackpot, and that her cat needed to be declawed, if Lucia might be able to spare a few dollars. Her furniture was torn to shreds, Joyce lamented. Perhaps, if she herself footed the veterinarian bills, Lucia might want to lend her some money to buy a new sofa for her den.

There was Joyce in the bathroom; Hank Slovania in the lunchroom, who simply had to give her his best wishes and chew her ear off about how his wife was threatening to leave him if he didn't buy her a pearl choker for Mother's Day; Walter Chass in the lounge, who hinted loudly that the coffee maker had seen better days, and it sure would be swell if someone who could afford it would donate a new machine to the company; and Rhonda Toomey, who insisted that her daughter's buckteeth were much worse than Barry Simon's son's, and did Lucia have any idea what orthodontists charged these days?

Lucia counted the seconds until she could leave for home. However, her apartment proved to be anything but a safe haven. Her mailbox was crammed with dozens of letters from societies, clubs, individuals, each with a pathetic story to tell and a vow that her money would be put to good use if she chose to contribute to their cause. And the telephone rang until Lucia's skull throbbed, each caller ebulliently outlining some wonderful project or moral purpose that required an infusion of funds from a benefactor, if Lucia might be interested.

She tried to maintain her sanity by organizing herself. She sorted the letters into three piles: legitimate charities, questionable charities and individual requests for money. She also kept an up-to-date list of each telephone call, the time, the caller's name, the agency or program the caller represented. By Thursday evening, three days after she'd won the jackpot, her stacks of letters had climbed to an altitude of nearly a foot apiece, and her list of phone calls extended to four legal-size pages.

Lucia was exhausted. Charities she'd previously considered valid and worthwhile fell from favor when they sent her pleading letters full of heartrending claptrap about how fine they were and how much needed to be done. Whooping cranes still faced extinction, Lucia was told in one letter. Children still suffered from kwashiorkor, she learned from another. The Chinese-American Chess Exchange could promote world peace, she was informed, if only they could afford to buy artistic chess sets instead of having to rely on chintzy plastic sets. Also in a position to promote world peace were the Inter-European Council on Drug Use, the Society for the Prevention of Eminent Domain, and the Tooth Fairy League. If only Lucia would care to help them in their struggles....

The ringing of her telephone drew her attention from the letter she'd been reading, which described the recent efforts of the Society to Reinstate Latin in Public Schools. She stacked it onto the questionable-charities file and went to her bedroom to answer the telephone. "What?" she answered churlishly. She was much too fatigued to be polite to yet another caller with yet another tear-jerking tale to tell.

"Lucia?" a shockingly familiar baritone greeted her ears. "Lucia Bowen?"

She sat upright and tried to ignore what had become a chronic three-day headache. "Who is this?" she asked.

"Malcolm Royce. Am I speaking to Lucia Bowen?"

"Malcolm?" She closed her eyes and offered a silent prayer that he, of all people, didn't have a son in desperate need of braces or a lawn mower on the blink. Somehow, she knew intuitively that he'd never ask for money to attend therapy sessions at the Masters and Johnson clinic.

"Are you all right, Lucia?" he asked. "You sound wretched."

She sighed, then attempted a faint chuckle. "I *am* wretched," she confirmed. Her chuckle erupted into a full-fledged laugh as she realized how absurd her life had become in the past few days. "No, Malcolm, I'm all right," she reassured him. "Just a little frazzled."

"Oh?"

"Malcolm..." She suddenly felt an urge to unburden herself, to share her ridiculous predicament with someone she believed would understand. Malcolm would understand. She didn't know why she was sure of that, but she felt it in her heart. He'd understand. "Malcolm, I have been harassed for three long days by fund-raisers and lunatics. They all want a piece of my winnings. I'm going crazy, Malcolm. You're the ninth caller tonight. I was afraid you were another lunatic wanting to tell me about how you're an agent for the Society to Rid the World of Plantar Warts, and you need some money for television advertising."

Malcolm's silence disarmed her. Maybe he didn't understand. "Has it been that bad?" he finally asked. The husky quality of his voice, so gentle and generous, informed her that he did understand, after all.

"It's been worse than that," she told him. "Whoever printed my address on the front page of the Newark newspaper deserves to be drawn and quartered."

"I'm sorry you've had such a rough time," he remarked softly. "I was hoping that you'd have a few days to reflect in peace before I contacted you. I was concerned about your doing something rash with your winnings before you'd had the opportunity to think things through."

"Why should it matter to you?" she asked, sounding less accusing than puzzled.

"Because I—" he hesitated "—because I like you."

"You hardly know me," she pointed out, feeling a strange rush of warmth fill her.

"I'd like to get to know you," he told her. "I'll be finishing up in Atlantic City tomorrow, and I thought it would be nice if we could have dinner together in the evening. Are you by any chance free?"

Her mind detoured briefly to the string of unwanted dinner invitations she'd received from Rick Lansing at work. As far as he was concerned, she'd never be free.

But for Malcolm... "Yes, I'm free," she heard herself say.

"Good." His pleasure was obvious in his hushed yet certain voice. The single word expressed more than all of Rick's palaver about her lovely eyes.

"What were you planning?" she asked.

"Well, either I can come to your place or you can come down here. I should be finished with my work by around six o'clock, and then after I freshen up...I guess I couldn't get to your apartment before eight-thirty or so. Would that be too late?"

Lucia considered. The way her life had been proceeding lately, she'd probably be ready to hit the sack by ten. "It might be," she warned him.

"The other option is that you can come down to the hotel," he outlined for her. "I'd be available by six-thirty, if you could get here by then. If you'd like, I can arrange to have a limo pick you up."

"A limo?" Lucia considered his offer, then rejected it. All she needed was for someone to see her traveling in a limousine, and she'd be inundated by a zillion more requests for money. "No, Malcolm, I can drive down there."

Malcolm was insistent. "Let me send a car for you, Lucia. I'm enough of a gentleman to think I ought to provide the transportation when I invite a woman to dinner."

Lucia reconsidered the idea. If she herself drove to Atlantic City, she'd have to drive back home again. Either she'd have to endure two long hours of driving at some ungodly hour, or else she'd have to end their evening early in order to remain alert during the trip home. If Malcolm sent a limousine, she could sleep in the backseat and let the driver worry about remaining alert.

"Okay," she conceded. "Send a limo. What the heck. I'm a quarter of a millionaire."

"That's the spirit," he concurred. "What time do you want to be picked up?"

Lucia shut her eyes and did some mental arithmetic. If she left work on time, went home, showered and changed, she wouldn't be ready until five-thirty at the earliest. With two hours of driving time added to that, she wouldn't be arriving in Atlantic City before seven-thirty, which might be a stylish hour for dinner, but was awfully late for someone as practical as Lucia. "I tell you what," she mused aloud. "Have the car come for me at five. I'll take off from work early."

"Good idea. Take off early," said Malcolm, then playfully repeated, "What the heck, you're a quarter of a millionaire." Lucia shared a laugh with him. "There's a fine restaurant on the top floor of the Shangri-la," he told her. "Good food, and as far from the casino as we can get. Would that be okay with you?"

"Sure. Dressy?" she asked him.

"Reasonably."

"As dressy as the Baccarat Room?" she asked, recalling how debonair he'd looked in his formal attire.

He chuckled. "Not that dressy. I won't be wearing a tux." His laughter waned. "I'm glad you're coming, Lucia. I can't think of anyone I'd rather spend my last night in Atlantic City with than you."

"I'll see you tomorrow," Lucia said before bidding him goodbye. She hung up the phone, stared at it for a minute, and then returned to the living room, where she gathered up that day's mail and sorted it out on the coffee table. Malcolm's parting words resounded inside her as she went back to her bedroom and prepared for bed. If he was leaving Atlantic City on Saturday, she might

never see him again after tomorrow. There was no room
for a relationship between them, she acknowledged, nor
much reason to believe that one could exist, even if he
remained in New Jersey. He seemed so different from
her, so worldly, so sophisticated, so self-assured...so
different.

But he wanted to spend his last night in Atlantic City
with her. That was enough for Lucia, enough for now.
He wanted to spend his last night with her. And, she admitted with her first genuine smile in days, she wanted to
spend his last night in Atlantic City with him, too.

IT HAD BEEN AN EXHAUSTING WEEK for him, but sleep
eluded Malcolm as he sprawled out on the king-size bed
in his suite and reran his telephone conversation with
Lucia for the umpteenth time. He had endured an incredibly taxing week: daytimes spent plowing through
computerized records, hound-dog sniffing in search of
waste, vehement arguments with Devane and the ac-
counting staff over billing procedures and unlabeled expenditures. Malcolm had endured working breakfasts,
working lunches, working dinners. The realization that
tomorrow night he would have a pleasurable dinner
elated him.

But as tiring as his week had been, Lucia's had apparently been worse. Malcolm had been dismayed, upon returning to the hotel at nearly 3:00 A.M. Tuesday, to be
informed by Devane that the Shangri-la had already released information about Lucia's jackpot win to the wire
services. "We didn't use our photos," Devane had explained. "Turns out one of the casino guests was a re-
porter for the Newark *Star-Ledger*, and he got some good
on-the-spot photographs. We decided to cut him a break
and use his material instead. Hey, Mr. Royce, you know

we've got to exploit this situation for all it's worth if we want to draw customers.''

Malcolm understood that well enough. But he hated the possibility that Lucia herself was being exploited along with the situation. When he'd seen the write-up in the paper later that morning, complete with her address, he'd been incensed.

Still, he'd contained his anger. It was part of his job to encourage Devane to promote the casino in any way he could. Lucia would simply have to cope with her position. Malcolm had resisted calling her until Thursday night, hoping that, by then, she'd have recovered from her shock and grown accustomed to her new status as a famous jackpot winner.

But the Society to Rid the World of Plantar Warts? He hadn't thought it would be that bad.

If Lucia wasn't cut out for wealth, she was even less cut out for publicity of this sort. Someone else—someone like Polly, for instance—would adore the notoriety. Sinking into the pillow, Malcolm recalled Lucia's dazed attempt to make herself presentable for the casino's photographer. Polly would have swept regally into the bathroom and emerged, a half hour later, looking like a cover girl, her face exquisitely painted and her hair perfectly coiffed. But that was Polly's nature. She was obsessed with appearances, with surfaces.

At one time Malcolm had found such an obsession peculiarly fascinating, but not anymore. After three years of marriage he'd come to loathe it. He'd come to despise attending elegant galas with Polly on his arm and listening to people tell him how lovely she looked, how lucky he was to have a wife like her, how envious they were that he got to make love to such a spellbinding woman every night. That he wasn't the only man making love to her had been the least of his problems.

But he didn't want to think about Polly. At long last she was receding from his world—fewer desperate telephone calls, fewer pleas for money, fewer tear-drenched conversations about how she needed him, how sorry she was, how, if he'd give her another chance, she'd be a better wife. Polly was gradually fading from his life, and he didn't want to think about her.

He wanted to think about the woman with the exotic name, with the wry sense of humor and the honest eyes, the woman who was so unsophisticated that she'd rather give her money away than invest it. He wanted to think about a woman who was disgustingly noble, who preferred simplicity to shrewdness. A woman like Lucia could do wonders to restore Malcolm's trust and eradicate his cynicism. He needed someone like her in his life.

He didn't know how his date with her the following night would go, whether they'd be comfortable enough with each other for him to explain his feelings to her. He didn't want to scare her away, and she seemed like the kind of person who could easily be frightened. He'd play it by ear, see how things proceeded, see what happened.

He suspected that she trusted him, at least subliminally. But after the harassment she'd received from plantar warts people and the like, she might be less apt to expose herself to Malcolm and to accept him. There was so much he wanted to tell her and to share with her, but he'd have to hold back. She'd been overwhelmed enough this week.

He'd play it cool to start, keep things light until he knew she was ready for him. They'd talk about what her life had been like since winning the jackpot—and perhaps she'd laugh about it. Maybe he could discuss with her the fact that she should consider all her options before ridding herself of the burden of her money. He could tell her about various investments and show her that she could be both intelligent and disgustingly noble when it came to dispersing her cash. Yes, that was the approach he'd take—friendly, concerned, willing to help.

And then, if he saw the glow in her eyes, the glow he'd seen in the casino that first night...if he was certain that she was receptive not only to his dispassionate counsel but to his passionate self, he'd tell her that he needed her and that he wanted her. Then he'd show her that she could trust him completely.

Chapter Four

Lucia used her Friday lunch hour to shop. She didn't own a "reasonably dressy" dress to wear with Malcolm, at least not one newer than three years old. It was high time for her to buy something new. She could afford it.

Not that she was going on a spree, she assured herself as she drove to the nearest shopping mall and found a parking space near an exclusive boutique. One new dress did not a spree make. Not a real spree, anyway. She wasn't just buying to buy; she was being practical.

When she glimpsed a few of the price tags dangling from the sleeves of the dresses in the boutique, she paused to wonder whether shopping in that particular store was practical at all. But, once again, she reminded herself that she could afford the shop's outrageous prices, and she resolved to buy something there and suffer no qualms about it. Surely, spending money on herself was as valid as donating money to the Tooth Fairy League.

She pulled a few dresses from a rack and carried them into the fitting room. She felt oddly self-conscious about trying on such expensive garments. When Lucia was a child, her wardrobe had consisted primarily of hand-me-downs from her sister. Only on those rare occasions when her father was between bankruptcies would her mother buy her something new—on sale, of course. "We probably won't have the money to buy it next week," her mother would whisper conspiratorially. "So let's buy it now, before the bills from your father's mail-order business come due."

Shaking off the memory, Lucia studied her reflection in the mirror. The dress she had on was a simple sheath of peach-colored silk, with spaghetti straps, a blouson top and a straight skirt. Unable to give it a fair appraisal in the dimly lit booth, she left the fitting room for the three-way mirror at the rear of the shop. As she pirouetted before the hinged glass panels and tried futilely to glimpse herself from the back, a saleswoman hovered nearby, admiring her. "That dress looks fabulous on you," she murmured enviously. "I wish I had a figure like yours."

"I'm too skinny," Lucia complained, wondering if her exposed shoulders appeared bony in the dress, and if her chest appeared underendowed.

"Who was it who said that it's impossible to be too thin or too rich?" the saleswoman wondered aloud.

Whoever it was, she was wrong, Lucia mused, giving her repeating reflection a critical inspection. She was both—too thin and too rich. But the dress was lovely, and if she'd bothered to keep up with fashions, she probably would have known that bony shoulders were currently considered stylish.

Glancing at the price tag, she winced. To consider that spending such a staggering amount on a single dress was practical was as ludicrous as to claim that spending eighteen dollars on a junket to Atlantic City was profitable, as Evvie had maintained. Lucia reluctantly granted that that junket *had* turned out to be profitable, but that didn't negate the fact that the peach silk dress was obscenely overpriced. Lucia moved back to the dressing room, slipped out of the dress and hung it on its hanger, determined to make her purchase at some store that specialized in reasonable prices.

She slipped her own skirt over her head, and as she adjusted it around her waist, her gaze settled on the dress again. It really was attractive, she thought. And she wanted to wear something special tonight, something special for Malcolm, who claimed that he liked her and that her soul made her beautiful.

All right, she resolved. Just this once she wouldn't be practical. Just this once she'd splurge a little. Feeling surprisingly carefree, she swung out of the dressing room and brought the silk dress to the counter.

Once she'd paid for it, she realized that she would need new shoes and a purse to go with it. She strolled through the mall and entered a shoe store. One hundred dollars later, she was the proud owner of a pair of delicate white leather sandals with sinfully high heels, and an envelope purse to match.

"That's it for sprees," she scolded herself as she locked her purchases in the trunk of her car and headed back to the research center. "That's absolutely it for extravagance, practical or otherwise. Any more shopping expeditions like this, and I won't have enough money left to pay Josephine Taggart's fare to the Masters and Johnson clinic." Chuckling, she parked in the employee lot and dashed inside, eager to get a chemical reaction set up in her laboratory right away, so she'd be able to leave work early.

The spate of begging on the part of Lucia's colleagues at work had slowed to a trickle, much to her relief. Joyce Dailey found a way to bring her cat's claws into every conversation she had with Lucia, and Tom made more than enough comments regarding what his neighbors would say about the scraggly condition of his front yard if he didn't get a new lawn mower soon, but for the most part, Lucia's coworkers left her in peace.

Except for Rick Lansing. He showed up at her lab at four-fifteen, just as she was packing up for the day. "A little early to be leaving, isn't it?" he commented, gliding into the room.

Lucia turned from her desk and grinned. "A little, yes, but I've got an early date tonight, and I've got to go home and get ready. I'm leaving my hood on over the weekend, Rick. Make sure you tell the security staff. I don't want some bozo switching off the exhaust over the weekend."

"No, we can't have that," Rick agreed, wandering to her hood, a ventilated workbench where most of her experiments were run. The hood's pumps drew fumes into a purification system, and its impermeable walls offered some protection against explosions.

Rick examined the reaction she'd set up, searching for a safety violation to carp about. Finding none, he turned and watched Lucia remove her lab glasses and massage the bridge of her nose. "An early date, huh?" he said.

"That's right."

"Maybe you and I could have a late date."

"Sorry." Lucia ran her gaze up Rick's athletic body to his blandly attractive face. "When are you going to give up?" she asked sweetly.

"Never," Rick swore.

Lucia laughed. "What if I told you I gave all my gambling winnings to the Chinese-American Chess Exchange, so they could buy new chess sets? What if I told you, Rick, that I'd sent the entire jackpot to Grand

Master Liu of Beijing and Grand Master Bandolini of Woonsocket, Rhode Island, in order for them to promote world peace through chess? Would you still want to have a late date with me?''

Rick eyed her dubiously, then scowled in indignation. "Lucia, do you think I've taken an interest in you because of your money?''

"As a matter of fact, yes," she replied with a serene smile.

"Well, you're wrong," he maintained, striding toward her. He clasped her elbows in his hands and studied her intently. "You—you haven't given all your money to some Grand Master in Woonsocket, have you?'' he asked.

Lucia succumbed to another laugh. "Gotta run, Rick," she said as she latched her briefcase and headed for the door. "Have a good weekend."

She hoped that Rick would give up on her in time. The rest of her fellow workers at Parker Chemicals had more or less stopped trying to get their hands on her money. In time Rick would, too. As she braked to a halt in front of her apartment building and removed her purchases from her trunk, she laughed at his obviousness. How in the world could he win the affections of the secretaries in the patent department, she wondered. He really was an idiot, his purportedly sexy smile and bedroom eyes notwithstanding.

Inside the building's vestibule, Lucia unlocked her mailbox and jumped back a step as the expected volume of envelopes spilled out. She scooped them up from the floor and flipped through them. Nothing important, nothing personal. Just another fourteen pleas for money. She sighed and carried the letters upstairs to her apartment.

She showered, washed her hair and then dressed in her new outfit. Examining her reflection in her bedroom mirror, she wasn't certain at first whether she liked the dress as much at home as she had in the boutique. She twisted this way and that, readjusted the narrow shoulder straps and fluffed out the bodice. Yes, she decided, she *did* like it. As much. Maybe more. She simply wasn't accustomed to seeing herself looking so elegant. But now that she was a jackpot winner, a bit of elegance on her part wouldn't hurt, especially during a date with an elegant man like Malcolm.

The sandals looked perfect with the dress, as did her gold-stud earrings and the S-linked necklace her sister had given her for her birthday a few years back. She twisted her hair in a variety of ways before deciding to let it hang loose. There were limits to how sophisticated she could possibly look, she decided. At least her hair was clean and glossy as it dropped in loose waves down her back.

She opened that afternoon's delivery of supplications while she waited for the limousine to arrive, reading each letter before she stacked it on one of her three piles. As she was stuffing the last one into its envelope, the chauffeur rang for her.

Relaxing in the roomy back seat of the limousine, gazing out the window at the traffic and listening to the soft classical music the chauffeur had turned on for her, Lucia offered thanks to Malcolm for having talked her into taking the limo. She didn't quite feel like herself, dressed as she was and traveling in such a classy vehicle, but she couldn't deny that she was enjoying the experience. She wouldn't want to make a habit of it, but just this once the glamour surrounding her seemed appropriate.

Nestling deep into the seat's cushions, Lucia thought about the last time she'd ridden in a limousine—the only other time in her life she'd ridden in a limousine. Malcolm had been beside her then, exuding his disturbing warmth, sending her indecipherable messages with his stunning eyes. Agreeing to spend the evening with him was at least as uncharacteristic for Lucia as was wearing a silk dress. Maybe she'd been impulsive in accepting his invitation. Maybe their evening together would be horrible…or worse, maybe it would be spectacular, and then tomorrow he'd be gone, out of her life forever.

He'd sounded so friendly on the telephone the night before that Lucia hadn't hesitated in accepting his invitation. But now, without the challenges of driving in the rush hour to distract her, she had the opportunity to question the wisdom of meeting him for dinner. What if he was after her money? What if he wanted to seduce her? She knew nothing about him, except that he worked for some investment firm named Advent and that he didn't suffer from athlete's foot. The more she considered it, the more she realized that she was taking an enormous chance in spending the evening with him.

But the last time she'd taken a chance, on an impulse, without stopping to think about it, she'd wound up getting a whopping return on her investment. What had her father said the other night on the telephone? She had the Midas touch. The gamble she'd chosen to take with Malcolm this evening might be riskier to her than stuffing silver dollars into a slot machine, but…maybe she'd get lucky again.

The limousine reached the underground garage of the Shangri-la Hotel and Casino fifteen minutes late. The chauffeur chivalrously accompanied Lucia to the elevator and pressed the first-floor button for her, once she'd stepped inside the car. The elevator doors slid shut before she could thank him, and she was whisked up to the lobby.

As soon as she emerged from the elevator, she spotted Malcolm ambling across the thick blue carpeting toward her. He wore a superbly tailored suit of lightweight gray wool that picked up the gray hue of his eyes. His eyes shimmered with delight as he neared her, and his smile expanded, cutting attractive dimples into his cheeks. "Hello," he said, drawing to a halt beside her.

"Hello, Malcolm," she greeted him shyly.

He gazed at her for several seconds, evidently trying to decide whether to kiss her. He chose not to and, instead, took her hand in his. He started to shake it, then stopped awkwardly. Lucia wondered whether he was as aware as she was of the swift reawakening of the erotic energy that had connected them the last time they'd been together. Suddenly, an amiable handshake didn't seem suitable. So he only held her hand. "How was your trip down?" he asked politely.

"Fine," Lucia replied. Staring into his multicolored eyes, she forgot about the doubt and apprehension she'd entertained during the drive. She forgot about everything but the electricity that sparked between them, the fiery charge of energy that drew them together. "Were you waiting in the lobby a long time? We got held up in rush-hour traffic and ran a little late," she apologized.

Malcolm smiled. "The chauffeur contacted the front desk on his mobile phone as soon as he crossed the bridge, and the clerk reported your E.T.A. to me."

"Nifty," Lucia commented, impressed. Obviously, she still had a lot to learn about limousines.

Malcolm signaled for the elevator and ushered her inside once it arrived. His eyes roamed down her body and his smile deepened. "That's a very nice dress," he said to her. "You look beautiful."

She suffered a twinge of nervousness at his use of the word "beautiful." "You know, you were right, Malcolm," she declared as the car ascended to the hotel's penthouse floor. "I've recently learned that some men think money makes a woman beautiful."

"Oh?" He angled his head quizzically. "Should I be jealous?"

"Jealous?"

"That other men are calling you beautiful."

She grinned and shook her head. "I didn't tell you that to make you jealous," she explained. "I only told you so you'd know that the minute you call me beautiful, my defenses rise."

"Ah." His smile mirrored hers. "In that case, I'll steer clear of the term. The last thing I want to do is to make your defenses rise."

His remark made her defenses rise even higher, but she bit her lip and fought off her uneasiness. She remained silent until the elevator door opened onto the restaurant on the roof of the building. Lucia's tension disappeared completely as she scanned the dining room, which was protected from the elements by a dome of glass. The early moon, the fading daylight, the dark ocean and the glittering lights of other casinos along the boardwalk were fully visible through the dome. "Wow," she whispered. "This is incredible."

Malcolm smiled and slipped her hand through the bend in his elbow as the dining room's host approached them. Malcolm gave his name, and the host led them to their reserved table alongside the glass wall overlooking the water. The ocean appeared both gray and green, with flashes of phosphorescence giving it an unreal luminescence. Gray and green and glittering with life, like Malcolm's eyes, Lucia mused, momentarily transfixed by the glorious view.

The waiter's arrival to take their drink orders forced Lucia's attention from the window. "Why don't we get a bottle of wine?" Malcolm asked.

"Fine."

"Do you like champagne?"

Lucia smiled and shook her head. "Not really," she admitted. "The bubbles tickle my nose. They make me want to sneeze."

Malcolm seemed amused. "We'll have a Médoc," he told the waiter, who nodded, set two menus on the table and departed.

Lucia wanted to ask him what sort of wine Médoc was. All she knew about wine was that the yellow variety was called white and the maroon variety was called red, and that dry wine was wet and sweet wine was sickening. She wondered whether as a newly wealthy woman it was her duty to learn about wines. She wondered whether Malcolm's knowledge of wines marked him as a man of wealth.

Possibly; possibly not. What it marked him as, she decided, once the waiter had served the wine, was a man of good taste. "This is delicious," she praised the crisp red wine after taking an experimental sip.

"And no bubbles," Malcolm added, lifting his crystal goblet to hers.

"What are we toasting?" she asked. "The fact that you're all done auditing this joint?"

"That would be a reasonable toast," Malcolm granted. "But I'd rather toast your jackpot. You never really drank a toast the night it happened."

Lucia's smile waned slightly. "I'm not sure that's worth toasting," she grumbled, though the wine was so tasty she couldn't resist sipping some anyway.

"Has it been that bad?" Malcolm asked, leaning back in his chair and studying her. The single pink rose in the bud vase in the center of the table obscured his view of Lucia, and he nudged it to one side. "Lots of mercenary men coming on to you?"

"That's the least of it," Lucia groaned. "Just today, for instance—" She cut herself off with a sheepish grin. "Maybe we ought to order first."

Intrigued, Malcolm passed her one menu and opened the other. Lucia scanned its calligraphic listings and tried to remain nonchalant as she noted the prices. In the context of this restaurant, her new dress seemed a veritable bargain. When the waiter returned, she ordered veal cordon bleu, and Malcolm requested medallions of beef. The waiter nodded and left with their menus.

Malcolm fingered his wineglass for a moment, then drank, his eyes never leaving Lucia. "Now tell me," he coaxed her. "Today, for instance?"

"Today, for instance," Lucia obliged, "I received fourteen letters from people asking me for money. Let's see, there was the Association for Pigeon Banishment— A.P.B., and the Acne Cure and Medication Experiment—ACME, and, oh yes, the Bronx-Brooklyn Governance for Unity and Nurture—B.B.GUN. Acronyms are very popular in the nonprofit-organization world." She sipped her wine and sighed. "Actually, one of the letters I got today piqued my interest. It was from an outfit named CEPTA—the Committee to End Pay Toilets in America. Now that's a cause I can believe in."

Malcolm laughed. His laughter was contagious, and she succumbed to a chuckle. "CEPTA," he murmured, shoving a drooping lock of hair back from his face. "I love it. Who do I make the check out to?"

"I know it sounds funny, Malcolm," Lucia conceded. "But believe me, after a few days it becomes pretty irritating. The letters are bad enough. The phone calls are worse. 'Hi, I'm Clarabelle Clunk from Nix-Mizz,'" she recited in a nasal voice. "'Would you be willing to donate to our worthwhile cause?'"

"Nix-mizz?" Malcolm echoed, bewildered.

"They're a group trying to get rid of 'Ms'. Not the magazine, the title. Apparently they feel they need fifty thousand dollars so they can take out full-page ads in all the major newspapers, explaining why the word 'Ms' is hard on the ear and potentially damaging to the sinuses. They want me to contribute."

The waiter delivered their salads. Malcolm waited until he and Lucia were alone again before speaking. "What have you done with your money so far?"

"It's in the bank."

He weighed that information, then nodded. "I suppose it's safe there for now."

"What do you mean, 'for now'?" Lucia asked, her eyes glowing mirthfully. "Did you invite me down here so you could give me a spiel about your investment company?"

"No," Malcolm replied. "Of course not. But—" he tendered a hesitant smile "—you're losing out if you leave your money in a savings account. You're earning the lowest possible interest there."

"Which suits me just fine," Lucia countered. She tasted the endive salad and smiled. Having skipped lunch to go shopping that afternoon, she was quite hungry now. She devoured her salad, then lifted her eyes to Malcolm, who had ignored his salad in order to watch her eat. Her cheeks colored as she considered how gluttonous she must have seemed to him. "I'm famished," she explained herself with a contrite grin.

"Don't apologize," Malcolm murmured. "I love a woman who can eat with gusto." He consumed the remainder of his wine and refilled his glass. "Why do you hate money, Lucia?"

"I don't hate money," she argued, but her voice lacked conviction. Malcolm's smile faded, and his unnerving eyes bore down on her until she felt compelled to tell him the truth. "Okay, I *do* hate money. It's the root of all evil, isn't it?"

He continued to study her curiously, then shook his head. "No. Human beings are the root of all evil, Lucia. Money's just a tool by which we measure wealth. A ruler measures length, a scale measures weight and money measures wealth. That's all it is, a tool. There's nothing evil about it."

Lucia pondered his words. She forgot about how hungry she was, ignoring the waiter as he carried their entrées to the table and cleared away their salad dishes. A tool to measure wealth? Was that what money was? Lucia had never thought about it that way. To her, money had always been something her family either didn't have or hoped to have—or had and then lost. It was the fuel that drove her father, the curse that plagued her family: money—dreaming of it, getting it, losing it.

"How can you say money isn't evil?" she questioned Malcolm, eager for him to clarify himself. "Just go downstairs to the casino here and see what money does to all those dazed gamblers."

"Money doesn't do that to them," he disputed her in a soft, steady voice. "They do it to themselves. Their greed does it. Their laziness."

"Laziness?"

"Sure. They want wealth, but they don't want to go to the trouble of earning it. So they gamble. They hope it'll come easily and painlessly to them. The majority of them are probably thinking about how, just last Monday night, a central Jersey women walked off with a quarter of a million dollars on a single bet. If she could do it, it must be easy. They want money the easy way, so they gamble for it."

"But Malcolm—" Lucia floundered for a moment, trying to sort her thoughts "—you said you were a bigger gambler than the people in the casinos," she reminded him. "Your firm gambles when it arranges investments."

"Yes, but those gambles aren't easy. They aren't blind. We aren't banking on luck. Instead, we inform ourselves about the market, we make projections, we forecast trends. We don't toss money into a slot machine, Lucia. We make careful evaluations. We'd never invest our clients' funds in any game where the odds are skewed against the player."

He sliced a bite of steak and speared it with his fork, then paused before eating it. "I'll tell you something," he added. "If those gamblers downstairs took the money they were planning to blow in the casino—whether it's five dollars in quarters or five thousand in chips—if they took that money and gave it to a firm like Advent to invest for them, they'd come out way ahead. But that might not be easy enough for them. It might take patience; they might have to wait for the market to recover from a temporary downturn, or for a bond to reach maturity. They don't want that. They want the excitement, the Super-Jackpot siren, the thrill of believing that they've been blessed with good luck."

Lucia was enthralled by his speech. "You've thought this out pretty thoroughly, haven't you," she observed.

"I've had to," he said. "It's part of my job."

She ate in silence for a while, reflecting not only on what he'd said but on the understated passion in his speech. She wondered why he cared so much about converting her to his view of money as something benign. "So it's human nature, then," she murmured as she set down her silverware.

He refilled her goblet with wine. "What's human nature?" he asked.

"The root of all evil," she explained before sipping her wine. "All I know is, I've never met an evil person, but I've met a lot of people who've been made insane by money. They lose their rationality at the mention of it. They lose their perspective, their sense of self-preservation. Maybe money isn't evil, but it's toxic. It does terrible things to people."

Malcolm folded his hands before him on the linen tablecloth and gazed into Lucia's eyes. "Who?" he asked. "What people?"

She absorbed the sharp, clean lines of his face, the powerful angle of his jaw, the sensuous firmness of his lips, the welcoming light of his eyes. He seemed so earnest, so genuinely interested, that she heard herself reply, "My father. My father and my mother and my sister. None of them are evil, Malcolm. They're just weak, too weak to resist the lure of money."

Revealing the truth about her family was not what Lucia had intended to do during her dinner with Malcolm, and when she realized what she'd said, she cringed. Her hands instinctively tensed on the table. Malcolm reached for one and ran his fingers over her knuckles. "And you're strong?" he asked.

At that moment, with his thumb massaging the back of her hand, she didn't feel strong at all. She felt her muscles weakening, her flesh softening. Disconcerted by the sensation, she slipped her hand from his and hid it in her lap. Malcolm didn't comment on her rebuff. He simply left his hand lying on the table between them, inviting her to take it if she changed her mind.

"I'd like to think I'm strong," she whispered, wondering on how many levels he would take her statement.

"Because you want to give the money away instead of making it work for you? That doesn't seem strong to me, Lucia."

"All right." She laughed nervously. "You said you had some brochures. I'd be delighted to read them. Right this minute, if you'd like. You don't happen to have them in your hip pocket, do you?"

"They're upstairs in my room. We can get them later." Her failure to return her hand to his was clearly beginning to frustrate him, because he started to fidget with his dessert spoon. "The brochures aren't important right now, Lucia. I—I'm still trying to get to know you, trying to understand you. That's what's important."

"Oh?" She dared to lift her eyes to his and found him studying her with acute fascination. She couldn't deny being flattered by his interest, but it didn't make sense to her. He was a suave, sophisticated man, someone who clearly knew what he was about and what he wanted. She was, in a nutshell, "Central Jersey Woman Wins Record Jackpot." "Why?" she asked, realizing the question wasn't tactful, but figuring that since this date was probably a one-shot deal, she didn't have much to lose by being blunt.

"Why?" Her lack of finesse amused him. His mouth arched into its dazzling, dimpled smile as he settled back in his chair and tilted his head to appraise her. "Because I've been thinking about you for days now. I knew you were special from the moment you started making eyes at me in the casino."

"Me?" Lucia objected. "Making eyes at *you*? Let me set you straight, Malcolm. *You* made eyes at *me*."

A deep, velvety laugh filtered up from his chest, and he shook his head. "You found me before I found you," he maintained. "But it's not worth arguing over." Reading her disgruntlement, he laughed again. "All right," he relented. "Whoever made eyes at whomever... When I spotted you leaning on the railing by the Baccarat Room, well, you looked totally out of place in the casino. It was amazing to see someone like you, so fresh, so natural, so... so wholesome." Lucia burst into laughter at that description, but Malcolm only smiled. "I wanted to talk to you, but then you ran away, and the next thing I knew you were being buried under a blizzard of jackpot dollars. And at that point—" his eyes glazed with memory, and he chuckled "—you looked dangerously ill, and I knew you needed someone to get you out of the casino before you threw up."

Lucia shared his memory and grinned. "In all honesty, I wasn't sure whether I was going to throw up or pass out," she related. "Both seemed like possibilities at the time."

Malcolm nodded, still reminiscing. The waiter cleared the table, then wheeled over a tea cart of pastries. Lucia and Malcolm accepted coffee and skipped dessert. The dinner itself had been filling enough.

He waited until they were alone before speaking again. "Lucia, when I saw how you were reacting to your big win... Anyone else would have been thrilled, giddy, crazy with joy. I've never met a woman who seems to loathe money the way you do. You pique my interest. You really do." He reached for his coffee and smiled. "And then, to top it off, you're really quite beautiful. Especially tonight, when you don't look nauseated at all."

Lucia felt a touch of anxiety rear up inside her. Ever since Malcolm himself had warned her about how men considered rich women beautiful, she couldn't accept the word without suffering a pang of doubt. "I'm really not," she protested softly.

"I like your nose," Malcolm asserted. "I like your eyes and the fact that you wear no makeup. I like your hair, your figure, your hands. I'd like to be holding one right now."

"You're embarrassing me," Lucia mumbled.

"I'd like to kiss you," he continued, embarrassing Lucia even more. His voice was hushed but steady, not a hint of falseness in it. "I haven't stopped thinking about you since we met. I got your telephone number from Paul Devane on Tuesday morning, and the only reason I didn't phone you until yesterday evening was that I wanted to give you a couple of days to unwind. But when I realized that I'd be finished with my business here today, I knew I had to go ahead and call you. I'm very glad you were free on such short notice. I don't mean to embarrass you," he concluded.

"I am embarrassed," Lucia said, though she managed a timid smile.

He gazed at her, his eyes gentle, a soft, smoky gray as they coursed over her downturned face. "How about a stroll by the water?" he suggested. "It was raining the last time you were here, so you probably didn't get to take a walk on the boardwalk."

"Do I get to pass 'Go' and collect two hundred dollars?" Lucia quipped, alluding to the Monopoly game that had been designed around Atlantic City in its pre-casino incarnation.

"Not only don't you get to pass 'Go,'" Malcolm teased, "but you don't get to pass the Shangri-la Casino and risk collecting two hundred *thousand* dollars."

"In that case, I'd love to take a walk on the boardwalk," Lucia said.

Once Malcolm had signed the bill, they left the restaurant and rode the elevator down to the lobby. Ignoring the clamorous activity of the casino just beyond the desk, Malcolm tucked Lucia's hand into the crook of his arm and guided her outside the building. A broad driveway separated the hotel's oceanfront entrance from the boardwalk, and they wove between the cabs in the driveway to reach the plank walkway lining the beach.

The boardwalk was nearly vacant; evidently, most Atlantic City visitors were in town to enjoy the gambling rather than the seashore. It was almost too dark to see the ocean; a pale froth marked its rhythmic waves as they curled and broke against the sand. The air was heavy with the smell of the sea. Lucia filled her lungs with the distinctive fragrance and smiled.

They walked without speaking for a while, simply enjoying the mild May night, the sprinkle of stars overhead and the constant whisper of the tide. "Did you spend any time on the beach while you were here?" Lucia asked.

"I've been working all day, every day," Malcolm answered. "Business is business. This wasn't a vacation."

"Maybe now that you're done with your business, you can enjoy the beach tomorrow."

Malcolm shook his head. "I've got a home to go home to," he noted. "I've had my fill of Atlantic City for now."

"Where's home?" Lucia asked.

"Manhattan."

"Oh, that's not too far from—" *From where I live,* she nearly said, but caught herself in time. In spite of Malcolm's lavish compliments upstairs in the restaurant, Lucia didn't want to sound overly excited about the possibility of seeing him again after tonight. "That's not too far from here," she said. "You can always come back some other time if you want to go swimming."

A brisk breeze gusted off the water and tangled Lucia's hair. She turned from the ocean and ran her fingers through her glossy brown locks, pushing them back from her face. Without awaiting permission, Malcolm assisted her, sliding his hands to her temples, fanning his fingers along the sides of her head and digging his fingertips into her wind-tossed hair. "I still want to kiss you," he murmured, running his thumbs along her hairline.

She felt the dark rush of yearning that she knew would come whenever he touched her, whenever he looked at her a certain way, the way he was looking at her now. His eyes were a little less gentle, a little more golden than gray, searching her face, questioning. Lucia didn't know what to say. All she knew was that she wanted to kiss him, too.

He lowered his mouth, and the light touch of his lips against hers was enough to deluge her with the fierce, hot fullness of her desire for him. Her hands reached tentatively for his shoulders and held them. He slid his fingers deeper into her hair and moved his mouth over hers in an unhurried way, savoring the soft texture of her lips and the eager pressure of her teeth behind them.

His tender, quiet kiss seemed destined to last forever, and Lucia felt oddly disoriented when he drew back. He examined her flushed face, her radiant eyes and rapid breath. "You're not like any woman I've ever met before," he commented in a soft, husky voice.

"You're not like any man I've ever met before, either," she whispered, her fingers curling reflexively over the lapels of his jacket.

"Oh? What kind of men do you usually meet?" he asked.

"Chemists," Lucia told him. "Test-tube jocks and the like."

"Obviously I'm not like them," he said with a smile.

"What kind of women do you usually meet?" she dared to ask.

His thumb wandered over the delicately chiseled arch of her cheek to the hinge of her jaw, and then down to her throat. "Greedy," he answered. "Grasping. You're not like them at all." His thumb reached her collarbone, exposed above the upper edge of her dress, and he traced the graceful bone to her shoulder. "Are you cold?" he asked.

The shore breeze was chilly, but Lucia's skin burned wherever Malcolm touched it. "I don't know," she answered honestly.

He touched his lips to her forehead. His hand continued its journey over the ridge of her shoulder, around her arm to its underside and along the smooth silk of her dress. By the time he reached her waist, Lucia knew she wasn't cold. On the contrary, she felt feverish, consumed by a throbbing heat. Seeking relief, she angled her head back, presenting him with her mouth.

He took what she offered, this time not gently but forcefully, his lips softening hers until they parted for him. His tongue filled her mouth, stroking against its partner, drawing back to her teeth and then surging deep inside her again. She was unable to breathe, unable to think, unable to do anything but drown in the sublime sensation of wanting Malcolm, wanting this sensual man who fascinated her at least as much as she fascinated him.

His hands tightened on her waist, and he drew her snugly against him. She felt his hips moving subtly against hers, his hard chest crushing the soft spheres of her breasts as their bodies discovered a natural alignment. "We could go to my room," he suggested, his voice thick and hoarse as he reluctantly pulled his mouth from hers.

She rested her head on his shoulder and tried to clear her mind. This was awfully quick, awfully sudden. Yet she'd known, as soon as Malcolm had telephoned her, that things might happen quickly and suddenly between them. She'd known it even before then, she admitted to herself—she'd known it from the moment their eyes had met across the Baccarat Room. She'd known that something strong and compelling existed between them, drawing them together, connecting them. She'd known all along that something like this might happen if she accepted Malcolm's invitation to join him in Atlantic City tonight.

She wanted him as much as he wanted her, but to go to his room with him would be to take an enormous chance. He hadn't mentioned anything about wanting to see her again after tonight. He hadn't so much as implied that he was looking for a relationship with her.

But Lucia wanted to trust him. She wanted to believe in him, to believe that Malcolm was respectful not only of her but of the strange force that linked them together. She could chance it. She had the Midas touch; this gamble might pay off.

"I understand you've got some brochures upstairs that you want to show me?" she whispered, smiling slightly.

He mirrored her smile, his eyes shining with pleasure. "Mm. They're far more interesting than etchings, I promise you." He grazed her cheek with his mouth, then curved his arm around her shoulders and ambled back with her to the hotel.

Chapter Five

It wasn't until they were in the elevator, soaring to the fifteenth floor, that Lucia came to her senses. Yes, Malcolm had a hypnotic effect on her. Yes, his kisses unleashed an unfamiliar, astonishing longing within her. Yes, she was a different woman now than she'd been a week ago. She was rich. She was wearing a silk dress and dainty sandals. She was enclosed in an elevator with an incredibly sexy, appealing man—the sexiest, most appealing man she'd ever met.

But that didn't mean she should be going to his hotel room with him!

She groped for the stop button on the control panel and slammed her palm against it. The elevator halted so abruptly that Lucia felt her ears pop. Abashed about having brazenly misled Malcolm on the boardwalk, she kept her gaze fixed on the panel and waited nervously for him to speak.

He cupped his hand over her shoulder and rotated her to face him. "Cold feet?" he asked, his eyes glittering with an unreadable emotion.

"Cold everything, I think," she mumbled sheepishly.

The corners of his mouth twitched upward. "Perhaps I could warm you up," he suggested.

She lowered her eyes and focused on her toes, visible through the delicately woven straps of the sandals. "I'd rather you didn't, Malcolm," she whispered shakily. "I'm sorry. I'm—I'm just not the sort of woman who goes to a hotel room with a man she hardly knows."

He mulled over her claim. His smile didn't disappear, but it didn't reach its full dazzling force, either. "You're not the sort of woman who wins jackpots at Atlantic City," he noted.

She flashed him a bewildered look. "What's that supposed to mean?"

"That's supposed to mean," he drawled, "that this week has been an unusual one for you, and things have changed in your life, so you might as well accept the way things are and come to my room."

She tried futilely to make sense of his enigmatic half-smile. "That's the dumbest line I've ever heard," she decided.

He laughed. "It isn't a line," he defended himself. "We don't have to go to bed just because we're going to my room. We can go to my room and have a drink and talk about investments if that's what you want."

She eyed him skeptically. "Is that what *you* want?"

"No," he admitted honestly. He shrugged and offered a whimsical grin. "I'm flexible, though."

A strident buzzing informed them that someone wanted to use the elevator. Lucia tuned out the sound as she wrestled with her thoughts. If she agreed to go to Malcolm's room to discuss investments, would he assume that her presence in his room was a green light for him to try to seduce her? If she didn't agree to go to his room, would he be insulted by her failure to trust him? *Did* she trust him?

The buzzing continued, and Malcolm made up her mind for her by pressing the start button on the panel. The elevator's motor revived with an airy hum and they were swept up to the fifteenth floor.

At least he was staying in a suite, Lucia thought anxiously as they moved down the corridor to his door. At least they wouldn't be marching directly into his bedroom. In the environment of his sitting room she could exercise a certain degree of control over the situation. She could sit stiffly on one of the velour sofas and chat sedately about mutual funds. She hoped she could, anyway—if Malcolm kept his distance, if they kept their attention on finances, if he kept his hands to himself.

He unlocked the door and they entered the suite. As soon as he shut the door behind them, he loosened his tie. "Would you like something to drink?" he asked, moving to a small cabinet. "I have some brandy here, or I can call room service if you'd prefer something else."

"Actually, I'd just as soon skip. Three glasses of wine with dinner is more than I usually drink."

"Does that mean you're in a weakened state?" he asked, his eyebrows arching roguishly.

"Absolutely not," Lucia warned him.

He chuckled. "You can't blame me for trying, Lucia," he declared, gesturing toward a sofa. As she sat, he crossed to his desk and riffled through some papers. "Here," he said, carrying three thick pamphlets to her. "My etchings."

She smiled wryly and took the pamphlets from him. One was titled "Advent Money-Market Fund," one "Advent Hanover Fund" and one "Advent Discovery Fund." She flipped through the money-market pamphlet and found every page filled top to bottom with tiny print. Her lip curled reflexively. "I'm supposed to read all this gibberish?" she asked.

"Letting me make love to you would probably be a lot more interesting," Malcolm pointed out. "More fun, too."

She glanced up at him and scowled. "So that's your strategy, is it?" she grumbled. "I'll agree to anything just so long as I don't have to read this stuff. Well, forget it, Malcolm. I'm a scientist, thirsting after knowledge. There's nothing I'd rather do right now than learn everything Advent has to tell me about money markets."

Malcolm's eyes twinkled with humor. "Whatever turns you on," he conceded, ambling back to the desk. "If it's all right with you, I'd like to make a call while you're reading. I want to hook into my answering machine at home and see if there are any earthshaking messages on it. I didn't have time to do that earlier today."

"Be my guest," Lucia offered. She propped her feet up on the coffee table, then turned to the first page of the money-market brochure and began to read.

Malcolm shrugged off his jacket and draped it over the desk chair. While waiting for an outside line, he pulled a pen and notepad toward him. He dialed a series of numbers, then listened.

Lucia tried to concentrate on her pamphlet, but it was impossible not to be distracted by Malcolm. She couldn't help observing the way his crisp white shirt followed the contours of his back, tapering down to the waistline of his gray pants, or the way his fingers plied the pen as he jotted a few words on his pad. She couldn't suppress her awareness of him, of his lanky legs, of the strong wrists and forearms he revealed when he rolled up his sleeves. Tucking the phone between his ear and his shoulder, he turned to Lucia and caught her staring at him. He smiled. "Why aren't you boning up?" he chided her. "There's going to be a quiz at the end of the hour."

Before she could respond, his brow darkened and his grin vanished in reaction to something on his answering machine. He muttered an oath and turned away from Lucia.

She watched him curiously, noticing the tense clenching of his shoulder muscles beneath his shirt. She heard him curse again, and he pounded his fist lightly against the desk. After hanging up, he remained with his back to Lucia, glowering at his notepad.

"I'd ask you if something was wrong," she ventured quietly, "but I don't believe in asking a question when you already know the answer."

He issued a sour laugh. "It's not a major tragedy," he reassured her. "Just a minor pain in the neck." He meditated for a moment, then lifted the receiver. "Keep reading, Lucia. I've got to make another call."

"Yes, sir." Lucia obeyed, making a point of rattling the page noisily as she turned it.

She couldn't help overhearing as Malcolm again requested an outside line and dialed a long-distance number. After a pause, he said, "Polly? What the hell was that all about?" His voice was gruff, clearly edged with anger. "You know what I'm talking about. So help me, if you've ruined my credit rating..."

Polly, Lucia contemplated. A girl friend? If Malcolm had seriously intended to seduce Lucia, he wouldn't have wasted time telephoning some other girl friend first. Maybe his claim that Lucia was safe in his suite was true, after all.

Yet she couldn't help feeling a twinge of jealousy as he spoke with his lady friend. Even if he was furious with the other woman, the fact that he'd interrupt a date in order to call her from Atlantic City and yell at her indicated to Lucia that they had a fairly intense relationship.

"Listen to me," he was saying in a barely tempered growl. "Shut up, Polly, and listen to me." Lucia had never heard Malcolm speak so rudely before. He seemed to have been transformed into a totally different person from the polite, polished man she'd thought him to be. Whoever Polly was, she obviously brought out the worst in Malcolm. "You are never, never to use my credit cards again. Do you understand? I don't care that they humiliated you. You had it coming." He exhaled roughly. "Whenever I think about our marriage, Polly, do you know what I think of? I think of how many times I've had to explain the limits to you. I think of how many times we've gone through this territory. When on earth are you going to grow up?"

Our marriage? Lucia registered. Malcolm was married? Her fingers grew icy, and the pamphlet dropped forgotten to the table. Malcolm was married.

Of course. Why shouldn't he be? He was away from his wife for a week of business—and pleasure, if possible—in Atlantic City. He had to return home to New York tomorrow, and his only chance for an extracurricular romp behind his wife's back seemed to be with a slightly nauseous jackpot winner who'd made eyes at him one evening.

Of course. Why not? He wouldn't want Lucia to visit him when he was in Manhattan, even though Manhattan was much closer to her home than Atlantic City was—and he knew it, because he'd seen for himself where she lived. No, he couldn't entertain Lucia in New York. He could only be with her now, while he was in Atlantic City, away from his wife.

If Lucia had been slightly nauseous the night she'd won the jackpot, she was extremely nauseous now. Unable to sit still, she prowled to the window and gazed out at the seething ocean below. It was almost invisible, as dark as the night sky above it, the breakers catching faint glimmers of light from the lamps lining the boardwalk. Lucia stared out into the darkness and tried to ignore Malcolm.

"I don't want to have to go through this with you anymore," he was saying. "If it happens again... All right." He sighed, suddenly sounding weary. "All right. Call Mike Lopez tomorrow and tell him what happened. I don't want to deal with it tonight. Good-bye, Polly." He dropped the receiver into its cradle and sighed again.

Lucia continued to face the window as she waited for him to say something. When he remained silent, she risked a quick glance at him. He was at the cabinet, pouring himself a brandy and looking miserable.

As well he should, she mused. Some seduction scene, complete with the ultimate irony—an interruption for an argument with the little lady back home. "That was your wife?" Lucia half asked, with a nod toward the phone.

Malcolm nodded vaguely. "I'm sorry about that," he said, corking the brandy bottle. Then he paused and opened it again. "Are you sure you wouldn't like a drink?"

"I'd rather go home," Lucia announced, heading for the door.

Malcolm reached out and snagged her arm. "Go home?" he asked innocently. "Please stick around and cheer me up. Even discussing investments would cheer me up right now."

"Are you kidding?" she blurted out. "You made a pass at me earlier this evening, or have you forgotten?

You invited me to your room, and *not* to discuss investments. And then—and then you talk to your wife on the phone, and you expect me to cheer you up? What are you, nuts?''

He frowned slightly. "My wife?"

Lucia pointed an accusing finger at the telephone. "You just said that was your wife."

"She *was* my wife," Malcolm clarified himself. "She isn't anymore."

Lucia weighed his statement and smiled sardonically. "I never doubted your ability to think on your toes, Malcolm. That's a clever explanation, but—"

His frown deepened. "Clever? It's the truth, Lucia. I'm divorced." Looking infinitely wearier, he let out a long breath. After taking a swig of brandy, he set down his snifter and gave Lucia a steady, solemn gaze. "My ex-wife hasn't yet figured out how to curb her excesses and live on her alimony. Evidently, she had a little adventure at Macy's today—she tried to use one of my credit card accounts when the store refused to honor hers. We had a joint account there when we were married, and Polly stupidly thought she could sneak through a charge on the joint account. She couldn't. They humiliated her, she said. They accused her of attempted fraud. She sounded hysterical on my answering machine, and when I realized she might have fouled up my credit standing, I..." His voice faltered as he appraised Lucia's stony expression. His eyes glimmered with unspoken thoughts, imploring her to believe him. "It could have waited until tomorrow, I guess," he said contritely. "But Polly has a way of pushing my buttons and making me so angry." His hand softened on Lucia's arm, but his eyes held her immobile, pleading silently with her.

"Malcolm," she said, relenting only the slightest bit. "Why on earth should I believe you? You made it very clear earlier that you wanted to go to bed with me."

He didn't deny that. "And?" he urged her to continue.

"And so you'll probably say anything to get me to stay."

He pressed his lips together and searched her face for a sign of softening. "Lucia," he murmured, running his fingertips gently over her bare upper arm, "if I was still married to her, why would she leave me a message on my answering machine?"

"How should I know? To surprise you? To try to catch you off guard while you're busy entertaining a woman in your suite? You tell me, Malcolm."

His thumb moved as far as her elbow and he let his hand drop from her. "If you don't believe me, then there's no point in your staying," he said hoarsely. He stalked to the phone and requested that the limousine be brought around for Dr. Bowen, who would be downstairs shortly. Hanging up, he turned back to Lucia. His eyes were clouded with disappointment as he gazed across the room at her. "Is this what you want?" he asked softly.

"Yes," she said, wishing he didn't look so sad, so wistful, wishing she didn't find him so handsome, wishing she could despise him for his attempt to deceive her. "Thank you for dinner," she added dully.

"Thank you for coming." He strode to the coffee table and gathered Lucia's purse and pamphlets. "Take these with you, read them when you have a chance," he advised her. "Read up on some other investment firms, too. Advent isn't the only money-management firm in the world. You might find another one better suited to your needs. But for heaven's sake, Lucia, don't do something stupid.''

Coming to Malcolm's room was undoubtedly the most stupid thing Lucia had ever done in her life. But she appreciated his recommendation nonetheless. She definitely didn't want to do any more stupid things.

"Can I see you to the car?" he asked.

"No, thank you," Lucia refused the offer as she reached the door. "So long, Malcolm."

He took her hand and pressed it to his lips. "I still want you," he whispered.

Shaken that she could respond to his light kiss and his suggestive words even after learning that he was married, she eased her fingers from his grip and hastened down the hall to the elevator. He remained in his doorway, watching until the elevator arrived and she ducked inside.

But even after hours passed, even after the long drive home, after she'd waved off the limousine and climbed the stairs to her apartment and locked herself inside, even after she'd crawled into bed and shut off the light and lay alone in the darkness, her hand still burned from his parting kiss.

DAMN. HOW LONG HAD HE STOOD staring at the elevator door, hoping against hope that it would slide open and Lucia would step back into the hall? "Malcolm," she'd murmur, "Malcolm, how silly of me to be upset. I believe you. I believe you're divorced; I believe you're honest; I believe you're a gentleman, an upstanding person. I know you'd never lie to me."

An hour? Two? It felt like forever to him. But she didn't come back.

He'd been an ass to return Polly's call. He should have known that Lucia would react badly. But when he'd heard Polly's plaintive message on his answering machine, whining that Macy's had accused her of fraud because she'd used his credit card—she'd *had* to use his credit card because he was too cheap to maintain her account, he was nickel-and-diming her on the alimony, they had *understandings* and he wasn't abiding by them—he'd acted reflexively, worried not about Polly but about his stupid credit rating, when he should have been worried about Lucia.

Lucia was the sort of woman who would never interrupt an imminent seduction to worry about credit cards. Well, maybe a seduction wasn't imminent; Malcolm couldn't be certain. She'd backed off from him in the elevator, she'd had second thoughts. Her sudden retreat hadn't really surprised him. She clearly wasn't the sort of woman who would engage in an affair lightly. In fact, Malcolm wouldn't even have invited her to his room—or at least not with the intention of making love to her—if she hadn't responded so warmly to his kiss on the boardwalk. She wasn't casual about sex, he knew that. But whatever it was that burned between them was very real and very strong. Once he had kissed her, he knew that she wanted him as much as he wanted her.

He wanted her. Still. The first time he saw her, and every time he thought of her, and tonight, when she'd stepped into the hotel lobby in that spectacular dress, with her magnificent shoulders and swanlike neck bared to him, and her shapely legs enhanced by those bewitching sandals, he'd felt an imperative desire for her. He'd felt it all through dinner, and on the boardwalk, and in the elevator when she admitted she had cold feet. He hadn't been sure he'd have her, but he'd wanted her, and he'd taken her to his room.

And then he'd heard Polly's message about what had amounted to an attempted theft, and in his rage he'd momentarily lost track of Lucia. Lucia wouldn't have lost track of him. Even when she was backing off from him, she must have been aware of the unspoken passion between them. No matter what happened, no matter what interruptions befell them, no matter how cold her feet or how many disturbing phone messages she might have heard, Malcolm knew she would never have let her awareness of him slip, even for an instant.

That was one reason he liked her, one of the most important reasons. Maybe she was impractical, maybe she was even a bit irresponsible when it came to finances. But to Malcolm, her unrealistic attitude toward money was one of her most endearing characteristics. He wished he could be that way, so detached from money that nothing, not even a frenzied message from his ex-wife about credit card abuse, could upset him.

He doubted he'd ever be able to emulate Lucia, though. Years of breeding and grooming had made him perpetually conscious of and careful about his wealth. The one time in his life he'd let his emotions interfere with his judgment, he'd wound up married to a pretty but avaricious woman who was in love with his wallet. That experience had taught him an important lesson: never to lose sight of who he was or what people wanted from him. Being a Royce had its obligations and its risks. When Malcolm had warned Lucia about how her wealth might prompt men to call her beautiful, he'd been speaking from personal knowledge.

It was no wonder that he was so strongly attracted to Lucia. Not only did he admire her lack of caution and her naiveté, but he treasured her apparent dislike of money. He himself didn't dislike money. As he'd told her over dinner, it was simply a tool, a measurement, as much a part of who he was as his height or his coloring. He'd been rich, literally, since the moment of his conception, for his grandfather had established a trust fund for the grandchild he anticipated. Malcolm had been raised to view his wealth as something to accept with responsibility. He regularly spent some of it in pursuits that Lucia might consider disgustingly noble, and the rest he invested soundly so that it would continue to grow. Not until his unfortunate marriage had he ever realized that his affluence could have a negative side.

Polly had wedded him for his money. That fact had become apparent within the first year of their brief marriage, and Malcolm had correctly chosen to blame Polly instead of his money for the breakup. But after they divorced, he seemed to keep meeting women like Polly, women taken by his wealth at least as much as by his personality. With his position as a partner of a successful investment firm, and with his social life consisting of service on the boards of various charitable organizations and attendance at galas and parties full of people who knew who Malcolm was and what he was worth, the life he led in New York simply didn't afford him the opportunity to meet different kinds of women.

If Lucia knew about the life he lived in New York, Malcolm surmised, she'd probably reject him. She didn't like money. During dinner, she'd made a cryptic remark about her family's weakness for money. Evidently she was determined not to succumb to whatever it was that made her parents and her sister weak. Malcolm respected her for that, though he knew that there was a great deal more to the matter of her family than she'd told him.

So he'd have to keep his wealth a secret from Lucia, at least until he'd regained her trust. He certainly couldn't pose as a pauper, but at least she wouldn't have to know what being a Royce entailed. Let her think of him as someone who lived well but temperately—which was pretty much the truth—and someone who was as decent and accessible as anyone else. Let her come to recognize him as a good, honorable man, and then his money wouldn't repel her.

He laughed ironically as he considered such a maneuver. There had been times since his divorce when he'd wished he could hide his wealth in order to learn whether a woman liked him for himself. But with Lucia, he had to hide his wealth because he believed she wouldn't like him if she knew how rich he was.

And he wanted her to like him. He needed that. He would do whatever it took to prove to her that she could trust him—even if that meant deceiving her about his affluence for a while.

PERHAPS MONEY WASN'T the root of all evil, Lucia meditated as she steered home with a trunkful of groceries. Perhaps money wasn't the root of all evil but, instead, the root of all stupidity. Because Lucia seemed to be suffering from a severe case of brainlessness ever since she'd won her jackpot nearly two weeks ago.

She'd received a frantic call from her father the previous weekend, claiming that her mother had gotten laid off from her inventory job and that until the juggling skunk enterprise took off, her parents would be squeezed to the limit. He'd sounded so panicked that Lucia had succumbed to a spasm of daughterly concern and sent him a check for ten thousand dollars. She didn't begrudge her parents the money if they really needed it; she wouldn't allow her mother to go through the indignity of having to flee town in the dead of night again.

But then, on Thursday, her mother had phoned to thank her for the generous gift and to ask why Lucia had sent it. "Dad's signed it over to the skunk business," she'd mentioned. "He's so happy—we just can't set aside enough from my earnings to build up the capital he needs for his juggling skunks."

Lucia had been railroaded. By her own father. She'd been lied to, cheated, embezzled from. By her own father! She knew he'd never view his action that way. He had no doubt felt utterly self-righteous when he'd extorted the money from Lucia. He'd probably raced to the bank to cash the check and congratulated himself on his shrewdness. *She'll see,* Lucia could imagine him saying to himself. *She'll see. This time I know what I'm doing, and she'll be glad I talked her into sending me the money. This time I'm going to make a fortune. This time it's going to work. This time I'm going to be lucky.*

It wasn't parting with ten thousand dollars that bothered Lucia. She didn't need the money. But she felt like an absolute fool for having been suckered by her own father.

Then, yesterday afternoon, to compound her idiocy, Lucia had agreed to let Rick Lansing escort her to the spring Sigma Xi dinner. Parker Chemicals' chapter of Sigma Xi, a science honor society, held catered dinners with guest speakers at area restaurants twice a year, and since Lucia had been planning to attend the dinner anyway, she didn't see the harm in letting Rick drive her to the restaurant. In fact, she entertained the notion that if she agreed to spend an evening with him, he might stop badgering her.

She was wrong. She was stupidly, brainlessly, idiotically wrong. Before they'd even reached his car, Rick was effusing about how beautiful she was, about the strong affinity he felt for intellectuals like her, about the magnificence of her eyes when she wasn't wearing her lab glasses. "I'm not an intellectual," she'd protested, "and the reason you always see me wearing lab glasses is that you're Parker's safety officer."

He'd fawned on her throughout the dinner. During the postprandial lecture, he'd repeatedly groped for Lucia's knee under the table, requiring her to slap his hand as if he were a frisky adolescent. She couldn't wait for the speech to end so she could go home.

But going home entailed spending more time alone with Rick, listening to him explain, in no particular order, that he intended to marry Lucia, that he had his eye on a wonderful vacation home in the Watchung Mountains, if only he could scrape together a down payment, that the secretaries in the patent department had their charms, but that there could never be anything lasting for Rick with one of them, that Lucia had beautiful eyes, and that a Mercedes was really a terrific bargain when you considered the quality you were getting for your money. Lucia had practically slammed her apartment building's door on Rick's nose when he'd tried to worm his way inside.

Grocery shopping she could understand, she thought as she pictured the three shopping bags in the trunk of her car. She liked doing the mental calculations necessary to determine which brand of cereal or detergent offered more ounces per penny. She liked clipping coupons and watching the cashier deduct their value from her bill. As the daughter of a woman who'd had to economize stringently in order to feed her family, Lucia found a special pleasure in putting into practice the lessons she'd learned from her thrifty mother.

A scratched decade-old Chevy was parked directly in front of the entry to Lucia's building when she arrived home. She grimaced as she wedged her car into a spot half a block away, annoyed about the extra distance she'd have to walk with her heavy bags of food. She didn't recognize the Chevy, but she resented it for occupying the spot she wanted.

She shut off the engine, climbed out of her car and smoothed the waistband of her cutoff denim shorts beneath her short-sleeved sweatshirt. The late May morning was simmering with a preview of summer's heat, and Lucia wished she'd pinned her hair up off her neck before she'd left the house an hour ago. She unlocked her trunk and lifted out one of the bags.

"Need a hand?" a husky male voice wafted over her shoulder.

She let the bag drop back into the trunk and spun around. Malcolm was standing on the sidewalk, dressed in faded jeans and a wrinkled oxford shirt, his hands in his pockets and his eyes concealed by sunglasses. She gaped at him for a long moment, wondering what his eyes looked like behind the dark lenses, wondering whether they were more gray or green or gold right now, whether they were sparkling with laughter or with desire.

She shook her head, determined not to let him trick her again. She'd had enough of her own recent stupidity. She wasn't going to let some married man beguile her with his lovely kisses, his gentle touch. "What are you doing here?" she muttered.

"I've got something to show you," he announced, pulling a thickly folded wad of paper from the hip pocket of his jeans.

"What? More Advent pamphlets?" Lucia asked.

He handed her the papers and she unfolded them. She vaguely recognized the legal format, the lines with names filled in in neat type: "Malcolm Singleton Royce" and "Polly Maguire Royce" and the name of a divorce court, and "Sworn to me this day..." and a judge's signature. "This is your divorce decree," Lucia mumbled in bewilderment.

"This is it," Malcolm confirmed. He flipped the page. "If you think Advent's brochures make scintillating reading, you'll get a bang out of all the clauses here. I'm only estimating, but I think the words 'heretofore' and 'hereinafter' appear at least a dozen times on every page."

"That's quite all right," Lucia said, refolding the papers. To read the details of Malcolm's divorce would be a terrible infringement on his privacy, even though he'd invited her to read them. She handed the decree to him, then turned to her trunk and stared hazily at her groceries. Finding Malcolm unexpectedly at her home left her shaken. She honestly didn't know what to do.

"How've you been?" Malcolm asked pleasantly.

She twisted to confront him. "Why did you come here, Malcolm?" she demanded. "Why did you just show up like this, without calling, without letting me know you were coming?"

"I wanted to see you," he said, providing the obvious answer. "I was afraid that if I called you, you'd refuse to let me come. I thought if I came with my divorce decree in my hand, you'd believe me."

"All right, I believe you. I believe you're divorced. But..." But she wasn't sure what. All she was sure of was that she'd been acting awfully foolish lately, and she didn't want to do anything foolish with Malcolm. She knew intuitively that he was much riskier than her father or Rick Lansing. Gambling on them—even when she lost—could never be as perilous as gambling on Malcolm.

Sensing that Lucia was having difficulty dealing with his sudden appearance, he bailed her out with a relaxed smile. "Let me just toss this thing back into my car, and then I'll help you with your groceries."

He pivoted and jogged down the sidewalk to the battered Chevy. After shoving the divorce decree into the glove compartment, he locked up the car and strode back to Lucia. "That's your car?" she blurted out, staring in astonishment at the dented, rusting car.

Malcolm assessed her surprise and grinned. "Why shouldn't it be my car?" he asked.

"Because...because when I think of you I think of limousines," she confessed, turning back to him. She associated him with limousines, and she associated him with skillfully tailored suits and tuxedos, not wrinkled shirts, well-worn jeans and scuffed sneakers. He definitely didn't look like James Bond at the moment. He looked more like a handyman, the gorgeous sort of handyman a rich, bored woman would invite inside on a hot day like today.

That image caused Lucia to giggle inwardly, but when her eyes took in Malcolm's towering frame, his fine build with its inordinately long legs, her laughter died in her throat. "You seem very different here than you did in Atlantic City," she remarked hesitantly. "I mean, your car, your clothes..."

"Considering how things went in Atlantic City," he reminded her, "I'm probably better off approaching you differently this time."

"What do you mean, *approaching* me?" she asked suspiciously.

He chose to ignore her question. "Your ice cream's turning to soup, Lucia," he pointed out, hoisting two bags into his arms. "We ought to get this stuff inside."

Scowling, she lifted the third bag and slammed down the trunk door. Malcolm followed her up the walk to the building. He waited patiently while she pulled a stack of envelopes from her mailbox, and then they climbed the stairs.

They set the bags down on Lucia's kitchen table. Before she unpacked her food, she flipped through the envelopes to see if any contained personal letters. They all appeared to be junk, and she tossed them onto the counter. The flow of begging letters had dwindled over the past week, but it hadn't yet stopped.

Malcolm leaned against the counter while she emptied the groceries from her shopping bags. He pulled off his sunglasses and watched her for a while, then lifted the letters and scanned their return addresses. "Anything from the Committee to End Pay Toilets in America today?"

"I don't think so. It might just as well be from them, though. Those are all fund-raising pitches. I can tell without opening them."

"This one has a private return address," Malcolm commented, lifting an envelope to the sun-filled window to determine its contents. "It looks like a personal letter."

Lucia snorted and swung open her freezer door. "Don't bet the rent on it," she muttered. "Go ahead, open it. Be my guest. See for yourself what kind of pen pals I've accumulated in the past couple of weeks.''

Malcolm gave her a moment to change her mind. When she didn't, he opened the envelope and slipped out the letter. He read for a few minutes, then guffawed. ''Is this serious?''

''What?'' Lucia asked calmly. She'd received enough weird letters lately to have become blasé about them.

''It's from an unwed mother of four in Staten Island. She needs money to pay for having her tubes tied.''

Lucia shrugged and grinned. ''I've gotten worse. Go ahead, read another.''

Uncertain about prying into her mail, he hesitated, observing her as she folded the bags flat and stored them on a rack in her broom closet. ''Why does a woman as wealthy as you save paper bags?'' he asked.

''Call me a rich eccentric,'' she said airily. ''I've been saving paper bags all my life. I'm not going to change now.'' She shut the closet door and then opened the drawer where she kept her coupons filed. She proceeded to sort her unused coupons for her next shopping trip. ''Go on, Malcolm. Read another letter. See for yourself what drives a rich lady to eccentricity.''

Malcolm lifted another envelope and slid his finger beneath the flap. He pulled out a sheet of creamy stationery and began to read. ''Juggling skunks?'' he roared.

Lucia jumped, then twisted around. ''Give that to me,'' she gasped, snatching the letter from him. Perplexed, Malcolm watched as Lucia read the letter:

Dear Lucia,
    What is this stuff I hear about your donating ten thousand dollars to the juggling skunks? Honest to

God, that crackpot's been hitting on Arthur and me for funds for his stupid skunk business for months, and then you go off and send him ten grand? What's wrong with you?

The letter went on, including congratulations about Lucia's having won the jackpot, and unwanted advice about how she should spend her windfall:

Get yourself fixed up so you can attract a rich man like I did. Do something with your hair—you're really too old for the Raggedy Ann look, Lucia— and buy some new clothes, and for heaven's sake, don't bury yourself in some smelly lab! The money won't last forever, so use it wisely and you'll be set for life. As the Good Book says, "Give a woman a fish and you feed her for a day. Give a woman a rich husband, and you feed her forever.

The letter closed with a brief caution about not sending any more money to their father. It was signed "Celia."

Lucia reread it and sighed. That Celia was too lazy to write her return address wouldn't have vexed Lucia under ordinary circumstances, but today it did. She was embarrassed that Malcolm had seen the letter. She peered up and discovered him perusing her thoughtfully. "This one was personal," she mumbled, gathering up the other envelopes and carrying them into the living room to sort.

Malcolm followed her. She plopped herself down on the center cushion of her couch and methodically opened the rest of her mail, scanning each letter and then setting it on the appropriate pile. She had recently added a fourth pile to the table: information from investment companies. Malcolm immediately noticed the logo of one of his company's competitors on an envelope, and he lifted it and poked inside.

"You've been doing research, I see," he said, lifting the rest of the pile and thumbing through it. "Don't go with this company," he recommended, setting one of the envelopes aside. "It's a discount brokerage, which means you get no counseling on your investments at all. That's fine for someone who's up on the markets and wants to pilot his investments himself, but for now, Lucia, I think you could use a bit more guidance. This firm's good," he said, setting another envelope down. "These people are all right, but their money-market rates tend to be on the low side. This outfit is for the birds," he said, waving another envelope at Lucia and shaking his head. "Try calling them. You can't get through. Ever."

"I got through when I called to ask them to send me their literature," Lucia commented.

"Different phone number," Malcolm pointed out. "If you want to sign on with them, you can get through with no problem. Then call them up to ask a question, or to transfer some of your money into a different account, and all you get is a busy signal. Their customer service is horrendous. These people are pretty good," he said, assessing the final envelope in the pile and returning it to the coffee table. He took a seat on the far end of the sofa, not close enough to Lucia to impose on her, and eyed her speculatively. "So. You've been investigating various investment firms."

"Trying," Lucia admitted. "But all their brochures read like mumbo jumbo to me. I can't make heads or tails out of them. Why can't they write these things in plain English?"

"Every field has its jargon," Malcolm noted. "Remember the first time you tried to explain your research to me? You might as well have been speaking in Swahili, for all I understood of what you were saying. Chemistry has its own lingo. So does finance. You'll start understanding it in time."

Lucia studied him. His eyes appeared thoughtful and sweet to her, a soft greenish-gray, his smile gentle and inviting. He didn't seem seductive—or particularly debonair. He looked to her like someone she might have befriended anywhere but at a casino. "Of course, you're fluent in the finance lingo, aren't you," she murmured, slanting a glance at the letters from the investment firms.

"If you're looking for a translator, I'd be happy to volunteer." He paused, the green overcoming the gray in his eyes as his focus narrowed slightly. "Lucia, did you really donate ten thousand dollars to juggling skunks?"

She turned away and pursed her lips. "No," she replied tersely, her cheeks darkening.

Malcolm measured her reaction to his question before speaking. "I wouldn't have opened that letter, Lucia, if you hadn't told me to."

"If I'd realized it was from my sister I wouldn't have told you to," Lucia mumbled. "She changes her stationery all the time, and she never writes her return address. And she always types because her handwriting's abominable. She's an excellent typist; she worked as a secretary until she managed to hook her boss and marry him."

Malcolm struggled through Lucia's rambling remarks. Her ensuing silence provoked him to ask, "Why did she write that stuff about skunks, then?"

Lucia sighed, a low, ragged breath. She didn't want to reveal her father's empty-headedness—or her own stupidity—to Malcolm. But she had asked him to be her translator; she knew she needed his wisdom. If she was going to trust him for monetary advice, she might as well trust him with everything. He had already proved that he'd been telling the truth about his divorce. And he didn't seem like a powerful mogul wearing sharp clothing and riding in limousines right now. He seemed like a concerned friend. Nothing more, nothing less.

"My father," she began, then swallowed. She prayed that Malcolm wouldn't laugh. "My father has spent his entire life flitting from one supposed money-making venture to another. They always fail, always. This latest scheme of his is a band of descented skunks that juggle Ping-Pong balls."

Contemplating her solemn expression, Malcolm fought against a smile. "Ping-Pong balls," he repeated in disbelief. "And you invested in it?"

"No," Lucia insisted. "I sent him some money because I thought my folks were about to go broke. They've gone broke before, many times. They've been bankrupt, both with the courts and without the courts. When I was a child, every couple of years or so—" She cut herself off, not wishing to dwell on her dismal past and elicit Malcolm's pity. "Anyway, my father duped me out of the money by telling me my mother was losing her job and they were on the verge of going under. Then he took the check I sent him and frittered it away on his skunk business. Please don't say anything," she added, certain that Malcolm was about to admonish her for having sent her father so much money. She was looking at her lap, not at Malcolm, but she could sense that he was about to speak. "I feel like a jerk, and now my hoity-toity sister and her highfalutin' husband are making me feel like even more of a jerk, so I don't want to hear anything out of you. It's bad enough to throw money away on junk, but to get swindled out of it by your own father—"

Her voice dissolved into a sob. She didn't want to cry. She'd managed to remain remarkably strong and stoical so far, given the recent upheaval in her life. She'd kept down her dinner at the casino the night she'd won the jackpot. She'd listened patiently to her pathetic colleagues at work. She'd exercised great willpower in not giving Rick Lansing a fat lip when he'd pawed her knee under the table the previous night. She hadn't exploded with indignation at Malcolm when she'd mistakenly thought he was married. She'd kept all her emotions inside, carefully bottled up, in her effort to continue living normally.

But to be cheated by her father was too much. She should have cried about it when she'd discovered the truth a couple of days ago, but she hadn't. Now she couldn't suppress the tears anymore. She hated her money, hated her winnings, hated the fact that her sudden wealth had made her father lie to her. Why, of all the millions of people who were in Atlantic City that night two weeks ago, did she have to be the unlucky one to win the jackpot?

Her body shuddered as she covered her eyes with her hands and wept. She felt Malcolm slide toward her on the sofa and curl his arm consolingly around her. His fingers wandered through her hair, and his shoulder and chest absorbed her trembling as she sobbed.

It felt good to cry, she realized. It felt good to give in to this long-overdue release of tension. And it felt especially good to have Malcolm beside her, comforting her.

Chapter Six

"Your sister's wrong," Malcolm remarked.

They were driving aimlessly around town in Malcolm's Chevy. He had on his sunglasses; his window was rolled all the way down, and he rested his elbow on the door frame. The sleeves of his shirt were rolled up. The breeze drawn through the window tousled his hair. He looked young and carefree to Lucia, like a teenager cruising through the neighborhood in his very first car—proud, defiant and a bit rough around the edges. She had to exert herself to find in his current image a hint of the polished, debonair businessman he'd been at the casino the last time she'd seen him.

Back at her apartment, once she'd regained her composure, he'd behaved briefly like that businessman as he'd attempted to explain the pros and cons of the various investment plans she'd obtained literature on, and studied the estimated tax forms she'd received from the IRS. But when he realized that her eyes were glazing over and her attention drifting back to the letter Celia had sent her, he'd tossed the forms aside, hoisted Lucia to her feet, and announced that they were going for a drive to clear their minds.

She stretched her legs, then crossed them. She had more than enough room for them, since Malcolm had the seat adjusted as far from the dashboard as it could go, in order to accommodate his lanky build. Lucia studied her legs for a minute. Although she hadn't cropped her jeans into extremely short shorts, a lot of flesh was exposed between her midthigh and her sandaled feet. She was glad she'd shaved her legs before the Sigma Xi dinner last night.

"What's my sister wrong about?" she asked Malcolm.

"Your hair." As if on cue, a strong gust whipped through the window and tossed a wavy lock across her nose. She tucked it behind her ear and turned back to Malcolm. "It looks wonderful just the way it is," he said. "You shouldn't restyle it."

"You read Celia's letter," Lucia muttered.

Malcolm shot her a quick look to see if she was angry, then concentrated on the road. "You were crying for a long time," he pointed out. "And the letter was lying there on your lap, right in front of my eyes. It was hard not to read it."

Lucia felt a rush of indignation that Malcolm had snooped into the one personal letter she'd received, but she swallowed her anger and said nothing. His reading her sister's letter was no more unreasonable than Lucia's having listened to his telephone conversation with his ex-wife a week ago in his hotel suite. Lucia had been sitting less than ten feet from him that night. It would have been impossible not to eavesdrop.

She uncrossed her legs and recrossed them in the other direction. "Celia knows a lot about hair," she commented. "She's much more fashion-conscious than I am. Prettier, too."

"And she's married to a highfalutin' man?"

"He's rich," Lucia confirmed. "Very rich. Celia married him for his money."

Malcolm pondered the acerbic quality of her voice. "You sound as if you don't approve," he hazarded.

Lucia shrugged. "It's not my place to approve or disapprove. Celia did what she set out to do. She wanted financial security, and I can't say that I blame her."

Malcolm tossed Lucia another swift look, then steered around the corner and headed west. "Are you looking for a rich man to marry, too?" he asked cautiously.

Lucia rolled her eyes. "What do I need with a rich man?" She chuckled. "I'm a quarter of the way to my first million." Malcolm joined her laughter. "Nah," she mused, contemplating her sister's marriage. "Celia married for money, but her husband...God, Malcolm, he's so boring! I mean, he's a nice enough guy, and he's faithful to Celia; he doesn't hit her or mistreat her or anything. But he's the most boring person I've ever met. His only interest is business. He owns a bunch of office buildings in Chicago, and that's all he cares about. Rents, property taxes, maintenance, dealing with the unions— ask him anything, and he'll find a way to direct the conversation back to his holdings. Celia says she doesn't mind, because he leaves for his office at eight in the morning and doesn't get home until six-thirty or seven at night, so she doesn't have to see too much of him." Lucia shook her head sadly. "No, I'm not looking for a rich man to marry."

Malcolm mulled over Lucia's description of her brother-in-law. "'Give a woman a rich husband and you feed her forever,'" he quoted from Celia's letter. "That obviously means a great deal to your sister."

"She isn't fat," Lucia said, deliberately misunderstanding Malcolm. He smiled wryly, and she shrugged again. "I don't blame her, I really don't. My father's failures affected her differently than they affected me. Celia was never as good a student as I was, and she never gave much thought to becoming self-supporting. She had more dates than me, more guys chasing after her. If it weren't for my father's being broke, Celia probably would have been even more popular, but we were treated as pariahs by most of our classmates. Having a father who'd filed for bankruptcy wasn't the proper sort of background for a prom queen to have."

She toyed with the frayed edge of her shorts and lapsed into thought. She'd never discussed such things with anyone other than Celia before. She doubted that Celia had ever bared the anguish of her past to anyone other than her. Celia could never reveal such things to Arthur; he was much too pompous and egotistical to care about his wife's concerns.

Yet it was good to talk about these things with Malcolm. It was right. The trust she felt for him transcended his having shown her his divorce papers. It transcended her having decided to depend on him for financial advice. It seemed to have grown into something organic, something even stronger than the erotic tension she'd felt with Malcolm the last few times they were together.

She still sensed that sensual energy between them, but it wasn't as dominant as it had been. It was more a background hum, like the buzz of a fluorescent lamp or an air conditioner, an entity so low and constant that, after a while, it was no longer noticeable. Perhaps it *was* as strong as ever, Lucia considered, but other aspects of their relationship had come to take precedence over it. Glimpsing Malcolm's angular profile as he drove, Lucia found him as attractive as she always had, but she didn't feel the surging desire for him right now. Instead, she felt the spreading warmth of her trust in him, and that pleased her greatly.

"They're lovely names, Celia and Lucia," Malcolm broke into her ruminations. "Your parents showed creativity in naming their daughters."

"Anyone who believes there's a fortune to be made in restyling old shoes has to be creative," Lucia grumbled. "That was another of my father's ventures—restyling shoes. If you want to know the truth, I think our names are a bit grandiose, considering."

"Considering what?"

Lucia meditated for a moment, searching for the right words. "My father calls me 'princess' and Celia 'angel.' These are not the pet names one associates with girls in hand-me-down clothes who are commanded to pack all their belongings in one hour because they have to skip town overnight and lay low until their dad can reorder his life and pay back his creditors. Lucia is the name of a princess, not someone whose father's on his way to the debtors' prison." She sighed. "I guess that's why I don't mind when my friends call me Loosh."

Malcolm eyed her and grinned. "Loosh," he echoed. "My friends call me Mal. Malcolm seems so stuffy."

"I like Malcolm," Lucia argued. "It sounds dignified. It sounds like someone in a tuxedo, in a limousine." She caught a glimpse of an unfamiliar industrial complex and scowled. "Do you know where we are?"

"Somewhere, I suppose," he said, unconcerned. "Just being able to drive fifty miles an hour is a thrill for a city boy like me. You don't mind indulging me, do you?"

"I'd rather we didn't get lost," she claimed. "Turn at the next light, okay? I'd feel better if I recognized a few landmarks."

"So, your brother-in-law's in real estate," Malcolm reflected, obediently turning the corner when the light switched to green. "Have you given much thought to real estate?"

"As an investment, you mean?" Lucia laughed. "I don't suppose my little jackpot will buy too many office buildings in Chicago."

"No, but if you bought yourself a house you'd get some useful deductions for your taxes. Property taxes, mortgage interest and points—"

"Wait a minute!" Lucia interrupted him. "In order for me to write those things off, I've got to spend the money first. I don't see how I'll wind up ahead if I have to spend so much."

"You'd be building up equity," Malcolm explained. "If you buy wisely, your property will appreciate in value."

She shook her head. "Too complicated."

Malcolm studied her thoughtfully, then drove in silence for a while. At a new condominium development he slowed down and steered onto the driveway.

"Where are we going?" Lucia asked suspiciously.

"This place is new," Malcolm noted. "They must have some model units and prices. It'll give us an idea of the market."

"I don't want an idea of the market," Lucia protested. But Malcolm had already parked by a unit displaying a realtor's Open House sign. When he climbed out of the car, Lucia grudgingly swung open her door. They walked together to the model unit. "I don't like condos," she whispered as Malcolm opened the front door for her.

"We're only here to do research," Malcolm insisted. "That's something a scientist like you ought to understand."

The model's interior was decorated luxuriously, but not in Lucia's taste. Clear plastic runners protected the beige carpeting, a color that struck Lucia as dreadfully impractical, and the large living room was papered in a busy pattern that made her slightly dizzy. "I hate this place," she grumbled beneath her breath.

Ignoring her, Malcolm moved to the real estate broker and asked her for some brochures. The conservatively groomed middle-aged woman answered a few questions and then cast Lucia a dubious glance. Malcolm strolled back to Lucia and said, "This unit is one hundred and twenty thousand."

"Dollars?" she gasped.

Malcolm chuckled. "No, pesos. Of course dollars. We're only here to get some ideas about price."

"One hundred and twenty thousand dollars," she snorted, then grinned. "It gives me some ideas, all right. No wonder that broker keeps glaring at me. The way I'm dressed, I certainly don't look like someone who can afford a place like this."

"It's fun to keep them guessing, isn't it?" Malcolm joked, guiding Lucia to the stairs.

They wandered down the short second-floor hallway, Lucia swinging every door open and peeking nosily inside. The hall ended in a square master bedroom. "Only two bedrooms?" Lucia exclaimed. "For one hundred and twenty thousand dollars, you ought to get three bedrooms at least."

Malcolm moved through the master bedroom to the master bath. He peered in and grinned. "Here's where the price comes from," he surmised.

Lucia joined him at the doorway. The master bathroom was enormous, containing, in addition to the shower stall, a sunken Jacuzzi lined with ceramic tiles. "That's the biggest bathtub I've ever seen!" Lucia blurted out.

"It's not a bathtub," Malcolm told her. "It's a Jacuzzi. Haven't you ever seen a Jacuzzi before?"

"Never in person," she said, venturing farther into the bathroom. The Jacuzzi was empty, displaying the tiled bench lining its walls and the spouts which caused the water to pulse. "I've seen hot tubs on television—usually filled with half a dozen giddy people drinking champagne."

Malcolm approached her and nodded. "You don't have to fill a Jacuzzi up with half a dozen people," he noted. "If you ask me, the optimum number is two."

Lucia cast him a measuring look. He was smiling, his dimples long and enchanting and his eyes glimmering. "Are you speaking from experience?" she asked.

His eyes captured hers and captivated them with their dazzling sparks of light. "As a matter of fact, Lucia, there was a Jacuzzi in the bathroom of my suite at the Shangri-la. We could have tried it out."

"Complete with champagne?" She chuckled and turned away. "I would've wound up sneezing."

Malcolm remained behind her for a moment, his hand hovering above her shoulder. Then he let it fall to his side and stalked out of the bathroom. "Let's see what else one hundred and twenty thousand can buy in this part of New Jersey," he suggested in a quiet voice.

Lucia followed him downstairs and out of the model. She wondered about his sudden change in mood, from playfully suggestive to cool and withdrawn. Had she done something to turn him off? Was her joke about sneezing from champagne the wrong thing to say?

She was still steeped in thought as she got into the car and buckled her seat belt. Had Malcolm come to New Jersey to seduce her, she wondered. Had he come to see her, hoping to recapture what they'd had and lost in Atlantic City? If he had, why had he made no move to kiss her or touch her so far? What would she do if he did make a move?

"Malcolm." She turned to him. His gaze was riveted to the road as he exited from the complex and merged with the traffic on the main road. "Malcolm, how long are you planning to stay?" Hearing the question stated so bluntly made her cringe, but she couldn't very well retract it.

His eyes flickered toward her. Then his attention returned to the road and he smiled. "You mean, do I want to spend the night with you?" he asked, matching her in tactlessness.

She plowed ahead bravely, figuring that it was too late for discretion. "Do you?"

He tossed her another fleeting glance and chuckled. "Of course."

"There's no 'of course' about it, Malcolm."

"If you're asking whether I *want* to spend the night with you, the answer is, of course. If you're asking whether I *will* spend the night with you... well, I guess you know the answer to that better than I do."

Lucia considered his calm tone. "You sound resigned to letting me make the decision," she commented.

His smile deepened. "That depends. If you tell me I can't spend the night, I may put up a fight the likes of which you've never imagined before."

She couldn't tell whether he was kidding. She felt out of her depth with someone like Malcolm. "Put me in a lab and I'm in my element," she muttered half to herself. "Put me in a car with you, and I'm not."

He gazed curiously at her, then proceeded through an intersection. "Why not?" he asked.

Tact was definitely needed here, but Lucia didn't know how to go about getting some. Malcolm seemed more than willing to keep their conversation on the plane of brutal honesty. She didn't have much choice but to continue in that vein. "I don't know," she admitted, struggling to shape her thoughts into coherent sentences. "In Atlantic City you were so suave—"

"Me? Suave?"

"You looked good in your tux, Malcolm. You looked as if you belonged in the limousine. I'm not like that. To me, middle class is the height of social attainment. And now, here you are, in a pair of jeans that look as if they've got quite a history, and you're driving this rattletrap car, and . . . and I just don't know what to make of you."

He seemed to appreciate the candor in her words, as well as the difficulty she was having expressing herself. "Make of me what I am," he advised her. "I'm a Manhattan businessman; I'm unmarried, and I'm very attracted to you. I know how to behave when I'm trying to intimidate people who owe my firm money. If that means wearing a tux, I wear a tux. If it means riding in a limo, I ride in a limo. But on my own time, I dress comfortably and drive a rattletrap car. It's really quite simple, Loosh."

She smiled at his use of her nickname. "I still don't feel that I know you very well."

"What do you want to know?" he asked.

Her eyes ran over his face, his strong shoulders, his graceful fingers curved through the steering wheel, his long legs, ending in scuffed sneakers. She tried to picture him as the suave gentleman of Atlantic City, but it wasn't easy. "Are you rich?" she asked.

"Comfortable," he answered, then looked askance at her. "You said you weren't looking for a rich man to marry."

"I'm not," she assured him.

"So, I'm in the running, then?"

"What is this?" she asked with a laugh. "A marriage proposal?"

"No." He reached across the seat, laced his fingers through hers, and drew her hand to his lap. "I like you, Lucia. We'll get to know each other very well in time." He lifted her hand to his lips and kissed her wrist, then released her in order to steer into the parking lot of a small shopping center.

"What are we doing now?" she asked nervously. It seemed safer to focus on her immediate situation than to analyze his enigmatic remark about their getting to know each other in time.

He braked to a halt by a stationery store. "I'm going to buy a newspaper so we can check the real estate listings."

"I've got a newspaper at home," she reminded him.

"But we aren't home. Come on, Loosh, you're so rich you can afford two newspapers," he teased. "In fact, you won't have to afford two newspapers. I'll treat." Before she could argue, he was out of the car.

She watched him saunter into the store, and shook her head. The trust she'd felt for him, so cozy and warm, still existed, but the hotter passion was threatening to supersede it. If she was going to stick to brutal honesty,

she'd have to admit that she wouldn't mind his spending
the night with her. But that possibility rattled her. She'd
never considered herself a particularly passionate person. Malcolm's effect on her was something alien, and
she wanted to remain in control of things until she'd
come to terms with it.

He returned to the car within a minute, carrying a copy
of the local newspaper. Climbing in, he slid along the seat
next to her and opened the paper to the real estate listings. "Okay," he said, smoothing the paper across Lucia's knees. "What towns are we near? Where should we
look?"

"I don't think I want to buy a house," Lucia murmured uncertainly.

"You don't have to buy a house," he insisted. "You
just ought to look. It'll give me a good excuse to drive
around at fifty miles an hour."

He opened the glove compartment to get a pen and
Lucia glimpsed his divorce decree on the nearly empty
shelf. The folded document reminded Lucia of how little
she knew about him. Would they really get to know each
other very well in time? How much time? And until then,
what was supposed to happen?

He interrupted her thoughts by circling an Open House
listing. "Scotch Plains isn't far from here, is it?" he
asked. "We can look at this house, and this one..."

"Malcolm, those houses are listed at well over a
hundred thousand dollars," Lucia argued.

"Then let's hope they have more than two bedrooms."

"Or a Jacuzzi," she admitted.

Smiling, he shifted back to the wheel and started the
car. "You'll have to give me directions," he told her as
he steered out of the parking lot. Once Lucia had pointed

him in the right direction, he said, "I suppose you'll want to be living close to where you work."

"I like where I live now," she declared. "I thought I was just looking, not buying. The distance from Parker Chemicals isn't important if I'm just looking."

He nodded vaguely, then turned the corner in response to her command. "So tell me, Loosh, what exactly do you do at Parker Chemicals? Do you soak socks with drugs?" At her laugh, he persisted. "Come on. Describe to a scientific imbecile what a typical day is like for a budding Einstein like you."

"Einstein was a physicist, not a chemist," she corrected him. "A typical day, huh?" She thought for a moment, then smiled. "I arrive at nine. I go to my lab, put on my lab coat and my lab glasses, and set up a reaction."

"A reaction?"

"Sure, you know—an experiment. We call them reactions in the business. For instance, I'll put some starting material in a beaker and set it up in the hood and reflux it."

"Reflux? What the hell does that mean?"

Lucia laughed again. "It means boil."

"Then why don't you say boil?"

"Why don't those stupid pamphlets from companies like yours say things like, 'Here's the way it works: you invest this much, you get this much profit, you pay this much tax'? Don't complain to me about jargon, Mal."

He smiled sheepishly. "If the pamphlets were written in plain English, then you wouldn't need me to stick around and translate them for you. There's the realtor's sign." He parked beside the Open House sign, which stood in front of a large brick colonial.

"This house is much too big," Lucia muttered.

"Research, Einstein," Malcolm overrode her as he climbed out of the car.

The brick colonial was too big. The raised ranch they inspected after the colonial was too close to a highway. The split-level showed evidence of recent flooding in its basement. The secluded ranch house in a heavily wooded area seemed overpriced. By four-thirty, Lucia was tired. And hungry. She hadn't had anything to eat since breakfast.

"Enough research for one day," she announced as she collapsed in the car and groaned. She shuffled the information sheets she'd received from the brokers at each house and tossed them onto the seat. "If I don't get some food soon, I'm going to die."

"We can't let that happen," Malcolm declared, pretending to be horrified. With Lucia's assistance he navigated back to a main boulevard and coasted into the lot of the first restaurant he spotted, a fast-food joint. "How's this?" he asked.

"It's a far cry from the roof of the Shangri-la," Lucia noted with a grin. "But it'll do just fine."

They entered the hut-shaped eatery and scanned the listings displayed above the counter. "Does anything tickle your taste buds?" Malcolm asked.

"Everything does," Lucia confessed. "I'll have a cheeseburger and a small french fries, and...do you suppose they have Médoc here?"

Malcolm eyed her and grinned. "Something tells me they don't."

"Hm. Then I'll settle for a milk shake. Which should I go for, the red or the white?"

"The brown is reputed to be a superb vintage," Malcolm joked as he stepped up to the counter. "Three cheeseburgers, two large fries and two chocolate shakes," he recited to the waiting young clerk. At Lucia's questioning scowl, he explained, "The small order of fries is never enough. Go with the large."

After a brief wait the clerk had their order stacked on a tray. Malcolm paid and carried the food outside to one of the picnic tables beside the parking lot. He and Lucia took their seats on the bench in the shade of an overhead umbrella, and he divided up their food.

Lucia unwrapped her straw, plunged it into the thick milk shake, and took a refreshing sip. "This is the most nutritionally unsound meal I've had in ages," she said cheerfully as she unwrapped her burger.

"Then you'd better savor every morsel," Malcolm recommended. He consumed a long drink of his milk shake, forgoing the straw, and when he lowered the paper cup, his upper lip was coated with a pale, chocolaty mustache.

Lucia laughed. How different he was now from the way he'd been in Atlantic City. How carefree, how delightfully casual, how comfortable. She watched him run his tongue over his lips to clean off the milky residue and then take a hearty bite of his cheeseburger. She could easily trust him when he was like this, so natural and down-to-earth. She could trust him...and desire him. When his eyes lifted to hers, she instantly felt their magic pull, their kaleidoscopic glitter momentarily mesmerizing her.

"Thinking about that ranch house in the woods?" he asked as he tried to read her faraway look. "You liked it, didn't you?"

She shook her head and closed her eyes to break the spell of his gaze. When she dared to look at him again, she labored to remain composed and detached.

"What?" he probed. "What's on your mind?"

What was on her mind was his claim that he wanted to spend the night with her, and that if she refused him, he intended to put up a fight. What was on her mind were her warring instincts, the instinct to yield to the irrefutable sexual attraction she and Malcolm felt for each other, and the instinct of self-preservation. She was a scientist; she had to gather more facts before she could reach a conclusion.

"Tell me about your wife," she said.

His face hardened slightly, and then he shrugged. "What about her?" he asked in a bland voice.

"How long were you married?"

He devoured a french fry. "Three years."

"What went wrong?"

He studied Lucia for several silent minutes. She could detect his displeasure at her line of questioning, but he didn't object to it. Perhaps he knew that she was asking him only because there were certain things she needed to know. "What went wrong," he said slowly, "is that she didn't love me."

Lucia's eyebrows arched in surprise. Malcolm struck her as an eminently lovable man. "I don't believe that," she blurted out.

He discerned a compliment buried in her words and smiled tentatively. Then his smile faded. "Maybe she did love me—she claimed she did. But in all honesty, I don't think she's capable of loving anyone but herself."

"Does she try to use your credit cards often?" Lucia asked, recalling the argument she'd overheard in his hotel suite.

Malcolm toyed with an empty foil wrapper and sighed. "She believes she should be receiving more alimony from me. She's getting more than she deserves, but it isn't enough for her. We've been divorced for over a year, and she still calls me to complain that she needs more money. Or she has her lawyer call my lawyer—or she calls my lawyer herself. And complains." He sighed again. "While we were married, she had affairs with a few men, men who might have been willing to shell out the kind of money she wants. I wish she'd married one of them instead of me."

"Does she have a job? Or is she taking care of children?"

"Neither. She's perfectly capable of getting a job, but she doesn't want one. She'd rather have me support her."

Lucia picked at the few remaining french fries in the cardboard container, then shoved it away. "I don't mean to take her side, Malcolm, but women often get the shaft in divorce settlements. My friend Evvie—you met her in Atlantic City," she reminded him. "She's divorced. She put her husband through medical school, and now he's earning three times what she earns, but she gets no alimony because she can support herself as a lawyer. She made a lot of sacrifices for him, but the court didn't see the marriage as a partnership that she deserved a fair share from. If she hadn't been working at Parker Chemicals, she'd probably have received plenty of alimony. Instead, she gets nothing."

"My marriage wasn't a partnership," Malcolm retorted. "It was a mistake. Polly married me because she wanted someone to pay for her excesses, and she thought I could afford it."

"Can you?" Lucia asked.

Malcolm pressed his lips together. His dissatisfaction with her inquiry was quite obvious. "Nobody can afford Polly," he muttered.

"You're angry with me," Lucia guessed in a subdued voice. "You wish I didn't ask you about all this."

"It's not my favorite topic of conversation," he granted. His expression relented and he offered a hesitant smile. "Here I am, trying to win you over. I can't help thinking that telling you about a stupid error I made in my past is not the best way to do that."

His confession touched Lucia. It was the first time she'd sensed vulnerability in Malcolm—vulnerability to her. She reached across the table and covered his hand with hers. "Human beings make errors," she consoled him. "Your wife took you for a ride. My father took me for a ride. We both got suckered by people we loved. It hurts, Malcolm, but I don't think any less of you for it. I hope," she added, sharing his bittersweet smile, "that you don't think any less of me for letting my father sucker me."

"Of course not," he countered. "But I don't see how you can even compare the two situations."

"They're the same," she maintained. "Maybe money is just a tool, a measurement, whatever nice things you want to call it. But it makes people do hurtful things. It makes them selfish and cruel." She lowered her eyes and fought off her own bitterness about her father's duplicity. When she lifted her gaze to Malcolm again, she felt her anger dissipate. "I'm sorry if I'm nosy about your marriage," she apologized. "But I have a right to know certain things if you're going to spend the night with me."

His eyes brightened with optimism. "Am I?" he whispered.

"Yes." She didn't even think about her answer. What she had to know about Malcolm wasn't the painful details of his marriage or his divorce, but that he was human, that he was fallible, that he was as vulnerable as she was. Now that she knew that, she knew she could trust him completely. "Yes, I think you are," she murmured.

He twisted his hand to capture hers. Unwilling to release her, he gathered up their garbage with his free hand and strolled with her to the waste bin to dispose of it. Then they walked to the car. They didn't speak. They didn't have to. Malcolm continued to hold her hand as he drove to her apartment.

In her living room she stared at the stacks of letters on her coffee table and then at the real-estate materials she'd collected that afternoon. "Where am I going to put all this stuff?" she grumbled, wriggling free of Malcolm's clasp to make room on the table for a fifth pile.

"What are these?" Malcolm asked, lifting the pile of mailings from questionable charities. "Junk?"

"Funny junk," Lucia identified the hcap. "Those are from silly organizations. These are from silly individuals," she said, straightening up the pile beside it.

"Throw them out," Malcolm advised. "What do you need them for?"

"Laughs," Lucia replied. "I ought to save them. I might want to show them to my children someday."

Something flashed in his eyes as he glanced at her. "You plan to have children?" he asked.

"I guess I'll have to, so I'll have someone to show this stuff to," Lucia joked.

Malcolm didn't laugh. "Well, then, you'd better save it," he commented quietly. "Go find a box to store it in."

Lucia left the room. Malcolm watched her vanish into her bedroom and smiled. *Children,* he contemplated. *She wants children.* Polly hadn't wanted children; having children would have been too pedestrian an activity for a woman with grand plans like hers. Besides, she'd pointed out whenever Malcolm had broached the subject, having children might spoil her perfect figure. Malcolm liked her figure, didn't he? He wouldn't want her to become flabby and scarred with stretch marks, would he?

He would have loved such a thing, but that was irrelevant. By the time he'd entertained thoughts of having children, his marriage was already beginning to disintegrate. He hadn't been stupid enough to believe that having a child would solve their problems. But after a year with Polly, he'd come to need someone else in his life, someone who could accept his love and return it, someone too innocent to care about whether he was wealthy. Polly would chatter on and on about the dress she'd seen at Bloomingdale's that she simply had to have for the fund-raising gala at the Met, or about that little diamond trinket in the window at Tiffany's that would look so marvelous on her, and Malcolm would think, *Buy the damned dress, buy the diamond trinket, but give me a baby so there'll be some love in this family, in this home.*

That was behind him now, that rage and loneliness. In its place was a woman who could discuss having children as if it were as normal and acceptable as eating or sleeping or loving. Which was just as it should be. A woman like Lucia would make a splendid mother, Malcolm mused. There was no pretense about her, no phoniness, but rather sensitivity, humor, warmth, faith. If he had wanted her before, he wanted her even more now.

She returned to the living room carrying a shoe box. Malcolm helped her to cram the letters inside. She put the lid on the box and straightened up from the table.

His gaze settled on her face and his arms closed around her slender shoulders. As he tightened his embrace, the shoe box dropped to the floor, strewing the letters about the carpet. "Leave them," he ordered her before covering her mouth with his.

Her hands slid to his waist and gripped him as his tongue slipped hungrily past her lips. Merely the sensation of her fingers fanning along his sides filled him with an insane craving for her. He called up all his reserves of willpower to keep himself from tearing off her clothes and making love to her right on the living-room floor, surrounded by an ocean of letters from the Committee to End Pay Toilets in America and the folks of B.B.GUN and ACME.

He lifted his hands to her head and combed his fingers through the lustrous brown waves of hair that framed her face. Drawing back, he took a deep, steadying breath. "Maybe we should go to your bedroom," he suggested.

But before she could turn toward the bedroom, his lips were grazing her brow, and then her eyelids, her temple, her nose. With each light kiss she felt herself become more pliant, more receptive, more eager for his love.

As if in a trance, she broke away and led him to her bedroom. The minute they'd crossed the threshold, he had his arms around her again, his lips commandeering hers, one hand cupped at the back of her head and the other at the curve of her hips, holding her mouth and body to his, offering her no escape.

She moaned softly. She should have known, from the moment her eyes had met his in Atlantic City, that sooner or later they'd be making love. She should have known that the urgent passion binding them together was too strong to resist. But to have surrendered to that passion in Malcolm's hotel room wouldn't have been right.

Today was different. Today Malcolm had opened to her, and she'd opened to him. They'd each exposed their mistakes. Malcolm had offered her the forgiveness she'd been unable to give herself; he'd forgiven her for her idiocy in believing her father. And she'd forgiven him for the idiocy of having married the wrong woman, something for which he seemed reluctant to forgive himself.

Today she trusted him, trusted him enough to trust her own impulses. Her fingers reached for the buttons of his shirt and plucked them open. She stroked through the soft curls of hair that shaped a triangle across his upper chest, then pressed her mouth to the base of his throat. His hand clenched on her hip and he groaned her name.

She caught her breath and laughed faintly. "I'm not usually like this, Malcolm," she confessed.

He tilted her head back and stared into her eyes, probing them with his own, mining them in search of her soul. "You're not usually like what?" he asked.

Her lips flexed as she sought the right words and the strength to voice them. "So forward?" she attempted.

He grinned wickedly. "Forward? You consider this forward?"

"For me it is," she insisted.

He inched his hand under the edge of her shirt to feel the smooth skin of her back. "If you were forward, you'd have stripped me naked by now."

"Is that what you want me to do?" she asked timorously.

His smile grew gentle, and he kissed the tip of her nose. "I want you to be yourself," he claimed. "If tearing off my clothing is out of character for you, don't do it."

She appreciated his effort to defuse her anxiety with humor, and she impishly countered, "You don't mind staying dressed, then?"

He appeared temporarily shocked, then detected from the sly glimmer in her eyes that she was teasing. "I'll tear off my own clothing and yours, too, Loosh. That would be very much in character for me right now.''

She smiled, then shoved him away. ''I'll be right back,'' she promised before hurrying to the bathroom.

She shut the door and inhaled, trying to ignore the quivers of longing that burned through her as she rummaged in her cabinets. At last she found the blue plastic case she was looking for. When was the last time she'd used this thing, she wondered. When was the last time she'd been so desirous of a man, so crazy with want? It definitely was out of character for Lucia to be feeling what she was feeling for Malcolm right now.

As soon as she was ready, she returned to him. He was stretched out on her bed, his clothing still on but his sneakers and socks off. He leaned up on one elbow as she shyly entered the bedroom and closed the door behind her. She gazed across the room at him, seeing in his posture, in his expression, in his glowing eyes and his wistful smile the same longing that drummed through her body. For a moment all she could do was stand where she was, staring at him, savoring the sheer pleasure of wanting him.

''You aren't getting cold feet, are you?'' he asked.

She smiled slightly and crossed to the bed. Malcolm reached for her hand and drew her down beside him. ''Whom should I strip naked first?'' he asked. ''Me or you?''

''You,'' she answered.

He laughed. ''Forget it, Loosh.'' He tugged off her shirt and hurled it across the room. She wasn't wearing a bra—as small-breasted as she was, she didn't need one—and Malcolm's laughter faded. He studied her first with his eyes and then with his hands, tracing a line between the firm swells and then around them. ''Oh, Lucia.'' He sighed, easing her onto her back and drawing his fingers forward to caress one nipple. All traces of humor were gone, replaced by an almost reverent joy at the lovely texture of her skin and the responsive hardening of the pink crest as he fondled it.

He bowed to kiss the other breast. When his tongue flicked over the nipple, she gasped at the abrupt increase in tension that seized her. "Malcolm," she pleaded, pulling uselessly at the soft cotton covering his chest. "Mal. Take off your shirt."

"Uh-uh," he refused, kissing a trail down her midriff to her waist. He raised himself to unfasten her shorts. "You had your chance to strip me," he chided her as he lifted her hips and completed undressing her. "You blew it. Next time, you'll know better."

He tossed her shorts and panties to the floor and leaned back to scrutinize her. His unabashed appraisal of her embarrassed her, and she reflexively rolled onto her side and drew up her knees. He easily rearranged her on her back, shifting upward to hold her down by her shoulders. "Don't be ashamed," he whispered.

"I'm not," she argued weakly. "But when you look at me that way—"

"I look at you that way because you're beautiful," he murmured.

She eyed him skeptically. "You were the one who told me to beware of men who called me beautiful," she pointed out.

"I was referring to men who called you beautiful when they were looking at your money. I'm looking at you."

"You don't think I'm too tall and skinny?" she asked.

He sat back to assess her body. "You're slim and graceful," he assured her. "And as far as being too tall, well, given my perspective, nobody's too tall."

She grinned briefly, then grew solemn again. "What about my nose?"

"Your nose is gorgeous," Malcolm asserted. "And so is your hair. Your sister doesn't know beans when it comes to your hair." He lifted a heavy lock of it and touched it to his lips. "Was she the one who convinced you you weren't beautiful?"

"Nobody had to convince me," Lucia replied. "I've got eyes."

"Beautiful eyes," Malcolm whispered. "And a beautiful nose and a beautiful mouth." He fused his own mouth to hers in a leisurely kiss. After what felt like an eternity, he tore his lips away and gasped for air. "Am I really going to have to undress myself?" he asked hoarsely.

"I'll help," she offered.

While she tugged off his shirt, he applied himself to his jeans. Within seconds he was naked. His lean, hard body enthralled Lucia. Her hands journeyed over his muscular shoulders, down his streamlined torso to his rock-hard hips. He closed his eyes, relishing her delicate touch, and then opened them again as his hands began their own exploration of her. His fingers traveled over the small mounds of her breasts to her flat stomach, then lower, circumventing the silky thatch of hair between her hips to stroke her thighs. "I've been dreaming about touching your legs all day," he confessed.

She sighed as his palm toured the smooth curve of her calf then ran back up to her thigh again. "But you didn't," she whispered, his voice dissolving into a moan as he tantalized the inner flesh of her thighs. "You didn't touch me all day. I don't mean my legs—I mean anywhere," she added.

"I didn't want to scare you," he revealed, his hand inching higher. "I waited until I was sure you wanted me to." His fingers played through the soft curls, then discovered the moist flesh beneath. "You do want me, don't you?"

"Yes," she breathed, arching her hips in rhythm with his hand. She moaned as her body responded to his intimate touch. Her soul became fluid, melting, bathing her with heat. "Yes, Malcolm, I do," she vowed, her voice soft and tremulous.

"I love you, Lucia," Malcolm whispered.

Her eyes came into sharp focus on his face; his body was angled above hers, his gaze unmoving as he watched her. "You don't have to say that," she told him.

"I'm not saying it because I have to," he insisted. "I'm saying it because it's the truth."

Before she could dispute him, he kissed her, his body following up onto her. Her legs opened to him and he entered her with an eager thrust.

For an instant he didn't move. He remained welded to her, surrounded by her warmth, content simply to find himself within the haven of her body. He felt safe inside her, safe and certain. He had dreamed of something like this, not just since the evening he first saw her, but since he first wondered about love, since he first wondered what love could be like with a woman as pure, as selfless, as generous and honest as Lucia. He didn't want to move. He wanted to treasure this moment. He wanted to live in Lucia's arms, in her body, forever.

But then she moved against him, and he reacted. His hips found an instinctive tempo and followed it. He lifted his head to view Lucia and saw in her eyes the rapture he felt, the sublime joy of their joining, their sharing, their love. He watched as her breath grew shorter, as the light in her eyes intensified, as her teeth caught her lower lip. Her fingers dug imperatively into the small of his back and she arched higher, forcing him deeper, demanding everything from him.

He viewed the changes in her face and felt them in her body—the tension, the sudden stiffening, the hovering as she waited for the storm to break. Her mouth opened and her head fell back onto the pillow as the release swept through her in heavenly pulses of bliss. A soft cry filled the air, Lucia's cry of ecstasy, of satisfaction.

He loved her. He followed her into heaven, met her there, exploded with the truth of his own life.

Chapter Seven

Long after his body had become still, he continued to feel the changes in hers, the private tremors, the secret echoes of love that Malcolm could never begin to understand. She was a woman, mysterious, experiencing sensations he could only guess at, lost in a paradise he could never reach. Her eyes were distant, looking at him but seeing something else, something she alone could know. He was thrilled to have pleased her; he only hoped she remembered that he was a part of this and that, wherever she was, he had brought her there.

Then her hands moved languorously up his back, and her eyes came into focus on his face, above hers. She smiled. Her smile was indescribably lovely, a bewitching mixture of contentment and astonishment as she studied him. Her eyes glittered with tears, but she didn't look sad. "Mal," she murmured.

"I knew it would be this way," he whispered. He bowed to kiss her and her fingers curled through his hair, holding his head to her. "I knew it, Lucia, right from the start; I knew it would be like this with us." He fought against her hands, raising himself enough to be able to see her. "You knew it, too," he claimed, his voice hushed but certain.

She peered up at him, at the fine, strong lines of his face, lines that had intrigued her the first time she'd seen him, lines that would never stop intriguing her. Yes, she'd known it would be this way with Malcolm. Right from the start, from that first instant when their eyes met and an almost tangible longing arced through the air between them, she had known it would be this way.

She slid her hand forward and traced the angle of his jaw. It was marked by a faint stubble of beard, a measure of how long they'd been together. She ran her fingernails tenderly along the hair-roughened skin and grinned at the scratchy sound. "I'm glad you're here," she said.

He eased off her and settled on his side, rolling her with him so that they faced each other. "I'm glad I'm here, too," he confirmed, brushing her thick hair back from her face. "It's been a wonderful day. And I have every expectation that it'll be a wonderful night."

Lucia smiled briefly, then grew serious. "Was it really a wonderful day for you? I didn't exactly welcome you with open arms."

"I feel pretty welcome right now," Malcolm assured her.

Lucia wove her fingers through his and gazed earnestly at him. "I was so snippy when you sprang yourself on me, and then I sat around and blubbered like a baby."

"And then you dried your eyes, and it was a wonderful day. Didn't you enjoy looking at the houses? I did."

"It was interesting," Lucia conceded. "That last house we visited was kind of nice, actually."

"The ranch house? It was too small," Malcolm dismissed it.

"Who needs a big house?" Lucia argued. "The bigger the house, the bigger the heating bills. And the more rooms you've got to clean."

Malcolm opened his mouth and then shut it. What would Lucia think if she ever saw his home, he wondered. What would she say about the four-story town house he owned in the elite neighborhood of Manhattan's Upper East Side? What would she say about the spacious rooms, the high ceilings, the arching stairs? Would she say that his home was too big, causing astronomical heating bills, requiring too much effort to keep clean? He'd tell her that he could easily afford the heating bills, and that he paid a housekeeper to keep the place clean, and...Lucia would loathe him. She'd think he was money-mad and loathe him.

He couldn't let her find out about his house. He couldn't let her learn how wealthy he was. Not yet. Not until he was absolutely sure of her, sure that she could love him no matter what. Not until he was sure she loved him enough to believe that his money hadn't made him evil, that it hadn't corrupted him or allowed him to corrupt others. He didn't intend to lie to Lucia, but he saw no harm in keeping the truth from her for just a little while, just until he was sure of things between them.

She was waiting for him to say something, and he obliged. "I suppose that ranch could be expanded if you ever needed more room."

"I liked the land around it, too," said Lucia. "All those trees. It was almost completely isolated. You couldn't see any of the neighboring houses." She closed her eyes to conjure a picture of the property in her mind. "I liked that house, Mal. Not that I want to buy it," she added hastily, opening her eyes again. "It's much too expensive."

"For the size," Malcolm concurred. "But you could probably bargain the owner down some."

"I could?"

"Of course. There's almost always room to maneuver in house prices."

"What do you think I could bargain it down to?" Lucia asked eagerly.

Malcolm chuckled. "I thought you didn't want to buy it."

"I'm only asking hypothetically," she defended herself. "For the sake of argument, let's just suppose I did want to buy that ranch house. What would I have to do to bargain down the price?"

Malcolm eyed her dubiously, then chuckled again. "Hypothetically?" he teased. At her insistent nod, he proceeded. "All right. Hypothetically. First, you'd bring in a licensed inspector, who would in all likelihood find plenty of things wrong with the place."

"What kind of things?" Lucia asked.

"Maybe the roof needs repair. Or the furnace is about to die. Or the storm windows need caulking, or the gutters need to be replaced."

"I never realized so many things could be wrong without my even noticing them," Lucia muttered, her enthusiasm ebbing.

Malcolm smiled. "None of those things are that significant. They're bargaining chips. Every house has something wrong with it. You buy a house assuming that eventually you'll have to repair the roof or replace the gutters."

"It must get to be pretty costly," Lucia mumbled.

"Nothing a jackpot winner like you can't afford," Malcolm reminded her. "And besides all the shortcomings the inspection would uncover, you'd have other bargaining tools at your command. The size of the house, for instance. Commuting costs. You might tell the owner you would have to replace the electric range with a gas range. You might tell him you're also very interested in a four-bedroom split-level in mint condition that's listed at a lower asking price. You'd make the owner squirm. Eventually he'd come down in price."

"How do you know so much about all this?" Lucia asked, clearly impressed.

"I know a lot about a lot of things," he said with a modest shrug. "Maybe not about athlete's foot and all that chemical jargon you threw at me today, but when it comes to investments, I know a thing or two." He grinned mischievously. "I bet you only love me for my expertise."

"No, Malcolm," Lucia disputed him. "That's not why I love you, and you—"

She stopped abruptly, but the words had already been spoken. As she felt their full impact, she comprehended the irrefutable truth in them. She did love Malcolm.

His smile vanished as he studied her, waiting anxiously for her to retract what she'd said. She didn't.

He leaned forward to kiss her. His arms and legs enveloped her, drawing her body fully against his. His tongue filled her mouth, challenging its partner, engaging it in erotic combat. Lucia's hands molded themselves to his shoulders and then glided down to his ribs. She felt his hunger in the tensing of his muscles, the instinctive rocking of his hips to hers, and she matched his movements, as insatiably aroused as he was.

And then the telephone rang. Malcolm froze, then released her and cursed. "Ignore it," Lucia said, cuddling up to him.

It rang a second time. "I can't ignore a ringing phone," he complained.

"It's probably only some clown from the Society for the Preservation of Squid Ink," Lucia hazarded. "Ignore it."

"I can't." Malcolm drew back from Lucia and sat up as the phone rang a third time. He couldn't help himself; he was compulsive about telephones. If he were trying to escape a burning house and a telephone rang, he'd undoubtedly risk death by smoke inhalation to answer the phone and inform the caller, "You've caught me at a bad time. Can we talk later?" If he were unemployed, standing in an endless line and underlining want ads for sewer scrubbers—minimum wage, no experience necessary—while waiting his turn to pick up his compensation check, he'd ask the fellow behind him to hold his place in line while he raced to the pay phone in the hall and called his secretary at Advent. "Any messages for me?" he'd inquire. "I know it's been two years since I was canned, but I was curious."

And if he were about to seduce the most exciting woman he'd ever met in his life, he'd hand her a brochure to read and call up his answering machine to hear if there were any important messages on it. That was simply the way Malcolm was.

Sighing, Lucia lifted the receiver on the fourth ring. "Hello," she said, then scowled. "Oh, hello, Rick." She shifted away from Malcolm and sighed again. Her finger coiled impatiently through the springy wire as she listened. "There's a good reason for that," she said dryly. "I was out." She listened, and her frown deepened. "Well, I'm glad you had a nice time last night, but—no, I take that back, Rick. I wish you'd had a lousy time last night. *I* had a lousy time."

Malcolm slid across the bed to Lucia. Even frowning, she looked so beautiful, her back arched, her skin smooth and soft, her hair draping like a silk cape across her shoulders. He kissed her arm, and she tried to bat him away. "No," she said.

"Why not?" Malcolm asked, nibbling his way to her wrist.

"Not you," she mouthed, wrenching her hand from him and shoving him across the bed. Into the phone she said, "Looking for a house to buy. What's it to you? No, not in the Watchungs. I have no intention whatsoever of buying a house in the Watchungs. If you want a house in the Watchungs, I'm not stopping you." She whispered an oath. "I'm not stopping you. Whether or not you can afford—" She pursed her lips angrily. "Rick, I really can't talk right now. I've got company. I'll see you at work." She hung up and cursed again.

Malcolm moved back to her. He propped her chin up with his thumb, guiding her face to his. "My fault," he murmured contritely. "I shouldn't have made you answer it."

Lucia managed an unconvincing smile. "Forgiven," she said.

"Who is he?" Malcolm asked, angling his head toward the telephone.

"A man who thinks I'm beautiful," Lucia grumbled bitterly, her smile completely gone.

"Oh, God," Malcolm groaned. "I'm jealous."

"Don't be. He's only looking at my money when he says that I'm beautiful."

"But you went out with him last night," Malcolm surmised.

Lucia tendered a wry smile. "You know, maybe we ought to invest in a conference phone, so we could eavesdrop on each other's calls more efficiently. What do you think, Mal? Would that be a good idea?''

He was too absorbed by the thought of her dating another man to respond to her wisecrack. ''What happened last night?'' he persisted.

He looked so unnecessarily concerned that Lucia softened. Her smile returned. ''You heard what I told him. I had a lousy time.''

Malcolm appeared slightly hopeful. ''Why? What was lousy about it?''

''He was obnoxious. He kept pawing my knee under the table at the restaurant.''

''You're kidding.'' Malcolm turned to confront her knees. ''Not that I blame him,'' he added as his hand cupped over her kneecap. ''You have lovely knees.'' He traced the oval bone thoughtfully. ''You work with this fellow, then?''

''Unfortunately.''

''And you see him every day?''

She was momentarily distracted by the pattern Malcolm's thumb was sketching over her knee. He concentrated for an instant on the faint round scar at its center, a memento of a roller-skating fall from her childhood. Eventually his hand stopped moving, and she remembered to answer his question. ''Every day? No—or at least, I didn't see him every day until after I won the jackpot. He used to specialize in flirting with the secretaries. But ever since I came into some money, he's been hanging around my lab, telling me how beautiful I look when I take off my lab glasses.''

''I bet you look beautiful even when you're wearing your lab glasses,'' Malcolm mused. His fingers slid behind her knee to caress the skin there. Lucia had never suspected that the underside of her knee could be so sensitive to touch, but as he drew an abstract maze over her flesh, she felt a tender ache spread up her thigh. "What does he think about your buying a house?" Malcolm asked, as if he were totally unaware of what his hand was doing to her.

"He wants me to help him buy a vacation house in the Watchung Mountains," she whispered. "Malcolm—"

She reached for his shoulder, but he leaned away. "Is it nice there? Do you want to look at houses there tomorrow?"

"I want . . ." Her voice trembled, then dissolved into a moan when his hand ran back up her thigh to the soft curve of her bottom. Malcolm's playful smile disappeared as he discerned the yearning in Lucia's face, in her profoundly dark eyes. What she wanted now had nothing to do with vacation houses in the Watchung Mountains. And Malcolm was delighted.

SHE WOKE UP. The bedroom was cloaked in the night's darkness, and she waited until her eyes adjusted to the gloom before turning to look at Malcolm.

He was sleeping soundly on the pillow beside her. His eyes were closed, his lips relaxed, the bristle sprouting along his jaw a bit more visible than it had been earlier that evening. The lightweight blanket had slid nearly to his waist, and Lucia indulged in an admiring inspection of his athletic chest, with its sleek muscles and its triangular shadow of hair.

She returned her gaze to his face. He appeared so serene in sleep, she thought, so human. So accessible. So vulnerable. If she had never had the opportunity to see anything of him but the polished, authoritative gentleman he'd been in Atlantic City, she wouldn't have fallen in love with him. She would have found him interesting, no doubt, and attractive. But to love him, she had to see him as he was now, stripped down to human proportions, real and natural.

She had seen his humanity all day. It wasn't just that he wore clothing she could identify with, or drove a car that creaked and squeaked like hers. It wasn't that he had abruptly stopped being the businessman he was; he hadn't. They'd discussed investments, they'd looked at houses, he'd revealed his expertise.

But as she'd told him, she didn't love him for his expertise. She respected him for it, and relied on him for it, but that wasn't why she loved him.

She reached out and ran her fingers gingerly through the inviting mat of hair curling across his upper chest. He stirred, his head shifting on the pillow, but he didn't wake up.

She watched him and meditated. His body was magnificent, and his ability as a lover transcended anything Lucia had ever before dreamed, let alone experienced. But even that wasn't what made her love him.

She'd never really been in love before. There had been a couple of serious relationships. In college she'd dated a classmate steadily for two years, but when they'd gone their separate ways to attend graduate school, he in California and Lucia in Pennsylvania, their feelings didn't survive the distance. A similar thing had occurred in graduate school—she'd become involved with a man, they'd dated each other exclusively, and then they'd wound up taking jobs in different regions of the country, and their relationship hadn't survived.

Jeff had urged Lucia to reject the senior research position at Parker Chemicals and accompany him to Houston, maintaining that she'd find a similar job there. But she'd chosen not to turn down the offer from Parker

Chemicals. It had been her goal in life to get just such a job, working at a solid, well-established firm and receiving a steady, comfortable income. She'd never give that up to follow a man, even if he was willing to support her—*especially* if he was willing to support her. Lucia knew too well what happened to women who depended on men for support. Either the woman loved the man blindly, and therefore put up with all his selfish nonsense, as Lucia's mother did, or else the woman became addicted to the support and forgot about love altogether, as Lucia's sister did.

Lucia supposed that if she'd truly loved Jeff, she would have taken a chance on her future and followed him to Texas. But she hadn't. She didn't like taking chances that way. All the evidence she'd seen in her youth had indicated that taking those kinds of chances invariably led to failure and heartache.

Staring at Malcolm, contemplating the sleep-softened lines and angles of his face, Lucia acknowledged that for the first time in her life she loved a man enough to take a chance. In fact, she'd already taken chances on him, even before she knew she loved him. And today she'd seen her gamble pay off. In his hotel room a week ago, she'd been certain that she'd chosen the wrong man to bet on. But now, after chastising herself for days about having taken a foolish risk by letting him invade her life, she found herself flush with success.

She rested her head against Malcolm's shoulder and felt his arm tighten reflexively around her, holding her snugly to him. She felt luckier tonight than she'd felt when she won the jackpot. Winning money was no sign of good luck. Winning the love of a man like Malcolm—and discovering that she returned his love—was genuine good luck, miraculous luck.

They were roused Sunday morning at nine o'clock by the ringing of the telephone. "Ignore it," Lucia mumbled groggily.

Malcolm eyed the offending phone and groaned. He knew he ought to do something about his compulsiveness when it came to phones, and Lucia was just the sort of positive influence he needed to break the telephone habit. He yanked his pillow from beneath his head and plopped it onto the jangling phone to muffle it. "Move over," he grunted, attempting to appropriate part of her pillow for himself.

"Nobody told you to throw away your own pillow," Lucia protested with a laugh, clinging tenaciously to her pillow. "This one's mine."

"Loosh," he pleaded in a sleep-hoarse voice. "Come on. You're supposed to be disgustingly noble."

"If I was that disgustingly noble, I'd have answered the phone. It's probably someone calling from the American Association for Agoraphobics in desperate need of a donation."

"At nine on a Sunday morning?"

"You'd be amazed, Malcolm."

The phone stopped ringing, and Malcolm leaned across Lucia to retrieve his pillow. As soon as he lifted it, the phone began to ring again, and he dropped the pillow back onto it.

Lucia clung stubbornly to her pillow and rolled away from Malcolm. He looped a leg over her and straddled her, wrestling her onto her back. "Come on, Loosh, share your pillow," he wheedled, tickling her ribs for good measure.

She shrieked with laughter and tried to push Malcolm off her. But Malcolm pinned her hands to the mattress, and he stifled her laughter with a sudden devouring kiss.

Her eyelids fluttered, then closed as her senses concentrated their energies deep within her, gathering around the responsive center of her body, where drowsiness had burned away. Malcolm's hands relented about her wrists, then released her arms and slid to her head, plunging into her hair. His body adjusted itself above hers, shifting and then moving, sharing his arousal with her.

"I thought you were sleepy," Lucia whispered breathlessly.

"Not anymore," said Malcolm before kissing her again.

The phone stopped ringing, but neither of them noticed. They were lost in their own world of sensation, a universe where telephones went unanswered, where nothing existed but Malcolm and Lucia and their love.

The night before, when Lucia had made love to Malcolm, she hadn't been conscious that she loved him. But now she knew, and that knowledge informed her every response to him, her every motion and gesture. When he took the tip of her ear between his teeth, she moaned not only from the thrill that spun along her nerves at his gentle assault but also because she loved him. And when his hands floated down her abdomen and then up to cover her breasts, and then down again, stroking the length of her torso, she cried out, not only from the poignant frustration of wanting more but from love, love for Malcolm.

His fingers wandered lower and a choked sob broke from her. "What, Lucia?" he asked.

"I love you, Malcolm."

"You don't have to say that," he teased, repeating her words from last night.

Her eyes narrowed on him and she opened her mouth to protest that she *did* love him. But the motions of his fingers against her stunned her into silence. She sank weakly onto the mattress and sighed.

He drew his hand away. "Were you going to say something?" he prodded her, his lips curved in a wicked grin.

She opened her mouth again to tell him that she wasn't saying she loved him because she had to. But she was afraid her voice wouldn't function, and she knew that there were better ways to tell him of her love than with words. She reached for his hand, drew it up to her lips and kissed his fingertips. Then she urged him onto his back and touched her tongue to one of his small, dark nipples. It swelled against her teeth.

Malcolm drew in an erratic breath. "What are you doing?" he asked in a strangely rough whisper as she lapped at his other nipple.

"Saying something," she replied huskily. She nibbled a path to his navel and felt his muscles clench spasmodically in her wake.

The phone began to ring again, but Malcolm was too transported by Lucia's unexpected aggressiveness to care. Lucia herself was oblivious of the phone. She had never *made* love to a man before—she'd always been on the receiving end, being made love to. But now she wanted to give, to give everything to Malcolm. She loved him, and she wanted to tell him.

Her mouth moved lower, and Malcolm sucked in another uneven breath. He gripped her arm and dragged her face back up to his. Crushing his lips forcefully on hers, he twisted her onto her back and drove deep into her, his thrusts wild and potent, consuming Lucia with their immeasurable strength.

The phone stopped ringing, but Lucia's soul continued to resonate in its own distinctive rhythm, each of

Malcolm's surges feeding her, fueling her, propelling her toward the full splendor of her love for him. Her moment came, sweeping through her with its throbbing power, beckoning Malcolm to follow her over the edge.

They lay immobile for many minutes afterward, fighting for breath, fighting to regain their balance. Finally Malcolm raised himself from her and studied her. "Did I hurt you?" he whispered.

"Hurt me?" she echoed in bewilderment.

"You made me so crazy, Lucia, I just..." His voice drifted off as he viewed the blissful radiance of her face, the satisfied flush in her cheeks. "Oh, God. You're more than I bargained for."

She eyed him acutely, her smile fading. "What do you mean?"

"I mean—" he faltered for a moment, then laughed softly "—I mean, I thought you were a scientist, down-to-earth, no pretenses about you. Direct and honest. Disgustingly noble. You're all of those things, Lucia, but...but you're so much more. I can't believe the things you do to me. You're incredible."

The possibility that Malcolm could consider Lucia an incredible lover astounded her. And yet, with him maybe she was. It was nothing innate in her, no great experience or talent but, rather, Malcolm himself who liberated her to be incredible for him. "You love me for my expertise," she murmured slyly.

"Among other things," he allowed. He sat up and shoved his hair back from his face. Spotting his pillow on the telephone, he frowned. "Who do you suppose was trying to reach you?"

She shrugged. "If it was important, they'll try again. If it wasn't, who cares?"

"Well-adjusted, too," he added to her list of assets. "You're much, much more than I bargained for."

After dressing, they settled in her kitchen for a breakfast of English muffins, fruit and coffee. The spring sunshine pouring through the window washed across Malcolm's face, bringing out the bronze hue of his complexion. Staring into his eyes, Lucia was so transfixed by their facets of green-and-gold light that she almost forgot to eat.

"I don't have to be back in New York till tonight," Malcolm announced after draining his coffee cup. "What would you like to do today? Look at more houses?"

"No," Lucia said definitively. "I don't think I want to buy a house."

"Not even that tiny ranch house in the middle of the woods?"

Lucia grinned. "After you started pointing out everything that might be wrong with it, it lost its appeal," she told him. "I don't know, Mal. Buying a house seems so risky." Her grin disappeared as she reminisced. "My parents bought a house once, in Tucson. That was when my father was going to go into the shoe-restyling business. Needless to say, he couldn't make the mortgage payments. We had to skip town in the middle of the night. I don't want to go through that ever again."

"There's no reason to think that you would," Malcolm pointed out. "If you did buy a house, it would be as an investment. You'd buy something that you wouldn't have to take a loss on."

She shook her head and crossed the room to get the coffeepot. Refilling their cups, she said, "I think I'll pass on a house for now. I'll just send my money to Advent. You people can do the right thing with it." Taking her seat across the table from him, she added, "I'm not going to be taking a big risk if I do that, am I?"

"Some of our mutual funds are high-risk," Malcolm informed her. "But if you don't want risk, you'd be best off in our money-market fund. Or anybody's money-market fund," he went on. "You don't have to feel obliged to work with Advent just because I'm there."

"You mean, you didn't drive all this way to make a sale?" Lucia teased him. At his good-natured chuckle, she remarked, "I'd just as soon send my money to a firm where I know someone. Then if things go wrong, I can scream at you."

"Things won't go wrong," Malcolm assured her. "I'll tell you what—I'll have Blanche Richter call you tomorrow. She runs the consumer department of the money-market-fund division. She can give you the most up-to-date information and answer any questions you might have. Can she reach you during the day?"

"Sure," Lucia said. She located a notepad and pencil in a drawer and jotted down her work number.

Malcolm studied the sheet of paper, then folded it and stuffed it into his shirt pocket. "Parker Chemicals," he pondered aloud. "Why don't we go there today?"

"To Parker?" Lucia hooted. "Whatever for?"

"So I can see where you work," Malcolm explained. "I want to know everything about you, Lucia. I want to see the split-pea-soup lagoon, or whatever it is you're a creature from."

"Primordial soup," she corrected him with a laugh. "All right, if you insist."

Malcolm agreed to let her drive. She cruised through town to Parker's modern concrete building and circled the nearly empty parking lot. "Satisfied?" she asked, amused by Malcolm's interest in her workplace.

He lifted his sunglasses off his nose to examine the building. "There are cars here," he noticed. "Do people work Sundays?"

"Sometimes," Lucia answered. "If you're running a timed reaction, sometimes you've got to check it at regular intervals during the weekend. I've occasionally had to come in on Sundays."

"So we could get inside now?" he asked.

"You want to see my lab?"

He smiled. "I'd like to see where you work," he said. "That way, when I find myself thinking about you during the day I'll have a point of reference."

His unexpectedly romantic comment, combined with his endearing dimples, melted Lucia's heart. "All right," she conceded as she parked the car. "In we go."

The weekend guard scrutinized Lucia's identification card and then unlocked the door, issuing a visitor's pass to Malcolm. They headed down the corridor to the elevator, their footsteps echoing in the stillness. When they reached Lucia's floor, she led him down the hall toward her lab, stopping at a supply shelf to pick up an extra pair of lab glasses for him. "Am I supposed to wear these?" he asked.

"You bet. Everybody has to wear them in the lab." She doubted that anything would happen to Malcolm's eyes during their brief visit to her lab, but she didn't want a guard—or a fellow chemist—to come upon them in the lab and find them not wearing regulation safety gear. If that happened, Rick Lansing would hear about it, and Lucia didn't want to have him confronting her over safety violations.

Malcolm dutifully slipped on the goggles, and as soon as Lucia unlocked her office door and entered the cluttered room, she lifted her own lab glasses from her desk and donned them. Malcolm moved nosily around the room, peering at the metal framework above her lab bench and the mysterious flasks and piping rigged inside her hood. He said nothing.

"Well?" Lucia cued him.

He turned to her. "It's not what I expected," he allowed.

"What did you expect?"

"I don't know. Sweat socks or something. A row of sweat socks hanging from a clothesline." He frowned indignantly as Lucia succumbed to a giggle. "Hanging from a clothesline, each with a different chemical inside its toes. And a tray of mushrooms growing below them. Stop laughing at me, Loosh."

She was doubled over, clutching her stomach as she tried to ward off a laughter-induced cramp. "A clothesline? You've got to be kidding! A clothesline?" She leaned against her desk and removed her lab glasses in order to wipe the tears of laughter from her eyes.

Malcolm's frown grew gentle as he watched her laugh. "At the very least, you ought to have had a lot of funny-looking tubes with colorful liquids bubbling through them, and maybe some foul-looking bottle with smoke pouring out the top."

A fresh spate of giggles overcame her. "You mean dry ice?" she suggested.

"Dry ice?"

"Those ridiculous laboratories in the movies," she explained. "It isn't smoke. They use dry ice to make that vapor."

"Okay. Make me feel stupid," Malcolm grumped.

"No—no, Mal, don't feel stupid." She sniffled, eventually composing herself. "You've just seen too many movies.'' A private memory tickled her, and she colored slightly and grinned.

"What?'' he goaded her.

"I was just remembering. The first time I saw you, you reminded me of a James Bond movie.''

His eyebrows shot up and he guffawed. "A James Bond movie?''

"Well, the way you looked in your tuxedo, in the casino. Wasn't there a movie where 007 gets himself all duded up and goes to a casino?''

"Several, probably,'' Malcolm guessed. "But what does that have to do with me? I'm not a spy.''

"No, but you looked so swanky that night,'' she murmured, her laughter spent. "I felt so—so utterly outclassed, Mal.''

He scrutinized her carefully, noticing the pensive sheen in her dark eyes. "You should never feel outclassed by me, Lucia,'' he told her solemnly. "If anything, I should feel outclassed by you.''

"Why?''

"Because you're so basic, so disgustingly noble. Because you have such sound values and views.''

"So do you,'' Lucia said, her voice fluctuating into a question. "Don't you?''

"I'd like to think so, but sometimes…'' He crossed the room to her and hugged her. "Yes, I'd like to think so.''

His enigmatic comment confused her. He seemed to be looking for reassurance, and she endeavored to provide it. "Oh, come on,'' she said heartily. "You're as basic and sound as I am, Mal. You're a regular guy. If I've learned anything this weekend, it's that you're not swanky Mr. Bond. And I like you much better this way. I don't feel outclassed. Okay?''

He hugged her, then released her and turned away. "Okay, Loosh." He swung open the door and waited for her to join him.

She pondered his somber mood as she folded her lab glasses and set them on her desk. Perhaps he was just feeling a little put off because she'd mocked him so mercilessly about his ignorance concerning chemistry labs. "Did you grow up in Manhattan?" she asked as they strolled down the hall to the elevator.

Malcolm returned his borrowed goggles to the supply shelf and nodded. "Born and bred there," he replied. "Why do you ask?"

"I was just thinking that the school labs there were probably pretty poorly equipped. Bunsen burners and kids catching their hair on fire...I mean, the New York City public schools are always suffering from budget problems and all."

"I didn't..." Malcolm hesitated for an instant. "I didn't go to public school," he said quietly.

Lucia eyed him with curiosity. "Oh?"

"I went to a private school. Lots of New Yorkers send their children to private schools."

She took a moment to digest this. "A private school, huh?"

"That's right," he said, his gaze never leaving her face.

"With uniforms, snappy blazers with little emblems on them and all that stuff?"

"Something like that," Malcolm conceded, holding the elevator door as Lucia stepped inside.

"Your parents must have been loaded," Lucia surmised.

He attempted to gauge her reaction. "They could afford it," he said in a guarded voice.

Well, she couldn't exactly say the news astonished her. Malcolm was clearly a sophisticated, well-bred man. He knew how to wear a tuxedo; perhaps that was something students in New York City private schools were taught: how to handle high finance without quailing, how to know which wines were good, how to wear tuxedos. Still, the understanding that Malcolm had such a privileged background disconcerted her, particularly when she compared it to her own sorry childhood, with its overnight moves and foreclosed mortgages.

She remained deep in thought as they turned Malcolm's pass over to the guard and left the building. At her car, Malcolm touched her arm and rotated her to him. "Tell me what you're thinking," he demanded.

"I'm thinking, maybe we're too different," she admitted, focusing on the bone in his throat.

"No. We aren't that different," he told her. He tucked his hand beneath her chin and lifted her face to his. "Your parents didn't have much money, and mine did. That's all. My parents are wealthy, Lucia; but their money doesn't make them evil. Just wealthy."

"And you?"

He considered his words before speaking. "I get by," he granted. "But—even if I *were* wealthy, Lucia, what difference would it make? We're alike in all the things that count."

"You mean because I suddenly happen to be wealthy, too?" she asked. "Malcolm, it's not the same. I mean really wealthy people, private-school-type people...Malcolm, they're the ones folks like my father look up to. They're the ones folks idolize because they have money and most everyone else doesn't. It's people like you, upper-upper-crust people, who make all the poor slobs in the world dream their crazy dreams. It's people like you who drive my father to want so much, and to wind up with so little."

Malcolm's hand tightened on her arm. "Don't think that of me, please," he implored her. "I'm—I'm not upper-upper-crust, and I don't make poor slobs do anything. I'm *me*, Malcolm, Mal. I love you. Where I went to school doesn't matter. How rich my parents are doesn't matter. Money doesn't matter, Lucia. So, for God's sake..." His voice faded as he saw Lucia's troubled expression, her obvious discomfort at the thought that he could be from a social class so alien to her. "Lucia," he whispered, "I'm not that way, I'm really not. I don't worship money any more than you do." He folded his other arm around her shoulders and kissed her brow. "Money is irrelevant, Lucia. We both know that."

"Irrelevant?" she asked, her words muffled by his chest as he held her to him. "Then why are you so worried about my doing smart things with my money?"

"I know more about it than you do, that's all," he reminded her. "It's my profession. It's my field. If I had athlete's foot, I'd turn to you for advice, and I wouldn't feel outclassed at all."

"Just itchy," she commented wryly. She managed a crooked smile and swung open the car door. "Bear in mind, Mal, I've got a long, ghastly history when it comes to money. Maybe it didn't make your parents do weird things, but...but maybe it did. Private school uniforms," she mumbled dubiously as he took his seat beside her.

"I'm not rich," he said swiftly, almost anxiously.

She cast him a probing look, and he stared out the windshield. "You're comfortable," she reminded him, recalling what he'd told her. "You get by."

"Living in Manhattan isn't cheap," he pointed out. "And I'm paying alimony. So if I can manage to keep my head above water, I count my blessings."

Lucia lapsed into silence. Keeping one's head above water she could understand. She could understand comfortable much better than rich. She herself was comfortable now. Comfortable meant not being in debt; it meant living in a safe, decent building that wasn't infested with insects; it meant eating three squares a day. In some cases, apparently, it meant being able to live in Manhattan and pay alimony. She could understand that.

Just because Malcolm's parents might be rich didn't mean he himself was. As she steered onto the main road cutting through town, she tried to imagine Malcolm young, living in some ritzy penthouse, perhaps, with butlers and maids calling him Master Malcolm and stern parents requiring him to dress formally for dinner.

For some reason, she pictured Malcolm's father as a spiritual cousin of her sister's husband, Arthur. A rapacious urban landlord, tearing down tenements in order to construct more profitable skyscrapers, displacing poor people in his avid pursuit of greenbacks. Or maybe not a landlord. Maybe a corporate lawyer, pushing papers around and charging hundreds of dollars an hour. Or maybe just a fool like Lucia's father, only a slightly shrewder one, who'd chosen not shoe restyling, not juggling skunks, but some equally unnecessary gimmick that happened to catch on.

Maybe Malcolm's father had acquired his wealth through a twist of fate. Maybe he'd gambled a few dollars on some slot machine and won a jackpot.

"Do your parents get badgered by the Committee to End Pay Toilets in America?" Lucia asked.

The question startled Malcolm, and he took a moment to assimilate it. "No," he answered. "But they do get asked to donate time and money to various causes. They may not be disgustingly noble, Lucia, but they're moderately noble."

"And they think of their money as a tool, I suppose," she muttered. "As a measurement, like a scale and a ruler."

"They don't think of it much at all," Malcolm remarked. "It's just there."

"*That* rich, huh?" she grunted.

He reached across the seat to touch her arm. "I don't want to defend my parents to you. They aren't evil and they aren't corrupt. I know you have a long and ghastly history when it comes to money, Lucia, but wealthy people can be just as normal as anyone else." At her skeptical frown, he sighed. "Let's forget I even mentioned them, all right? All that really matters here is you and me."

Lucia nodded. Malcolm was correct; all that mattered was that he was himself, someone she could relate to, someone she could understand. Whatever his youth had entailed, he was currently no more a pampered elitist than she was currently a bedraggled waif sneaking through the night to evade a creditor. Their pasts were behind them. They were both adults now, neither rich nor poor, but comfortable, getting by, keeping their heads above water.

And they loved each other. As Malcolm had implied, that was all that really mattered.

Chapter Eight

Evvie edged the office door open just as Lucia was concluding her telephone conversation with Blanche Richter from Advent. Mrs. Richter had proven to be even more informative about the firm's money-market funds than Malcolm had been. "We have several different funds you can choose from," Mrs. Richter had explained in delightfully straightforward English. "Mr. Royce tells me that you're looking for a reasonably low-risk investment. Naturally, the fund with the lowest risk has the lowest interest, but for many people a smaller yield is preferable to losing sleep at night."

"That's the category I fall into," Lucia had said with a laugh.

Mrs. Richter had instructed Lucia to have her bank wire whatever amount of money she wanted to invest in the fund. "I'll handle your account personally," Mrs. Richter had promised Lucia. "That's what Mr. Royce wants."

"Is he your boss?" Lucia asked, as tactless as usual.

"Not really," Mrs. Richter replied. "He's in a different area altogether. But if he wants me personally to keep an eye on your money, I certainly will."

Evvie waited patiently for Lucia to get through the final niceties with Mrs. Richter and hang up the phone. As soon as she did, Evvie charged across the lab to Lucia's desk and leaned against it. "Well?" she asked. "How was your weekend?"

Lucia tugged off her lab glasses and rubbed the bridge of her nose. She could feel her cheeks warming as she eyed her friend through the shield of her fingers. "My weekend," she said, "was fantastic."

Evvie appeared surprised. "No kidding? You thought Friday night was going to be abysmal."

"Friday night was," Lucia confirmed. "But the rest of the weekend more than made up for that." She smiled meekly. "Evvie, I'm in love."

Evvie's surprise increased dramatically. "In love? Loosh, what are you talking about?"

"What do you think I'm talking about?" Lucia rejoined, her smile exultant. "I'm talking about love. As in a man and a woman, fireworks, holding hands, music in the air, all that kind of stuff. I know it's hard to believe, but—"

"That's putting it mildly," Evvie snorted, her eyes bearing down on Lucia. "Loosh, he isn't really your type, is he?"

Lucia leaned back in her swivel chair and grinned complacently. "Actually, he is," she informed Evvie. "You've only seen him in one context, so you don't know what he's truly like. You'll just have to take my word for it at this point—he's a wonderful man. Fantastic. He's a fantastic, wonderful man."

Evvie angled her head, as if a different perspective might clarify things for her. She sighed dismally. "Oh, Loosh. I'm having a lot of trouble believing this."

"What don't you believe? That I could be in love with him, or that he could be in love with me? That's the current status, Evvie. It's mutual. I love him and he loves me."

Evvie's eyes darkened and she gripped Lucia's shoulder. "What's the matter with you?" she scolded. "How do you know he loves you?"

"He told me."

"Lucia." Evvie groaned in exasperation. "A Ph.D. is no guarantee of brains, girl. Maybe he told you this weekend that he loves you, but last month he told Cindy Hawkins in Legal that he loved her, and at the last Christmas party he swore his undying love to Debbie Garvin from Analytical. I can't believe you could take him seriously for more than five minutes."

Lucia's bewilderment surpassed Evvie's. She sat upright and gaped at her blond friend. "What are *you* talking about?"

"Rick Lansing. Rick 'Don Juan' Lansing. Didn't he take you to the Sigma Xi dinner Friday night?"

"Oh!" Lucia erupted in laughter and shook her head. "Oh, no, Evvie, not him. Friday night was a disaster. I just told you that."

"Then who the hell are you in love with?" Evvie demanded to know.

"Malcolm," Lucia told her.

"Malcolm? Malcolm Royce? From Atlantic City?" Evvie's eyes grew round with astonishment.

"Actually, he's from Manhattan, but yes, that's the Malcolm we're talking about."

"But, Loosh, you told me he was married." Lucia had shared with Evvie the ghastly story of her dinner date at the Shangri-la. At the time, Evvie had consoled her with the observation that Malcolm was obviously a slick operator, his many charms notwithstanding, and that Lucia had acted wisely in removing herself from his room before things could get out of hand.

"He isn't," Lucia now informed Evvie. "He drove all the way to my apartment Saturday just to show me his divorce decree. Isn't that romantic?"

Evvie curled her nose. "My own experience with divorce decrees has taught me that there's nothing romantic about them. I sincerely hope there was more to your weekend with him than that."

"There was. Much more," Lucia murmured, then blushed and averted her eyes.

"I get the picture," Evvie said with a grin. "Well, like I said, the man does have his charms. He's head and shoulders above any of the blind dates I've set you up on, so be my guest and love him."

"Thanks so much for giving me your permission," Lucia joked.

A movement at the door provoked the women to turn. Rick Lansing filled the open doorway, looking rather like an owl in his oversized goggles. Lucia spun her chair back to her desk in time to see Evvie snatch her lab glasses from the blotter and slip them on. "Don't cite me," she called to Rick. "I'm protected."

"I'm not," Lucia muttered through gritted teeth as she took a swipe at her stolen goggles. "Give them back."

Evvie eased herself off the desk and plucked the goggles from her tiny nose. She handed them to Lucia and covered her eyes conspicuously with her arm. "I'm on my way, Rick," she announced. "Don't cite me." When he stepped through the doorway to allow Evvie to pass, she eyed Lucia mischievously and said, "Hey, Rick, have you heard? Lucia's in love." Before Lucia could scream, Evvie was gone.

Grimacing, Lucia shoved the lab glasses upon her nose with her thumb and pretended to be engrossed in the computer printout spread across her desk.

"Have you got a few minutes?" Rick asked.

"Is this a safety inspection?" she shot back. "If it is, you won't find any infractions."

"It's a friendly visit," Rick said, closing the door behind him and removing his goggles as he sidled toward her desk.

Lucia cursed beneath her breath. She resolutely kept her lab glasses on as she glowered at him.

"Are you really in love?" he asked, occupying the desk corner Evvie had just vacated.

"I don't think that's any of your business," Lucia retorted. Even before last Friday night's date, she'd lost her sense of humor about Rick's advances. She used to be able to laugh about his obtuseness and his lack of subtlety, but not anymore.

"Well, I was thinking maybe it *is* my business," he commented, not at all discouraged by her curt tone. "I mean, I'm going to marry you, so—"

"Oh, will you shut up?" Lucia snapped. "You aren't going to marry me. And while we're on the subject, I'm not going to buy you a house in the Watchung Mountains. So please leave me alone."

"Won't you at least just look at the place I've got in mind? You'll love it, Lucia. It's beautiful. It's as beautiful as you are."

"Spare me!" she protested. "I can't believe the secretaries in Legal fall for your garbage, Rick. You're so obvious about wanting to get your hands on my money. Well, that's not going to happen, and I'm sick and tired of your hassling me about it. Even Joyce Dailey and Josephine Taggart have stopped regaling me with sad stories about cat claws and sex therapy. It's about time you stopped too.''

"Sex therapy?'' Rick's attention perked up. "Joyce Dailey needs sex therapy?''

"No, her cat does,'' Lucia grumbled. "Please leave.''

Rick glanced at the door and then back at Lucia. "Was Hooper pulling my leg, or are you really in love?'' he asked.

Lucia sighed. "I'm really in love,'' she declared, hoping that that would dissuade him.

He pondered the news for several seconds. "How do you know *he* doesn't want to get his hands on your money?''

"Because—'' Lucia's jaw flexed with anger that Rick could insinuate such a thing about Malcolm "—because he doesn't need my money.''

"He's rich?''

"He's comfortable.''

"So am I,'' Rick pointed out.

"He's more comfortable than you,'' Lucia argued, then groaned. How in the world had she gotten caught up in such a ridiculous dialogue?

"So, he *is* rich?'' Rick guessed. "Now that you're rich, you don't want to have anything to do with the lower orders, is that it? You know, you never struck me as the snobbish sort, Lucia. In fact, you always struck me as the opposite.''

"I am the opposite,'' Lucia maintained. "I'm an antisnob. I don't like rich people. Okay? Are you satisfied?''

"Then he's not rich,'' Rick concluded. "In which case, he's probably after your money, just like I am.''

"This conversation is at an end," Lucia decided. She swiveled to her desk and stared at the computer print-out, praying for him to leave.

Rick hovered behind her, studying the jagged line etched across the page. "What does that peak mean?" he asked, trying to impress Lucia by demonstrating his rudimentary understanding of advanced chemical analysis.

"It means," she said coldly, "that if you don't leave this lab within ten seconds, you're going to get a face full of hydrochloric acid."

"This is why it's so important to wear your lab glasses at all times," Rick said piously, tapping his goggles with his index finger. At the if-looks-could-kill glare Lucia cast him, he hastened to the door. "I'm on my way, beautiful lady," he said. "But think about it, Lucia. At least I'm candid about what I want. This other guy...if he isn't rich, then ten'll get you twenty he's after your money."

"I'm not a betting woman," Lucia grunted. "Get out of here." With a supercilious smile, Rick departed.

Left in solitude, Lucia felt her shoulders slump as the tension she'd felt in Rick's presence ebbed from her muscles. How dare he impugn Malcolm? How dare Rick attribute his own grubby avarice to someone else? Just because Rick was crass didn't mean every man who took an interest in Lucia was.

After all, Malcolm himself had been the one to warn Lucia about men like Rick. Malcolm had been the one to caution her about men pretending to be taken by her while they were, in fact, planning to take her. Malcolm had been the one to tell her to beware of men who called her beautiful.

But he'd called her beautiful himself. The first night, when they were alone in the backseat of the limousine, he'd called her beautiful. And Saturday night, when she'd lain naked with him, he'd called her beautiful.

When he said it, it was different, she assured herself. When Malcolm called her beautiful, he was looking at her soul. She knew that.

And anyway, if he *were* after her money, he wouldn't have spent the weekend advising her to buy a house. Of course, Rick had spent much of Friday evening advising Lucia to buy a house—a specific vacation house in the Watchung Mountains. But that was because Rick wanted that particular house. Lucia didn't think Malcolm was personally interested in owning a house in central New Jersey. Why in the world would he want such a thing, when he lived and worked in Manhattan?

And hadn't he explained to her that the idea behind buying a house was to build equity, to invest her money in something sound? A vacation house in the Watchung Mountains didn't seem like such a sound investment to Lucia. But a house in the growing suburbs of central New Jersey... Lucia would certainly see her money appreciate if she purchased a house in the area.

That thought brought her up short. She yanked off her lab glasses and massaged her temples, trying to clear her skull. Since when did she care whether her money appreciated?

Since Malcolm had entered her life, that was when. Since Malcolm had made his intelligent-sounding suggestions about not throwing her money away but, instead, investing it, donating the interest while retaining the principal. Not until Malcolm had begun to advise her about how to handle her jackpot winnings had she ever thought in terms of investments and equity and things like that. Before Malcolm had shared his insights with her, Lucia had been planning to give the entire amount away.

Had Malcolm really changed her mind for her? No. He'd influenced her, she'd grant that. But receiving 149 letters from charities and individuals begging for donations had certainly had more than a little to do with Lucia's decision to keep her money. So had the one donation she'd made, under false pretenses, to her father. Without Malcolm's help, left to her own devices, Lucia was bound to make some drastic errors. That was why she was putting her trust in his financial counsel.

In any case, she could think of no good reason why Malcolm would want her money. As he said, he was comfortable, he got by, he kept his head above water, even while living in Manhattan and paying alimony to a woman whom nobody could afford. Yes, he'd said that to Lucia, too: "Nobody can afford Polly."

She pressed her fingertips deeper into her temples. She felt a headache taking shape behind her eyes, and she didn't like the notions that had spawned it. Damn Rick for having planted seeds of suspicion about Malcolm inside her, she railed inwardly. If Malcolm truly needed money—to pay for his unaffordable ex-wife or anything else—he had rich parents he could turn to. He didn't need Lucia's money.

Unless, of course, his parents refused to give him money. Who knew? Maybe they hadn't approved of his marriage, or of his divorce. The sort of people who'd sent their son to private school where blazers with breast-pocket patches were de rigueur might just be priggish enough not to help their son out financially when he needed it.

But even without his parents' assistance, Malcolm clearly wasn't destitute. "Comfortable" in Manhattan meant "rich" anywhere else. Evidently, he had a decent job—Blanche Richter had sounded appropriately deferential whenever she mentioned Mr. Royce. He must be some sort of upper-level manager at Advent, and that would mean he earned a more than respectable salary. So, he drove a dilapidated Chevy years past its prime. So, he couldn't afford a fancy car. Perhaps he could if he didn't have to fork out so much in alimony every month.

Lucia groaned. Her headache was reaching fruition, and she frankly didn't like the route her thoughts had taken. Not once all weekend had her faith in Malcolm slipped, not once had her trust been shaken. Why should she allow a creep like Rick Lansing to undermine her confidence in Malcolm? Rick had made his nasty remarks because he was envious and resentful. Why should Lucia waste her time weighing them for possible accuracy?

She managed to remain focused on her work until closing time, and before she'd been home more than ten minutes, Malcolm telephoned her. The mere sound of his voice instantly erased all her doubts. "Hello, Loosh," he greeted her in his low, husky voice. "I missed you last night."

A heady warmth rippled through her at his compliment. "If you really miss me so much, Mal, you could drive out to see me now," she invited him.

"I'd love that, Loosh, but I can't," he complained. "I've got a working dinner at seven o'clock tonight." He sighed. "I wish I could play hooky and see you, but I can't."

"Of course," she agreed, touched that he'd even consider playing hooky to be with her. She arranged herself comfortably on her bed, which seemed cavernous to her without Malcolm in it. "Your pal Blanche Richter called me today, speaking of your work," Lucia related.

"Oh?"

"I'm supposed to have my bank wire my money to her tomorrow. She said she's personally going to keep track of it."

"Well, Blanche is excellent at what she does. You can be sure your money will grow while she's looking after it."

Lucia mused for a moment. "How come she calls you Mr. Royce when you call her Blanche?" she inquired. "She said you weren't her boss."

"I'm not," Malcolm asserted. "If I were talking shop with a friend of hers, I'd refer to her as Mrs. Richter. It's business etiquette. She doesn't call me Mr. Royce to my face." He exhaled. "Let's not talk about work, all right? I've had a rough day. Cheer me up."

"I'd rather cheer you up in person, but if you'd prefer to go to a business dinner, that's your problem," Lucia teased. "When can I cheer you up in person, Mal? This weekend?"

"I was hoping you'd say that," he readily concurred. "I've got 'Loosh' written in ink all over my calendar for Saturday and Sunday."

"Why not Friday, too?" Lucia suggested. "We could get together after work—"

"I can't," Malcolm cut her off. He sounded sorely disappointed. "I wish I could, but I've got—it's a long-standing engagement, and I can't back out."

"With another woman?" Lucia asked, then bit her lip and winced. She couldn't believe her own tactlessness sometimes.

Malcolm didn't seem at all rattled by her question, however. "No," he answered. "It's a family obligation.

A party of sorts. I promised my folks I'd make an appearance, and they're counting on me.''

Well, Malcolm already knew she was tactless, and it didn't seem to bother him. "Why don't you bring me along?" she suggested. "If it's a party, they probably won't mind if you drag along a date. As a matter of fact, I happen to own a decent silk dress. You saw it in Atlantic City."

"I remember," he murmured, his voice seductively soft. "I remember that dress very well, and I promise you you're going to wear it with me again, so I can see what it's like to pull those straps off your shoulders. The sandals, too. The whole outfit . . ." His voice dissolved into a guttural sigh. "But not this Friday. It's just not the sort of thing I could bring you to."

Lucia measured his words. "Are you angry that I invited myself?" she asked.

He chuckled. "Not at all. One of the things I love about you is that you aren't coy. You always say exactly what you're thinking. I like that. A lot. Damn," he grunted. "I thought talking to you would cheer me up, and instead it's making me miss you even more. Look, I can't really talk—I've got to get changed and meet my associates downtown for dinner. But I'll call you tomorrow night, all right?"

"All right," Lucia agreed.

"And I'll see you Saturday. I can drive out early—"

"Or maybe I could come to New York," Lucia commented. "I could spend the weekend with you, Mal. Wouldn't that be fun? We could go to a museum, or a show, maybe. I haven't been in the city in a long time."

"I . . . I don't know," he said. "I like getting out of the city for the weekend myself. But we can make plans after this week, okay? I'm really running late."

"Okay. Have a good dinner, Mal."

"I'd rather be with you," he insisted. "I love you, Loosh."

"I love you too," she whispered before hanging up.

MALCOLM STARED at the telephone for a full minute. He didn't like lying to Lucia. Well, he hadn't actually lied, he tried to console himself. But he *had* been evasive. He couldn't bring her with him to his parents' fund-raising gala Friday night, and he couldn't let her come to New York, not yet. He needed at least another weekend with her, away from all this, to make absolutely sure of things between them.

His gaze circled his massive bedroom, with its silk-papered white walls and heavy mahogany furnishings. He'd paid a small fortune to have the place redecorated after his divorce. Polly had favored pastels, lush lavender chaises and floral spreads, frilly girlish stuff that had never appealed to Malcolm, even when he thought he loved her. Once she'd moved out, he'd gotten rid of all the evidence of her taste that had marked his home.

He wondered what Lucia would think of his bedroom. She'd probably like the simple decor. Her own bedroom was plain, lacking in ruffles and frippery. It had a hominess that pleased him, and he wanted to think his bedroom would please her.

It would, he knew. She'd like the style of it—if she ever reached the bedroom level. But more likely than not, she'd be so disconcerted by Malcolm's obvious wealth that she wouldn't make it as far as the master bedroom. She'd probably turn and bolt before they reached the stairway at the end of the first-floor foyer.

He didn't have time to think about that now. Hastening through his dressing room to the bathroom, he applied a razor to his five-o'clock shadow and tried to concentrate on the business dinner he had to attend. In time, he hoped, in time Lucia would understand how things were when one was a Royce. In time she'd accept his wealth as easily as she accepted him.

In time, he prayed, she'd even accept attending fund-raisers for the Royce Collection, one of his parents' pet projects. The Royce Collection raised money to purchase art for public museums. It was a noble pursuit, but not the sort of charitable activity Malcolm chose for himself. He generally preferred to donate his time and money to projects for the handicapped. Polly used to hate his projects—she thought they lacked glamour. "Who wants to watch a bunch of retarded kids run in a race?" she'd whined, during his participation in a Special Olympics organizing drive. "Do you really need to give money to that program where people read novels onto cassette tapes for the blind? At least, if you were hiring professional actors instead of just any old readers, we could mingle with some exciting people." Polly had greatly preferred the social obligations of raising money for the Royce Collection.

But as much as Malcolm appreciated art museums, he felt he could make more important contributions elsewhere. Not because he was disgustingly noble, but because he was a Royce, privileged, and he owed it to those in the world who had less than he had.

Polly would have shone at his parents' upcoming gala, he knew. She lived for such parties; she flourished at them. It was no wonder that his parents approved of her, even after her adulteries became known. "Every woman has her faults," Malcolm's father had pointed out. "But Polly *is* an asset to you, Mal. She's a lovely woman to look at, and she complements you well—in terms of how others see you. Appearances are important, Mal. You ought to bear that in mind before you do anything rash."

He'd borne it in mind. His divorce hadn't been rash. If anything had been rash, it was his wedding, but it took him three long, miserable years of marriage before he'd severed things with Polly. And still the nastiness continued. His lawyer, Mike Lopez, had phoned him at work that afternoon to inform him that Polly's lawyer was making noises about increasing his alimony payments to her. She couldn't afford to live the way a Royce—or an ex-Royce—ought to be living, her lawyer had contended. Polly Royce had an image to project, and Malcolm wasn't living up to his end of the bargain.

"The hell I'm not," he growled at his freshly shaven reflection in the mirror above the double sink. Polly had reneged on her end of the bargain long before Malcolm had. She'd promised to love, honor and cherish him, and she hadn't. She'd only loved, honored and cherished his wealth. Her inane affairs were the least of it. By the time she began betraying him physically, she'd already betrayed him many times emotionally.

He arrived at the downtown restaurant to meet his colleagues within a few minutes of the appointed hour. Somehow, he managed to talk intelligibly about business matters with them, even though a portion of his mind devoted itself to Lucia. He wanted to be with her now. He wanted her to love him no matter what. He wanted to reach a point with her when he wouldn't have to hide anything from her, when she could put on her lovely silk dress and attend Royce Collection functions and not see them as something evil. He hoped that would happen soon.

In the meantime, when he had dropped the car off at the Rent-A-Wreck office Sunday morning, he'd made arrangements to rent the Chevy for the following weekend. It was really silly for him to be renting a decrepit car when he had a perfectly nice Jaguar parked in the garage under his town house. But if he'd played hooky from the business dinner that evening and driven to New Jersey to see Lucia, how would he have explained the expensive car? "I borrowed it from a friend for the evening," he might have mumbled. "I borrowed it from Blanche Richter." Fat chance Lucia would believe a fib like that!

Soon, he resolved, soon he'd tell her the truth about himself. He couldn't conceal his affluent circumstances forever. He loved Lucia too much.

The dinner didn't end until ten-thirty. Much to his relief, Malcolm's associates didn't mention his preoccupied state. But then, he'd disguised his distraction well. He was, above all else, a consummate businessman. Even during the upheaval of his divorce, to say nothing of the strain of his difficult marriage, the people he worked with were never aware of the disarray in his personal life.

He caught a cab uptown to his town house and climbed the stairs to his bedroom. Any day that had begun at eight in the morning and ended at nearly eleven at night would have been exhausting, but Malcolm was doubly tired because his mind had been torn into pieces—one piece on business, one angry piece on Mike Lopez's call concerning the alimony payments, and one piece, brooding and churning, on Lucia, on how much he wanted her, how much he wanted to have faith in her ability to have faith in him.

He undressed, collapsed on his king-size bed and stared at the ceiling. Merely lying on the crisp sheets evoked a memory of the night he'd spent in bed with her. His attraction to her had been undeniable from the start, but he'd never imagined how marvelous making love with her could be. It was obvious to him that she wasn't particularly worldly when it came to men, that she didn't have a wild history of lovers. She wasn't even on the Pill. She was clearly a bit shy about sex, a bit reserved, even hesitant.

And yet...God, how she'd satisfied him. She'd known intuitively just how to touch him, how to please him, how to unleash his passion and let it overtake him. He'd satisfied her, too, and while he'd never considered himself selfish with women, satisfying Lucia had been more important to him than it had ever been with any other lover. He'd suspected that he and Lucia would be good together in bed, but he'd never imagined how indescribably good.

Impulsively he clicked on the lamp on his nightstand and reached for his telephone. He dialed her number and listened. The phone rang twice, three times, seven. He knew she had to be home; when he'd spoken to her earlier that evening she hadn't sounded like a woman about to race off to an assignation with some clown who wanted to buy a vacation house in the Watchung Mountains. But the phone continued to ring—twelve times, thirteen.

She knew how to ignore phones, he remembered. Maybe she was asleep; maybe she'd already received a dozen calls from representatives of Nix-Mizz and the like, and she was stubbornly refusing to answer any more calls. But Malcolm was at least as stubborn as she was. He was determined to outlast her.

She answered on the twentieth ring. "What?"

"Loosh? It's Mal," he murmured, hoping he sounded suitably contrite about having disturbed her.

"Mal?" She hesitated, then cleared the sleepy roughness from her throat. "Do you know what time it is?"

"It's late. And I miss you."

"Oh, Mal." All the rancor vanished from her voice. He'd apparently said the right thing. She forgave him. "How was your dinner?"

"Boring. You would have gone cross-eyed from all the jargon, Loosh. *I* went cross-eyed from it." He paused. "I'm sorry I woke you up."

"You didn't."

"You're not in bed?"

"I'm in bed, but I hadn't fallen asleep yet," she told him.

"Are you wearing pajamas?" he asked amorously.

"Oh, for heaven's sake, Malcolm," she scolded, though she was laughing.

"The phone rang so many times, Loosh, I was afraid you might have thrown your pillow over it or something."

"That's your trick, not mine," she reminded him.

"What's your trick?"

She laughed again. "I don't have a trick. I just ignore the ringing. Unless it rings twenty times. Then I figure it must be important." She mused, then added slyly, "So, you'd better make this important, Mal. Asking me whether I'm wearing pajamas is definitely not twenty-rings important."

"Okay, I'll be important," he obliged. "I don't want to wait until Saturday to see you. When can we see each other before then?"

"Any night this week," she cheerfully told him. "How about tomorrow night? We could get together after work. You could come out here for dinner."

"Perfect. I'll leave straight from the office, and—" he stopped and worked through his thoughts "—I'll have to take a train," he said. "I won't have the use of the car tomorrow."

"Why not? Do you share it with someone?"

Not a bad guess, he silently praised her. "It's—it's in the shop."

"I'm not surprised," she noted. "It was making a suspiciously squeaky noise on Saturday."

"There's nothing wrong with it," he defended the rented Chevy. "It's just getting a tune-up." *Enough!* he reproached himself. No sense embroidering a lie. "I haven't got a train schedule. Can I call you at work tomorrow and let you know what train I'll be taking?"

"Sure. You can even spend the night if you'd like. You know, Mal—" her voice became velvety soft "—there are people in Edison who commute to Manhattan for work every day. Oh, brother!" she interrupted herself. "I can't believe I said that."

"What's wrong with what you said?"

"It's so forward. Honestly, Mal, if I were the only person living on a desert island, I wouldn't nominate myself as ambassador. I'm the most tactless person I know."

"And I adore you for it," he assured her. "I probably won't spend the night, Lucia. I've got a busy week scheduled. But I'll definitely come for dinner."

"I won't have a chance to cook anything," she warned him. "Although I suppose I could brew up some mushrooms in lab—"

"We'll go to a restaurant," he cut her off with a chuckle. "I'll talk to you tomorrow about my arrival time."

"All right, Mal. Now, if you don't mind, I could use some sleep."

''Good night, Loosh,'' he whispered before lowering the receiver to its cradle. Her sweet voice echoed inside him as he nestled into the pillow. He smiled. He could happily endure a million jargon-laden business dinners if he knew that Lucia's voice, Lucia's love, would be waiting for him when he got home.

LUCIA HUNG UP and shook her head. She hoped she hadn't sounded too annoyed when she'd answered the phone. She hadn't exactly been in the best of spirits when Malcolm had called.

She'd been trying to rest, but sleep had eluded her, thanks to another call she'd gotten earlier that evening, from her mother.

Her mother had tried to reach Lucia Sunday, but Lucia hadn't been home. Where on earth had Lucia been at nine o'clock on a Sunday morning? She'd tried her number again and again. ''Where were you?'' she'd demanded to know, as if Lucia weren't a mature woman of twenty-nine, but a naughty teenager who had to account for her whereabouts and receive parental permission.

Lucia had explained that she had, in fact, been home, but that she'd chosen not to answer the phone. That was her prerogative, she'd declared. Her privacy had been invaded often enough in the past few weeks; she had a right not to answer her phone if she didn't feel like it.

Her mother hadn't sounded terribly mollified by Lucia's feisty defense of her actions. But she'd called with more important matters to discuss than Lucia's weekend whereabouts. It seemed that Lucia's father had left Indianapolis for Los Angeles with his partner in the juggling-skunk enterprise. He'd contacted Lucia's mother from a motel they were staying at, informed her that they were *this* close to lining up an audition for the skunks with a talent agent who claimed he had an inside connection with Merv Griffin's people, but that the agent required an auditioning fee before he'd see the skunks. They were *this* close, if only they had an extra five hundred dollars. They'd traveled all that way, spent money on the motel room, and all they needed was five hundred dollars.

"No way," Lucia had stifled her mother. "Absolutely not. Try Celia."

"I already did," Lucia's mother had reported. "Arthur answered, and he said such terrible things about your father. I just couldn't bear to listen to him say such things. Your father tries so hard, Lucia, and he's so close to realizing his dream with the skunks."

"No." Lucia had remained firm. "Mom, I'm not sending him any money. He's already swindled me out of ten thousand dollars."

"He didn't swindle you, dear," her mother had quibbled. "He probably meant to explain to you what he was planning to do with the money, and—"

"He swindled me. He bilked me, Mom. He lied."

"Lucia," her mother had argued, "it's thanks to that ten thousand dollars you sent him that he's gotten this far. How can you leave him hanging when he's so close, when he can almost taste it?"

"I wish I hadn't sent him the ten thousand dollars," Lucia had muttered. "Then he wouldn't be almost tasting it now. He cheated me, Mom. My own father. Maybe if he'd been honest about the ten thousand dollars—"

"If he'd been honest, you never would have sent it to him, would you?" Lucia's mother had pointed out. "Honey, he's your father, and he loves you. Think of all he's done for you."

Sure, Lucia had fumed in seething silence. All he'd done for her was to uproot her time and again during her youth, run her family ragged with his asinine schemes, throw away money that might have gone to the mortgage or the rent, or to a single new dress for Lucia once every five years. He'd thrown the money away like gamblers at Atlantic City, not with logic or wisdom, but with blind faith that maybe this one time he'd get lucky, the window would fill with three black bars and he'd win. He had brains; he had a healthy body, but all he'd done for his family was to take crazy chances. And lose.

"Mom," Lucia had said softly, her voice quivering with bitter memories, "I want to do something for him—the most loving thing I can do for him. Do you know what that is? It's to tell him to grow up and face reality. It's to tell him to take responsibility for himself and for you. It's too late for him to be a responsible father, but at least he can be a responsible husband. He can go home to Indianapolis and get a job doing something normal, and stop being an idiot. That won't happen if I send him money. I think I'm doing the right thing by saying no."

"You're breaking his heart," her mother had announced. "For once in your life you're in a position to help him, and you're refusing him. This is going to break his heart. I hope to God it doesn't kill him. Goodbye, Lucia."

How could Lucia have expected to fall asleep after that? Was her father really going to die of a broken heart if he didn't get his juggling skunks onto national television? Or had her mother only implied that to make Lucia feel guilty?

This was why Lucia hated money. Malcolm could say all sorts of pretty things about it, that it was a tool, a measurement, a scale. Lucia knew better. Money was what made madmen tick; it was what tore families apart. It bred guilt and recriminations, greed and grudges. It broke hearts. If that wasn't evil, Lucia didn't know the meaning of evil.

She thought about the money sitting in her local bank, the money she planned to have the bank wire to Advent tomorrow during her lunch hour. What was the point in her keeping it, she wondered. She didn't want it. If she gave it all to her father, he'd fritter it away on skunks or audition fees or whatever, and she'd be done with it. Was that less reasonable than her sending it to any of the other ludicrous charities she'd heard from lately?

But no, she'd been correct in telling her mother that refusing to send her father money was the most loving thing she could do. Compulsive gambling was like a disease, and even if her father never went to casinos, he was a compulsive gambler. If he were an alcoholic, would she be demonstrating her love for him if she gave him liquor when he demanded it? If he were suffering from cancer, would she be demonstrating her love by supplying him with cigarettes when he claimed he was desperate for a smoke?

Assuring herself that she'd done the right thing by refusing her father the money didn't make her feel any less guilty, though. If only she hadn't won the jackpot; if only she hadn't suddenly become rich, a target for her father's demented yearnings; if only some other fool had slipped five dollars into the Super Jackpot slot machine before Lucia had and applied the proper flick of the wrist while pulling down its lever... If only Lucia had never let Evvie talk her into going to Atlantic City in the first place...

But then she never would have met Malcolm.

She would see him tomorrow. She would pick him up at the train station, and they'd go to a restaurant and talk, and her world would brighten. He would reassure her that she'd done exactly what she should have done with her father, that wiring the money to Advent and letting Blanche Richter nurture it in the money-market fund was the wisest course to take. He would erase her guilt. When it came to money, he was sane and knowledgeable.

Lucia trusted him. Rick Lansing might have insinuated some nasty things about Malcolm in her office that afternoon, but he couldn't shake her trust in Malcolm. So what if he wasn't rich, but only comfortable? So what if he couldn't afford his ex-wife? He had seen Lucia's beauty by looking into her soul. And he loved her so much that telling her he missed her was twenty-rings important.

How could she help but trust him?

Chapter Nine

The train-station parking lot was already fairly crowded when Lucia arrived to pick up Malcolm. She braked to a halt at the end of a row of cars and climbed out to join the numerous people, mostly women, awaiting the return of their spouses from the city.

What a perfectly domestic suburban scene, Lucia thought as her gaze took in the charming old station house with its peaked roof, shingled walls and twelve-pane windows. It was flanked by a recently constructed concrete platform lined with billboards touting liquor, magazines and Broadway shows. She felt oddly as though she belonged there with the other wives, eagerly awaiting her triumphant hero's return from the battlefield of the city.

Lucia had stopped home before driving to the station. She'd wanted to wash her hands of the faint chemical smell that permeated her latex work gloves, and to change from her prim professional attire into something more feminine: a flowered skirt and a lace-trimmed white blouse. She'd also rearranged her hair, removing it from its ponytail and pinning it back from her face with tortoiseshell combs. The delay while she freshened up her appearance after work had almost made her too late; by the time she reached the sidewalk, the train was creaking into the station.

As if by magic, the once-vacant platform was suddenly swarming with commuters, most of them men wearing suits and carrying attaché cases and newspapers. Lucia scanned the crowd and spotted Malcolm without any difficulty. Although he, like his fellow passengers, was dressed in a tailored suit, his jacket slung over his shoulder and his tie loosened, and although he also carried an attaché case of belting leather and a folded copy of *The Wall Street Journal*, his height, his dark coloring, his striking attractiveness made him stand out among the crowd of otherwise indistinguishable men.

When he located Lucia, his face lit up. He jogged through the mob to her and wrapped her in his arms. "Hello," he murmured before commandeering her mouth in a consuming kiss so sensuous that Lucia soon became oblivious of the many people around them engaging in their own far less passionate reunions.

By the time Malcolm released her, the lot was nearly empty. "Hello," she whispered breathlessly.

"This was a wonderful idea," Malcolm announced as she led him to her car.

"What? Kissing me that way?" she teased.

"Coming out here for dinner. It wasn't that long a trip at all." He tossed his briefcase and newspaper into the backseat before settling himself in her car.

Lucia took her place behind the wheel and started the engine. "I didn't think it would be," she responded to his critique of the trip. "Lots of people do it every day."

Malcolm nodded. "I noticed there were a number of regulars on the train. Two bridge games were going on in my car, and many of the guys greeted each other by name." He attempted to stretch his long legs out in the narrow floor space before him. "Where are we going for dinner?"

"I was thinking of a Chinese restaurant in town. It's a nice place—not as elegant as the Shangri-la, but much more reasonably priced. And much more elegant than the last place we ate at," she added, grinning as she recalled their take-out burgers.

He apparently recalled that meal as well. "What do I have to look forward to? Médoc or milk shakes?"

"Tea," Lucia answered, steering to the end of the lot and joining the flow of traffic. "Although I suppose you could get one of those funny drinks with a paper parasol sticking out of it, if it strikes your fancy."

Malcolm eyed her appreciatively. "*You* strike my fancy," he commented. "Why bother with drinks when I can get high on you?"

She felt her cheeks color at his flattery. Even if it was just a line, she couldn't help responding to it. "If you want," she suggested softly, "we could buy some take-out and bring it back to my apartment."

His eyelids drooped slightly and his smile expanded, increasing the delectable length of his dimples. "Don't tempt me, Loosh," he scolded her wistfully. "If I went to your apartment, I'd never leave."

She said nothing as she parked in front of the restaurant, which was situated at the end of a shopping center. They entered the restaurant and the host seated them in a booth. Malcolm surveyed the interior, which featured trite Oriental-looking murals and fake lanterns, and then the place settings of willowware and mismatched stainless steel. "Takeout," he considered, smiling seductively. "Your kitchen has better ambience than this place. So, for that matter, does your bedroom." He shook his head and lifted a menu. "I shouldn't even let myself think along those lines," he reproached himself. "I've got a hectic day at the office tomorrow. We'll eat here."

Lucia was undeniably pleased that Malcolm could consider visiting her home so dangerous a temptation. "The food here is better than the ambience," she assured him, making light of his suggestive remarks. "I recommend the sweet-and-sour chicken, and the egg foo yong. They're both excellent."

Malcolm scrutinized the menu and shrugged. "Pretty pedestrian," he assessed it. "The Chinese restaurants in New York City have much more exotic fare. Have you ever tried Szechuan cuisine?"

Lucia shook her head. "I've heard of it, but I don't know much about it."

"It's very spicy," he declared. "The chief seasonings are ginger and pepper. You can go through five pitchers of ice water, but it's worth it."

"Maybe we could—" She bit her lip to stifle herself.

"Maybe we could what?" Malcolm asked.

She smiled sheepishly. "I was going to say that maybe we could go to a Szechuan restaurant in New York someday."

"I'd like that very much," said Malcolm.

"But not this weekend?"

His mouth flexed, but he was spared from responding by the arrival of the waiter to take their orders. Malcolm took Lucia's recommendation to heart and requested the sweet-and-sour-chicken dinner. She ordered the egg foo yong. The waiter poured their tea and removed their menus from the table.

Lucia studied Malcolm intently. He appeared haggard to her, and despite his erotically charged words about what would happen if he dared to go to Lucia's home with her, he seemed too fatigued to do much besides eat-lng. His eyes weren't sparkling as brilliantly as they sometimes did, and a vague tension gnawed at the corners of his mouth. She wondered whether he was truly exhausted, or whether her allusion to the upcoming weekend had for some reason rankled him. "Malcolm, why don't you want me to come to New York?" she asked bravely.

"I never said I don't want you to come to New York," he protested.

"But not this weekend."

"I told you, I've got to attend a function at my parents' behest on Friday. By Saturday morning, all I'll want to do is escape from the city for a couple of days."

She gave him a measuring perusal. It wasn't that she didn't believe him. But she couldn't shake the weird notion that Malcolm was hiding something from her. "Are you sure that's why you don't want me to come?" she asked, surprising herself with her persistence.

He eyed her cautiously. "What are you driving at, Lucia?"

She lowered her gaze to the intricate blue-on-white pattern of her plate. A nervous laugh slipped past her lips. "I don't know, Mal. If you hadn't shown me your divorce decree..."

The waiter approached the table carrying bowls of wonton soup. Malcolm waited until he and Lucia were alone again before asking, "If I hadn't shown you my divorce decree, what?"

"I'd think you had a wife in the city."

His spoon clattered against the bowl as he glared incredulously at her. "What the hell is wrong with you, Loosh? How can you say such a thing?"

His anger seemed way out of proportion to what she'd said. Evidently, his former wife was a sensitive topic with him. Lucia wasn't sure why she'd even raised the subject. Her comment went way beyond her usual tactlessness, and she regretted having said anything at all. "I'm sorry, Mal. I didn't mean that the way it sounded."

"Don't you trust me?"

"Yes, of course I do," she said hurriedly. "How can I not trust you, when I've seen the document with my own two eyes?"

He stirred his soup listlessly, then added some soy sauce to the broth. He ate in moody silence for a moment, and his fury gradually abated. "Ah, Lucia," he said, sighing. "I'm having a rough time with Polly at the moment. I'm sorry if I overreacted."

"A rough time? Has she been fooling around with your credit cards again?"

Malcolm pressed his lips together, apparently reluctant to discuss the matter. Yet Lucia's concern was genuine, and her touch of doubt was troubling enough that he felt compelled to explain. "I spent an hour on the phone with my lawyer yesterday, and another hour today. Polly's decided she wants more alimony from me."

"Oh?" Lucia ate her soup, but the bulk of her attention was on Malcolm. "Can she do that? I mean, doesn't she have to accept the terms of the divorce?"

"She wants to take the settlement back to court and get a readjustment."

"Do you think she's got a good case against you?"

Malcolm scowled and set down his spoon. "Whether or not she's got a case is irrelevant," he muttered. "If I decide to fight her in court, it's going to take a lot of time and effort. We'll have to dredge up unpleasant memories, and I just don't know whether I want to go through all that. And I'll wind up paying a fortune in legal fees, even if I win on the alimony issue. Either way the situation's going to cost me."

"I could lend you some money if you need it," Lucia offered.

Malcolm's eyes glittered with astonishment. "Don't be ridiculous," he said.

"I wasn't being ridiculous, Mal. If you need money to fight this thing—"

"Lucia, you amaze me," he cut her off. "You're very generous, but no, I don't need your money." He reached for her hand and squeezed it. "Thank you," he murmured.

She returned his tenuous smile and lapsed into silence as the waiter cleared away the soup bowls and delivered their dinners. Her offer of money had astounded her as much as it had astounded Malcolm. But it had been a natural outgrowth of her love for him. If he needed money and she could supply him with it, why shouldn't she?

"I really don't want to talk about it, it's such a mess," he concluded. "Let's talk about you. How's the sock business these days?"

Lucia tasted her food and smiled. "Status quo. No major breakthroughs."

"Doesn't it get frustrating waiting for breakthroughs?" he asked. "Or boring?"

"Frustrating, yes. Boring, never," she replied. "I don't have a chance to get bored. There's always a meeting, or some more journal articles to read, or an unexpected safety inspection."

Her mouth curved reflexively into a grimace as she recalled Rick's visit that afternoon. As he'd done on Monday, he'd once again made all sorts of slimy insinuations about Malcolm, about how the man Lucia claimed she was in love with was undoubtedly after her money, just as Rick himself was. She'd been too disgusted to defend Malcolm to Rick, and she'd demanded that he leave. Before he did, he'd decided to cite her for not wearing steel-toed shoes—the first time he'd ever mentioned such an infraction. It was simply spite on his part, Lucia had assumed. She hated wearing steel-toed shoes, even though she was required to have a pair on hand at all times in the lab. The shoes were ugly and heavy, and she felt like Frankenstein's monster when she wore them.

Her thoughts circled back to Rick's mean-spirited remarks about Malcolm. She knew she oughtn't to dwell on them. Malcolm was a much finer man than Rick. If he was facing a temporary financial setback because of his ex-wife's selfish demands, why shouldn't Lucia help him out? It wasn't as if Malcolm were after her money. The very fact that he'd declined her offer proved that he didn't want to take money from her.

Besides, he loved her. Rick might insist that he wanted to marry her, but he'd never once breathed a hint of love. All he'd done was to call her beautiful. So had Malcolm, but when Malcolm said it, he meant it. Lucia was sure of that.

"This isn't bad," Malcolm appraised his meal. "It's not Szechuan, but for what it is, it isn't bad. I *will* take you out to dinner in New York," he added earnestly. "I promise."

"I bet this place is much less expensive than those fancy New York restaurants," she pointed out.

"Yes, this is much less expensive," Malcolm concurred. "Everything costs more in New York."

Including ex-wives, Lucia pondered silently. "I bet you've got to pay an astronomical rent, too," she mused.

"Well, housing isn't cheap there," he agreed. "A dollar doesn't buy much floor space. No argument there."

Lucia peered quizzically at him. Was that why he was hesitant about letting her see where he lived? Was he fearful that she'd be disappointed in the puny apartment he could afford on his "comfortable" income? "Malcolm," she ventured carefully. "Are you ashamed for me to see your home?"

His eyes flickered with unreadable shadows. "Ashamed? Should I be?"

"I don't know," she admitted. "Maybe your place is much smaller than mine or something. Maybe it's dark and cramped. I know enough about housing in the city to know it's awfully expensive, and it's difficult to find something even remotely livable that's also affordable. But I don't care," she hastily continued. "I don't care where you live, or what it's like. I really don't. You don't have to be ashamed."

"I'm not," he said, then paused. "Maybe I am," he refuted himself in a distant voice, momentarily lost in a private rumination. His eyes shifted back to Lucia. "Yes, housing costs are astronomical in the city, but I get by. I can't complain."

"For the same amount of money," Lucia hazarded, "you could probably live like a king in an area like this. You were on the train; you saw how many people opt for the forty-minute commute so they can live in decent housing. I bet in New York you'd have to pay three times as much rent as I pay to get half the space I've got."

"Probably," Malcolm agreed. "But if I were going to suffer the commute—to say nothing of giving up easy access to good Szechuan food—I'd buy a house around here, rather than rent an apartment. That's something I could enjoy. A nice, roomy house with a yard, some trees, maybe a garden. If you're going to live in the suburbs, you might as well have a little property to show for it, right?''

Lucia felt an undeniable twinge inside her, a vague tension, a pang of worry. What had Malcolm said? A house in the suburbs. A little property. Was that what he wanted? Was that why he'd driven her all over the region last weekend to look at real estate for sale?

She didn't want to think that way. She didn't want to let Rick's vile comments distort her view of Malcolm. But there was that nagging twinge. She tried to define it, to fathom it so that she could conquer it. Her mind toyed with it, gauging its shape, its size, its content.

If Rick could desire a vacation house in the Watchung Mountains, why couldn't Malcolm desire a house in central New Jersey? He, not Lucia, had been the enthusiastic one when they'd toured the Open Houses. It had been his idea, not hers, his interest, not hers. She had told him she didn't want to buy a house. And he had told her, just now, that he would very much enjoy a house.

Yet, in his current plight, being harassed by his greedy ex-wife, he certainly couldn't afford to buy a lovely house in the suburbs. He was only getting by, keeping his head above water. Lucia was the one who was rich. She could afford a house. He couldn't. *Not without her money.*

Her hand began to tremble, and she set her fork on the edge of her plate and stared numbly at her half-eaten dinner. Her appetite had fled. She struggled desperately to fend off her apprehension, but it lodged itself firmly within her.

Just because Rick lacked subtlety didn't mean that Malcolm did. Malcolm could easily be the most subtle man she'd ever met. He had class, proper breeding and polish. He'd gone to prep school and worn a uniform with an emblem on the blazer's pocket. He was as accustomed to being diplomatic as he was to living well.

But far from being awash in money, he was presently in economic straits. His ex-wife had already tried to use his credit accounts; obviously she was an enormous financial burden to him.

Lucia fought through her memory of her entire relationship with Malcolm. The first night he'd seen her at the casino, he'd flirted wordlessly with her while he was in the Baccarat Room—perhaps playing with donated chips from the casino's manager, as he'd claimed, or perhaps gambling his own money, gambling like any other money-hungry fool at the casino. He'd caught Lucia's eye and smiled, and raised his glass in a silent toast to her. Nothing wrong with that.

But then she'd won her jackpot. It wasn't until *after* she'd won her jackpot that he'd latched on to her. Even before he knew her name, he'd known that she had come into possession of a quarter of a million dollars. With his knowledge of her windfall, he'd taken on the role of her self-appointed guardian, her savior, protecting her from the obnoxious casino manager and the crush of gawkers. He'd known nothing about Lucia, except that she was rich.

And ever since the moment she had abruptly joined the ranks of the wealthy, he'd been urging her not to give her money away, but to invest it, to hang on to it, to allow it to appreciate.

He didn't think money was evil; he thought it was a tool. A tool with which to pay for things. Like a lovely house in the suburbs, perhaps. Or an ex-wife's excesses.

And no sooner had he warned her about men calling her beautiful than he was calling her beautiful. "I'm looking at your soul," he'd said.

And Lucia had been stupid enough to believe him.

"What's wrong?" He broke into her thoughts.

"Wrong?" she choked out. "Nothing's wrong." She took a long sip of her tea to relax the clenched muscles of her throat.

"You've stopped eating," Malcolm observed.

"I—I'm not very hungry," she mumbled.

Malcolm searched her face, his eyes registering his concern at her evident distress. "Don't you feel well?"

"I feel fine, Mal. I'm just not hungry."

"Something's troubling you," he commented perceptively. "Please tell me what." When she remained silent, he asked, "Was it what I said about my ex-wife? That's not a very pleasant subject for either of us, Lucia. I shouldn't have talked about it at all, but I want to be as open as I can be with you about that." He contemplated her for a long moment. "It bothers you that I'm divorced, doesn't it?" he concluded.

"It would bother me more if you weren't," she noted dryly.

He conceded the point with a grudging smile. "Lucia, I wish I could come to you with no black marks on my record. I wish I could say to you that I never made a mistake in my life. But I'm only human, and I did make a mistake, and I'm paying for it. If you love me, you can accept that."

"Of course I can," she granted softly.

He ran his index finger across the back of her hand, and she tried to control her instinct to flinch at the contact. "It's *my* mistake, and I'll pay for it. But your offer to help me out was very sweet. You're an incredibly kind woman, Lucia, incredibly generous. That's one of the things I love you for. You're kind and generous, and sweet."

"Yeah, I'm a real soft touch when it comes to someone in need," Lucia muttered sardonically. "I'm a real sucker when women from Staten Island write to me and ask if I'll send them money so they can have their tubes tied."

"You haven't sent that lady money, have you?" Malcolm asked, his eyebrows arching.

"No," Lucia told him. "I may be a sucker, but I'm not exactly brainless."

"Far from brainless, Dr. Bowen." He captured her hand in his and drew it to his mouth for a kiss. Again, Lucia had to smother the urge to flinch. "Have you wired the money to Blanche at Advent?" he asked.

"During my lunch hour today," Lucia said with a nod, adding silently, *That should make you happy, Mal. You want to protect my money so you can get your hands on it, right?*

"The whole amount?"

She cringed, her anguish and doubt causing her abdomen to ache. "Most of it," she whispered. "I kept some in the local bank to cover my estimated-tax payment. I've got to send the IRS a check in a couple of weeks."

"You could always draw a check off your money-market fund," Malcolm reminded her. "Blanche explained the check-writing feature of the account to you, didn't she? You ought to send the whole amount there, so it'll be earning the maximum interest until you need it. Even two weeks of interest on that kind of money can make a difference."

"Well," Lucia said, forcing flippancy into her tone, "I wanted to keep some money handy, in case I decide to do something silly with it."

Malcolm smiled with curiosity. "Silly? What silly ideas have you got up your sleeve?"

She glared suspiciously at him. She had to admire his flair—he really did sound more fascinated than condemning. But then, as Evvie had pointed out, Malcolm was a slick operator. He had fooled Lucia up to now. He was subtle and slick. "I don't know," she said testily. "I was thinking I might want to send some money to my father. How's that for silly?" How was that, indeed? If she could consider giving money to Malcolm, why not her father? She'd known him longer, and they were bound by blood. Why not?

"Your father?" Malcolm exclaimed in bewilderment. "You mean the juggling skunks?"

"Sure. He's in Los Angeles now. He needs five hundred dollars in order to audition the skunks for some talent scout who claims to be buddy-buddy with Merv Griffin."

Malcolm scowled. "That sounds like a scam to me."

"It sounds like one to me, too, but if my father wants the money, why shouldn't I let him have it? He *is* my father, after all."

Malcolm was clearly puzzled. "Last week you were eating yourself up for having sent him ten thousand dollars."

"Right. Ten thousand dollars down the drain. What's another five hundred? Good money after bad. Why not? I can afford it."

Her derisive tone took Malcolm aback. He released her hand and settled back in his seat, assessing her disapprovingly. "You aren't serious, are you?" he asked.

"Why shouldn't I be serious? He's my father, for heaven's sake. If I don't send him five hundred dollars, he'll probably do something horrible like cash in his return airline ticket to Indianapolis. And then, how's he going to get home when the deal falls through? Anyway, it's none of your business what I do with my money, Malcolm, is it? It's *my* money, and I can do whatever I want with it, and it's none of your business.''

He couldn't help but discern the barely contained rage that underlined her every word. His brow furrowed as he tried to make sense of it. Unable to, he shook his head. "You're right," he said in a subdued voice. "It's none of my business. If you want to send your father five hundred dollars, go ahead.''

"Thanks. I will.''

"Would you . . .'' His frown deepened, and he rubbed his jaw thoughtfully as he watched Lucia. When he spoke, he enunciated each word carefully, endeavoring not to sound judgmental. "Would you mind explaining what made you decide to do this?''

Before she could answer, the waiter approached to ask them how their meal was. Malcolm glanced at Lucia's half-eaten dinner, then told the waiter to bring the check. Once they were alone again, Malcolm turned his attention back to Lucia and awaited her answer.

"Well,'' she said in a small voice, "I was all set to give you money. Why shouldn't I give it to my own father?''

"I didn't accept your offer,'' Malcolm pointed out. "Your father will.''

"And what if you *had* accepted my offer? What then? What if I decided to buy one of those houses we saw last weekend? Would you move in with me?''

He appeared utterly baffled. "Lucia, what are you trying to say?''

"I'm trying to say,'' she said, struggling to maintain her tenuous composure, "that from the moment I won the jackpot you've taken a much bigger interest in what I did with my money than I have.''

"Someone had to look after it," Malcolm defended himself. "All you wanted to do was get rid of it.''

"Yes, I'd still like that, I think. Maybe I'll send some to my father, and some to the Committee to End Pay Toilets in America, and some to the IRS, and whatever is left over I'll donate to Josephine Taggart so she and her husband can visit the Masters and Johnson clinic. And then I'll be done with it. The whole thing will be over with. How does that sound to you?''

"It sounds crazy," Malcolm said honestly. He eyed her speculatively, then shook his head. "It's none of my business, as you said," he remarked quietly. "Do what you want to do.''

"What I want to do is go back to being comfortable, keeping my head above water and no more. Just like you. Getting by. That's what I want." She examined his reaction—the light fading from his eyes, his lips growing progressively tighter, shaping a grim, straight line above his jaw. "Would you still love me if I did that?''

"Would I still love you if you did something stupid?'' he asked rhetorically. "Lucia, one of the things I love about you is that you're intelligent. The thought that you'd do something so completely mindless rattles me.''

"Good. I'm glad I rattled you, Malcolm. You're slick, I admit it; you're slick. But I'm intelligent enough to know that I'm tall and stringy, and I've got a big nose. You can call me beautiful from here to kingdom come, but I'm intelligent enough to see what's going on." The waiter arrived with the check, and Lucia rose from her seat. "Let's go.''

"Can I settle the bill first?" Malcolm asked helplessly.

"Are you sure you wouldn't like me to pay?" she snapped.

He shot her a scathing look before pulling a twenty-dollar bill from his wallet and tossing it onto the table. Lucia stormed ahead of him out of the restaurant.

The sun had nearly set, but the sky was still light and the air retained the day's warmth. Lucia felt tears rising to her eyes as she stalked across the lot to her car, Malcolm at her heels. She reached for the door handle, but before she could twist it, he grabbed her hand and spun her around to face him. His hands gripped her upper arms with an almost brutal force, and his gaze singed her face with blazing anger. "Would you please tell me what the hell's gotten into you?" he growled.

She blinked her eyes to keep the tears from seeping through her lashes. "Isn't it obvious, Mal?" she muttered. "What's gotten into me is money. And I hate it. You're the one who thinks money is great, not me. I think it's the root of all evil, and I want to get rid of it. And if you can still love me after that, then you're a better man than I've ever met before."

He seemed to be wrestling against the urge to shake her. "I *am* a better man than you've ever met before," he asserted. "I'm the best damned man in the world for you. When it comes to your money, your root-of-all-evil money, no other man would have your interests at heart the way I have."

"My interests, eh? And your own interests, too, Malcolm?"

"My interests, Lucia, entail looking after you when you haven't got the God-given sense to look after yourself."

"Yeah, sure." She tried to shrug free of his grasp, but his hands only held her more relentlessly. "And if I didn't happen to have a quarter of a million dollars, you wouldn't give a hoot about my interests at all, would you?''

He was so shocked by her words that he fell back, his fingers yielding, dropping from her arms. ''Is that what you think?'' he whispered hoarsely. ''Is that what you think of me?''

Lucia gazed defiantly up at him. ''What I think of you, Malcolm Royce, is that if you were so smart when it came to money, how come you're just getting by? How come your wife is taking you to the cleaners, and you can't afford her, and you drive a rattletrap car that's sitting in the shop right now? That's what I think.''

''Oh!'' He threw back his head with a caustic laugh. ''Oh, you mean you're so rich that maybe I'm not good enough for you, is that it? You want someone up there in the economic stratosphere with you? My rattletrap car isn't good enough for you?''

''Is it good enough for you?'' Lucia shot back. ''Stick with Central-Jersey-Woman-Wins-Record-Jackpot, and maybe there's a nicer car in it for you. To say nothing of a house, right? And all that money appreciating in Advent's money-market fund. All you've got to do is tell her she's beautiful and take her to bed, and the next thing you know, you've won your own record jackpot. Slick, Malcolm. Very slick.''

He gaped at her in disbelief. The dusk's rosy light played mysteriously over his face, emphasizing the lines of his cheeks and the canopy of his brow. His eyes radiated a disturbing metallic glimmer through the shadows. He seemed to have difficulty finding his voice, finding the words he wanted to say. ''No,'' he whispered brokenly. ''No, Lucia, it's not like that at all.''

She turned away. "It looks like that from where I stand," she said in a faltering voice. "You say you love me for my intelligence. I find that pretty ironic, considering how stupid I've been with you." She swung open her door and dropped onto the seat, where she surrendered to a miserable shudder.

Malcolm moved around the car to the passenger side and climbed in. He watched as Lucia jammed her key into the ignition and gunned the engine. "I'm rich, Lucia," he confessed in a quiet voice.

"I don't want to hear about it," she retorted as she backed out of the parking space and directed the car toward the train station.

"It's the truth. I'm very rich."

"But you can't afford a decent car."

"I rented that car," he told her.

"If you were so rich, you could have rented a better car than that," she sniffed.

"If I were so rich, I'd own a Jaguar. Which I do."

She chuckled sarcastically. "Of course. You own a Jaguar, so you rented a jalopy. Of course. How sensible."

"I was trying to impress you."

"I'm impressed, Mal. Very impressed. When does the next train leave for New York?"

"Damn it, Lucia, I'm telling you the truth. My family is old money. I was rich before I was even born. And I'm a partner at Advent, which means I earn a salary well beyond what I need. I was afraid that if you knew how rich I was, you'd back off from me. So I got a car from Rent-A-Wreck for the weekend. As far as not affording my ex-wife, Lucia, I could easily afford to pay her what she's asking and more, but I don't think she deserves it. She cheated me every way a woman can cheat a man, and

I don't think she ought to be rewarded for that. She wouldn't be hitting me up for more money if she didn't know I could afford it.''

"This is all quite interesting," Lucia said crisply. She steered into the lot of the train station and parked by the sidewalk. "Let me apply my intelligent, scientific mind to it and see how it computes." She clicked off the engine and struck a contemplative pose. "Either you're lying now, or you were lying last weekend. Yes, that's how it computes. One way or another, you lied to me. It doesn't look good for you, Malcolm, not good at all."

"I wasn't lying last weekend, Lucia," he defended himself. "I only wanted you to get to know me for *me*. I didn't want to scare you away, and I was afraid that if you knew how rich I was you'd be scared. I know what you think of money, and—" he struggled with his words "—I didn't lie, though. I only misled you a little," he confessed apologetically.

"You didn't lie, but you misled me." Lucia grunted. "So now we're getting into semantics," she snorted. "Maybe we ought to switch to jargon. I'll talk about refluxing and polymers, and you can talk about liquidity and capital gains. I think I hear a train whistle."

He touched her cheek with his hand. She felt hot sparks of desire spread through her face to her throat, and then down to her chest. As infuriated as she was, she couldn't deny her immediate physical response to Malcolm.

Perhaps that was all they'd ever had. She'd been willing to trust Malcolm because of the passion that drew them together even before she'd attained her unexpected wealth. Perhaps she'd been willing to trust him, to believe anything of him, to have faith in him, because the sensual pull between them demanded such trust and belief and faith of her.

But now he was sitting in her car, telling her he'd deliberately misled her. Whether he was lying now or had been lying last weekend no longer mattered. The bottom line was that he'd lied, and she couldn't trust him anymore.

"Lucia," he murmured. His husky voice stroked her nerves as his fingers stroked her cheek, igniting the same irresistible heat through her body. "Lucia, you're angry with me now, but in time you'll understand why I did what I did. If anything, I had more reason to distrust you than you had to distrust me. I've been loved for my money before, and now I'm being taken to the cleaners for it, to use your expression. I never thought you'd love me for my money, Lucia, but I thought you'd hate me for it. Can't you understand that?"

"However you look at it, money got in the way and spoiled everything," she mumbled. "I stand by my initial theory: it's the root of all evil."

"Lucia. Look. Why don't you come to the city? All right? You'll see where I live—and if I might have seemed ashamed of my home, it's because it's so extravagant, not because it's so shabby. You'll see where I live, and you can come with me to my parents' fund-raising gala for the Royce Collection Friday night. In your silk dress. I don't want to hide anything from you, Loosh. I want you to see for yourself how I live and decide whether you can stand it. I'm not evil, Lucia. I'm wealthy, but I'm not evil."

"You deceived me," she said uncertainly.

"Because I was afraid of losing you before you had a chance to love me. You told me you love me, Lucia, remember? You told me last weekend that you love me. That was the truth, wasn't it?"

"It . . . it was the truth then," she mumbled. "But that was when I believed everything about you. I don't know what to believe anymore."

"Well, think about it. That's all I ask. Think about it. Try to understand." A train glided into the station and braked to a squealing halt. "I'll take this train if you want me to, Lucia," Malcolm offered.

Lucia nodded mutely.

"Will you consider coming to New York on Friday?" he asked. When Lucia remained silent, staring blankly at the steering wheel, he groped in his pockets for a pen and a piece of paper. "Here's my parents' address," he said as he wrote. "The party starts at seven. And here's my home phone number, if..." Her obdurate silence caused him to falter.

Through the open window they heard a man's voice crackling metallically through the public address system, announcing the train's remaining stops on its way to New York City.

Malcolm absorbed Lucia's rigid posture and unyielding frown He sighed. "All right," he conceded, setting the slip of paper on the seat between them. "I want you to come Friday. I want you to see how things are. If you can't come to New York, if you *won't* come, I'll call you and we'll talk some more. In the meantime, Lucia, please don't do anything crazy; don't do anything you can't retract, okay? I love you."

He leaned toward her, and when she refused to turn toward him, he kissed her cheek. Then he reached behind the seat for his attaché case and newspaper. After casting her one final, worried look, he darted from the car and raced up the stairs to the platform.

Lucia sat motionless in the car, listening to the chug and hiss of the train's engine, then to the high-pitched song of the steel wheels along the rails as the train pulled out of the station. Eventually the train disappeared, its sound fading after it, and the world grew still around her.

Chapter Ten

Lucia walked in a daze to her bedroom. She felt battered and sore, as if she'd just endured a bout with some unknown disease for which there was no cure. To plummet from such exhilarating love to such excruciating doubt and confusion was wrenching. She didn't know what to do, what to think.

If Malcolm truly loved her, why had he misrepresented himself to her? How slick an operator was he?

She couldn't make sense of it. She couldn't make sense of her own sudden distrust of Malcolm, except that it frightened her. She no more wanted to believe that he was some supercilious, bourgeois businessman like her brother-in-law than that he was after her money. She wanted to believe that he was a kind, considerate man who found beauty in her soul and who understood her basic values. But somehow, she simply couldn't believe that anymore.

Well, he wasn't going to get her money, that much was certain. He wasn't going to get her to buy a house for him within commuting distance to New York City. And if he *was* as rich as he implied, he wasn't miraculously going to change her negative feelings about money into adoration for it. No matter how many jackpots she won, she'd never be able to feel like a member of the economic elite.

She dropped onto her bed and sighed. As her eyes circled the room, she recalled the weekend she'd spent with Malcolm, and the sublime experience of making love with him. Had that physical joy been enough to make her believe she loved him? She'd known so little about him; she'd been flying blind.

Yet the love she'd felt for him was as real as the bed beneath her, as real as the air she breathed, as real as the money she'd invested at Advent. That money had been wired to Advent from the bank, transferred electronically. Nobody had counted out two hundred thousand dollar bills; nobody had fondled the cash; nobody had folded it into a showy wad. Lucia had never even seen the money. She'd held a check, deposited it, signed papers, and then signed more papers to have the money transferred to New York. She had never actually felt the money, yet it existed—intangible but real.

Her love for Malcolm was like that: a matter of faith, not tangible fact. Just as Lucia had never touched her money, she'd never touched a concrete aspect of Malcolm's character or background. She'd accepted what he told her about himself, just as she'd accepted that this or that piece of paper told her she was rich.

Her gaze alighted on her telephone and she sighed again. No more than an hour ago, she'd been so in love with Malcolm that she'd offered to give him money. Giving a person money didn't necessarily mean one loved that person. Yet she hadn't really offered Malcolm her money—she'd offered him her help. That was where the love came in.

Her mind drifted to skunks, and to her impulsive statement to Malcolm that she'd as soon give money to her father as to him. Her father didn't need her money, either, but he needed her help. If she loved him, she would help him.

Drawing in a deep breath, she dialed her parents' home in Indianapolis. Her mother answered.

"Mom, it's Loosh," Lucia identified herself. "Have—have you heard from Dad since yesterday?"

"No," her mother replied, sounding both tired and agitated. "He can't very well call me every day from California, you know. That would be much too expensive."

"So you don't know whether he's raised five hundred dollars for the skunk audition, do you?" Lucia asked.

"Why? Are you going to send it to him?" her mother asked. "After last night, Lucia, I thought you'd wiped your hands of him."

"Of course not," Lucia defended herself. "I want to help him."

"Then you're going to send him the money?" her mother asked, her indecisive tone hovering between pleasure and concern.

"I—I don't know," Lucia admitted. "I don't know what I'm going to do. Can you give me the name and address of the motel where he's staying?" She rummaged in a drawer of her night table for a pen and notepad while her mother went to get the information Lucia needed.

Returning to the phone, her mother supplied the motel's address, and Lucia wrote it down. "Lucia, honey, if you send him the money. . . I don't want to tell you what to do. But if you send him the money, you'd make him so happy, so very happy. He makes mistakes, Lucia, but he has such dreams."

"I know," Lucia conceded. "Mom, I've got some thinking to do. I'll be in touch." She said goodbye and hung up.

For several long minutes she stared at the scribbled address. Her love for her father was as intangible as her love for Malcolm—and perhaps even more irrational. However unintentionally, her father had hurt her many times when she was growing up. He'd hurt her by pursuing his dreams, his sick, empty-headed dreams. Yet he was her father and she loved him. Loving a person meant wanting to help that person in whatever way one could.

But to feed her father's dreams, to send him money... Lucia shook her head. When she'd thought about it before, she'd likened such a gesture to giving an alcoholic a drink or a cancer victim a cigarette. She wanted to help her father, but not by supporting him in his foolishness.

Money was a tool, and for once in her life, she could use that tool to help her father. With a resolute shrug, she lifted the receiver and dialed Western Union. "I'd like to send a telegram," she told the woman who answered. She recited her father's name and the motel's address, and then her message: "Dear Dad—You need help, and I will help you. Forget about the skunks and go home. You have to grow up and face reality."

"You're paying by the word, ma'am," the clerk reminded her.

"Yes, I understand that," Lucia assured her. "Read me what I've got so far."

The clerk read the message back to Lucia, pausing questioningly at the word "skunks." When Lucia didn't correct her, she read the rest of the message.

"Okay," said Lucia. "Please continue: Find someone professional who can help you. I will pay whatever it costs. Do this for Mom and yourself. I love you. Lucia.''

The clerk read the message for her one more time, and Lucia requested that the fee be billed to her telephone number. Then she hung up.

This was the help she would give her father. So what if he was sixty-three years old; so what if he'd been chasing rainbows all his life? If it was too late to help him, Lucia would have lost nothing but money by trying. And if it wasn't too late, she would know that she'd put her jackpot winnings to the best possible use: helping someone she loved.

Her spirits lifted. She was still distraught about Malcolm, but somehow her confusion about him had led her to think clearly about her father for the first time in her life. If money was indeed a tool, a tool with which she could save her father, she was thrilled to have it.

Her satisfaction about what she had decided to do for her father kept her from sinking into an emotional miasma about Malcolm. She hoped that, in time, she'd discover a solution for dealing with him the way she'd discovered a solution concerning her father. She clung to that fragile hope until she fell asleep, and it continued to bolster her when she arose the following morning and prepared for work.

Her office phone rang at eleven o'clock. "Loosh? It's Evvie," her friend announced over the phone. "Can we have lunch out today? We've got to talk."

Intrigued, Lucia agreed to a twelve o'clock lunch date with Evvie. She spent the intervening hour perusing the latest issue of the *Journal of the American Chemical Society*, and when Evvie knocked on her door, she tossed off her goggles, shrugged out of her lab coat and joined her friend.

Evvie chattered about inconsequential things as they left the building and climbed into her car. She drove to a coffee shop not far from Parker Chemicals. Once they'd both ordered sandwiches and coffee, she fixed her big eyes on Lucia and smiled nervously. "Lucia, the strangest thing happened to me this morning," she confessed.

"Oh?" Lucia was glad to be discussing Evvie's life instead of dwelling on her own problems. "I'm all ears."

"Well..." Evvie traced her index finger around the rim of her coffee cup, her eyes flitting evasively about the restaurant. "Rick Lansing asked me to drive to the Watchung Mountains with him on Saturday."

Lucia hooted. "You're kidding!"

"No, I'm not."

"Rick Lansing? Rick 'Scorecard' Lansing?"

Evvie grinned sheepishly at Lucia. "I—I sort of said yes. Are you mad, Loosh?"

"Mad? Me? Evvie, I think the question we ought to be asking is, are *you* mad? As in crazy." She shook her head, amazed that Evvie would agree to go out with Rick after all the negative things she'd said about him to Lucia. "Do you know why he wants to take you to the Watchung Mountains? He's got some vacation house picked out—"

"Yes, he explained that to me," Evvie cut Lucia off. "He wants to say good-bye to it. He can't afford it, and he's not going to buy it, but he wanted to see it one last time and say farewell to it." The waitress delivered the sandwiches, and Evvie picked idly at the crust of her bread. "He asked me to keep him company and cheer him up on the drive."

"And you said yes?" Lucia exclaimed.

"Sort of," Evvie allowed. "Loosh, I know you think I'm crazy, but he was different than he's ever been before. He told me that when he was busy courting you—to get you to help him buy this vacation house—well, he said he realized that even though things would never be right between you and him, he found you much more stimulating than he'd ever found a woman before."

"Stimulating?" Lucia snorted. "All I ever did was tell him to leave me alone."

"He said...he said he had deliberately avoided educated women before, but when he was with you, he never felt bored. You were challenging, and he enjoyed you much more than he enjoyed giggly, vacuous women with big bosoms. He said he'd always found me attractive, but he'd stayed away from me because he figured I was an egghead lawyer, but now that he's seen the light, he thought we might get to know each other. And he *is* awfully good-looking, and I thought, well, just a daytime drive to the mountains, I mean, where's the harm in it, you know? I mean, it's almost like I'm getting a free vacation out of it, even if it's only a short trip—"

"Evvie," Lucia interrupted. "Evvie, you don't have to defend yourself to me. If you want to drive to the mountains with him, go ahead and have fun."

"You don't mind?" Evvie asked uncertainly.

"Why should I mind?"

"Well, he did ask you to marry him."

"With all the passion of a hibernating turtle," Lucia told her. "He's all yours, Evvie. You'd look good with him. You're both blond."

Evvie appeared enormously relieved. "I'm so glad you aren't angry, Loosh. I was hoping you wouldn't be. I mean, you and Malcolm Royce are tight, so I was hoping it would be no skin off your nose if Rick and I..." She fell silent at Lucia's perceptible stiffening. "Did I say something wrong?"

No longer distracted from her own dilemma, Lucia exhaled and set down her sandwich. "I don't know how tight Malcolm and I are," she said bleakly.

Evvie's eyes widened. "What do you mean? You told me on Monday—"

"That was Monday," Lucia groaned. "I saw him last night and...and he said things, and I don't know if I can trust him anymore."

"What things?" Evvie asked worriedly.

"At first he said things that made me think that he was after my money," Lucia began.

"No!"

"Yes, and when I called him on it, Evvie, he told me he was rich."

Evvie waited for Lucia to elaborate. When she remained silent, Evvie scowled. "So? He's rich and you're rich. Rick Lansing's blond and I'm blond. Relationships have been built on shakier foundations than that."

"Not rich," Lucia clarified. "*Rich*. Old-money rich. Rolling in it. He said he'd hidden his wealth from me because he thought I'd reject him if I knew he was wealthy."

"Would you?"

"I'm not sure," Lucia mumbled weakly. "But I can't shake the feeling that maybe he was just telling me he was rich so I wouldn't think he was after my money. Maybe he really isn't rich at all. I just don't know."

"Do you care enough to find out?" Evvie asked.

Lucia shot her friend a surprised look. For once, Evvie was the clear-sighted one, cutting through Lucia's muddleheadedness to the heart of the matter and asking the only question that had to be asked. If Lucia cared enough about Malcolm to find out the truth about him, she'd find out. If she didn't care enough, then whether or not Malcolm had been honest with her was irrelevant.

She *did* care enough. She cared enough about him to want to know what he was after, and why he'd misled her. She cared enough to be willing to face the truth about Malcolm, no matter what it might be, no matter that it might hurt her terribly.

"Evvie, you're brilliant," she declared with a tenuous smile. "If Rick Lansing's looking for an intellectual challenge, he's met his match in you."

"Don't be silly," Evvie said with a modest laugh. "I'm not the doctor here—you are."

"Doctor of Jurisprudence," Lucia corrected her. "Isn't that the degree you lawyers get these days?"

"Juris I'll go along with," Evvie agreed. "Prudence has never been my long suit."

Going to Malcolm's parents' party in New York might not be prudent, Lucia mused after she and Evvie returned to work. Pursuing Malcolm and opening herself to the possibility that she'd be deceived by him again didn't seem prudent at all. But no matter how imprudent Evvie thought she herself was, she'd made Lucia face the fact that she cared enough about Malcolm to learn the truth, one way or another.

She clung to that comprehension over the next couple of days. Doubt threatened to undermine her; she knew that many wrong things could happen if she went to New York. She might find out that Malcolm was indeed after her money. Or she might find out that he was superwealthy, and that she could never feel comfortable in his world. Either finding would ruin their relationship. But if she didn't go to New York, their relationship would be ruined, anyway. Regardless of Malcolm's promise to call her if she didn't show up at the party on Friday, she suspected that if she didn't show up, things would be over between them. By not calling her in the intervening days, Malcolm was leaving the fate of their relationship up to her.

She succeeded in ignoring her fear and anxiety until she found herself seated on a Manhattan-bound train at six-thirty Friday evening. She'd convinced herself that she ought to take the train so that she wouldn't have to worry about trying to park her car in the city. But she knew that the real reason she'd chosen to take the train was to give herself no opportunity to change her mind, to turn around and head for home.

She sat rigidly on the upholstered seat, smoothing the hem of her silk dress, crossing and uncrossing her sandaled feet, and fidgeting with her hair. She'd wanted to arrange it in a sophisticated style befitting the elegant party she'd be attending, but none of the exotic knots she'd twisted her hair into looked right on her. Seeing herself in the mirror with her thick brown hair piled dramatically on top of her head made her feel ridiculous rather than glamorous. The evening was sure to be a disaster, she decided silently. She ought to have stayed home. But she was on the train, doomed to attend the Royces' party.

At Penn Station, she briefly considered hopping onto the next train back to New Jersey, but she courageously propelled herself through the sprawling underground station and outside to summon a taxi. She'd come this far; she might as well go through with it. She cared enough.

She gave the cabbie the address Malcolm had written down for her, and he cruised uptown and east to Park Avenue. The traffic slowed them, and Lucia concentrated on the mechanical clicking of the fare meter so that she wouldn't succumb to uncontrollable nervousness. When the driver pulled to a halt in front of a luxurious building with an ornate canopy above the front door and a liveried doorman standing guard, Lucia sucked in her breath. Well, Malcolm had not lied about his parents being rich. She should have expected something like this.

She paid the driver, and the doorman opened the cab door for her. He ushered her into the lush, gilt-wallpapered foyer and asked her who she was. "I'm Lucia Bowen, and I'm here for a party at the Royces'," she said in as strong a voice as she could muster.

He nodded and pressed a button on his intercom. He spoke quietly into it, then hung up and pointed Lucia toward the elevator. "The twenty-first floor," he told her. "Apartment 2104."

She smiled meekly and stepped inside the elevator. Like the foyer, it was papered in glittering gold, with a crystal chandelier overhead. A chandelier in an elevator? Lucia was definitely in an alien environment.

She arrived at the twenty-first floor and located the door marked "2104." Her ring was answered by a balding gentleman in a subdued suit. He held a clipboard and a sterling-silver fountain pen. "Yes?" he asked imperiously.

Peering past him, Lucia saw a broad, elongated hallway whose walls were adorned with works of art. The hallway ended in a room filled with people dressed in gowns and tuxedos. Lucia gulped.

"Yes?" the man repeated.

"I'm Lucia Bowen," she said timidly. "I'm—well, I wasn't exactly invited here, but Malcolm told me I—that's Malcolm Royce, the Royces' son."

The man ignored her rambling explanation as he scanned a list on his clipboard. "Dr. Bowen," he said, making a check mark on the list and escorting her in-side. He shut the door and guided her down the gallery at a pace too rapid for her to examine any of the paint-ings. Lucia had learned what little she knew about art in an art-history survey course during her freshman year at college, and the paintings looked authentic to her.

As soon as she stepped from the gallery into the enor-mous living room at its end, the man with the guest list vanished. Stranded, Lucia scanned the room. She could scarcely see its decor for all the people milling about in it. The array of chic attire worn by the guests made Lucia feel almost frumpy in her overpriced silk dress. She spotted a string trio playing chamber music in one cor-ner. Several uniformed butlers and maids circulated among the guests, carrying trays of canapés and cham-pagne.

Lucia shifted uneasily as her eyes skimmed the room again. At the center of a cluster of men stood Malcolm. He was talking, his eyes fastened on his listeners, one hand moving gracefully through the air while the other held a glass of champagne. He was wearing a tuxedo, a pleated white shirt and a bow tie. Lucia recalled the first time she'd seen him in a tuxedo—the first time she'd *ever* seen him—and her understanding that he knew how to wear such apparel. She had that same impression now. Of course he was rich.

He paused as one of the other men spoke, and as his gaze drifted, he spotted Lucia. He froze for a moment, then set down his glass and excused himself from the group. He worked his way with astonishing speed through the swarms of people to Lucia's side. "You came," he whispered, extending his hand to her face. He hesitated for a moment, unsure of whether he should touch her, and decided not to. His arm dropped to his side, but his shimmering eyes remained fully on her.

"I came," Lucia confirmed softly.

He tendered a slight smile, one that reflected gratitude more than victory. "Can I get you something to drink? Some champagne? Or are you afraid it'll make you sneeze?"

Lucia grinned wryly and surveyed the room. "I'm afraid this whole setup might make me sneeze, Mal," she admitted. "Is this a typical Friday night at the Royces'?"

Malcolm shook his head and dared to take her hand. He slipped it through the crook of his elbow and escorted her into the room. "It's a fund-raiser. My parents sponsor the Royce Collection. They raise some money, buy a piece of artwork and donate it to a museum. Tax shelters in the name of altruism," he explained. "Their friends here all have similar projects. My parents go to their parties and write checks for their projects, and then they all reciprocate by coming to my parents' party and writing checks."

"You mean—I'm supposed to write a check?" Lucia asked, blanching.

"No, of course not. You're here as my guest, not as theirs. Would you like to meet them?"

"I don't know," Lucia demurred.

But Malcolm was already leading her directly to a handsome couple who were holding court beside a small velvet-covered table upon which stood an odd bronze sculpture that resembled a plump bird with stunted wings. The man was nearly as tall as Malcolm, with stunning silver hair and a friendly face aged with genteel creases. The woman was absolutely beautiful, Lucia thought—statuesque, with perfectly coiffed black hair and exquisite features. The man wore a tuxedo of a more conservative cut than Malcolm's, and the woman was clad in a luscious gown of plum-colored chiffon. They were chatting with another couple. "See?" Malcolm whispered. "They don't look evil, do they?"

"Looks can be deceiving," Lucia muttered skeptically.

Malcolm chuckled and urged her toward them. The other couple moved away, and his parents turned to him. "Mom, Pop, I'd like you to meet Dr. Lucia Bowen. Loosh, my parents."

The Royces took turns shaking her hand. "What a pleasure to meet you," Mrs. Royce said courteously, her smile warm and genuine. "Malcolm has told us a great deal about you."

"He has?" she blurted out, eyeing him curiously.

"I understand you're a chemist," Mr. Royce chimed in. "Something to do with mushrooms, was it?"

Lucia caught Malcolm's mischievous grin and laughed politely. "Something along those lines, yes," she confirmed. She could tell just by looking at him that Mr. Royce had never suffered from athlete's foot.

"This is the Leonard Baskin we've just purchased for the Hirshhorn Museum in Washington," Mrs. Royce boasted, gesturing toward the sculpture. "It's a marvelous piece, don't you think?"

"It's very nice," Lucia said. She honestly didn't care for it, but she thought that if ever she ought to be tactful, now was the time.

"Malcolm, why haven't you gotten Dr. Bowen a drink?" Mrs. Royce chided her son.

"She doesn't like champagne. It makes her sneeze," Malcolm explained, much to Lucia's chagrin.

"We can get you something else," Mr. Royce offered.

"No, thank you," Lucia declined. "I'm really not thirsty."

"As a matter of fact," Malcolm interceded, "we're on our way. We've got other plans for tonight."

Lucia opened her mouth and then closed it, too surprised to argue with him. His mother pretended to be exasperated. "I suppose we should thank you for deigning to drop by," she clucked affectionately.

"Save the thanks," Malcolm parried her. "Just send a check to the Special Olympics."

"Of course. You two run along and have a nice evening," said Mrs. Royce before kissing Malcolm's cheek. He shook his father's hand, then slipped his arm around Lucia's shoulders and steered her deftly through the crowd to the gallery. With a brisk nod at the fellow with the clipboard, Malcolm led Lucia out of the apartment.

"Were you ready to leave so soon?" she asked as they waited for the elevator.

"I was ready to leave before it started," Malcolm confessed. "But I waited, hoping you'd come."

Lucia weighed his compliment and decided not to comment on it. Instead, she asked, "What was that about the Special Olympics?"

The elevator arrived, and Malcolm ushered her into it. "That's *my* project," he explained as they descended to the ground floor. "We Royces are all disgustingly noble."

Okay, Lucia thought as they stepped out of the elevator and left the building. *Okay.* Malcolm was rich. They'd established that much. He wasn't after her money—unless he wanted her to donate some to the Special Olympics. Which would be fine with her, she thought. She'd much rather give money to the Special

Olympics than to the Society to Rid the World of Plantar's Warts.

Outside in the balmy evening, Malcolm linked her arm through his again, and they began walking south. She savored the feel of his strong arm beneath her fingers, but the physical pleasure of being with him wasn't enough to erase her edginess. "What other plans did we have for the evening?" she asked cautiously.

Malcolm peered down at her. A breeze ruffled through his hair, and although he was barely smiling, his dimples took hold. "We have to talk," he declared. "And you have to see where I live. You have to see who I really am."

"Wasn't I seeing who you really were at your parents' party?" Lucia asked.

Malcolm considered. "You were seeing Malcolm the dutiful son there," he explained. "You still have to see Mal the independent man who leads his own life his own way."

"What if. . . what if I don't like it?" Lucia asked dubiously. "What if it makes me feel queasy, or—"

"Or sneezy?" he suggested, trying to make light of her tension. "Let's just hope that doesn't happen." They turned the corner and ambled down a side street of charming brownstone houses. Trees had been planted along the curb, casting long shadows over the sidewalk as the sky deepened from pink to purple in the last throes of sunset. Malcolm covered her fingers with his free hand, pressing them snugly against his arm. "I'm so happy you came tonight, Lucia," he murmured, gazing at her downturned face. "I think I'm happier than you are. You're still angry with me, aren't you?" he asked.

"A little," Lucia allowed. "And confused. Relieved that you're not after my money, Mal, but confused. I still don't understand why you didn't tell me the truth—" She cut herself off as Malcolm led her up a short flight of steps to the recently painted black door of a pretty brick town house. He pulled out his keys and unlocked the door. "Is this where you live? It's very nice," said Lucia. "Is it a walk-up?"

"I beg your pardon?" Malcolm asked as he opened the door.

"I mean, what floor do you live on..." Her voice trailed away as she recognized that the building he'd brought her to hadn't been converted into apartments, as had so many of the city's town houses. There was no intercom in the entry, no row of mailboxes, but rather a stark, grand foyer with a couple of chairs and a pedestal table between them, a thick Persian area rug covering the floor and a sweeping stairway curving up and out of sight. This wasn't a collection of apartments but, in fact, was one single dwelling. Malcolm's. The entire building. His. "Mal?" she asked in a tiny voice, venturing meekly into the foyer. "You own this?"

He nodded, watching her reaction carefully.

"Oh." She couldn't think of anything else to say.

"There's more, if you think you can handle it," Malcolm warned her.

She nodded bravely and let him lead her up the stairs. They opened into a vast living room, tastefully furnished, with a sunken conversation pit around a fireplace. Sliding doors opened into a cozy library at one end and a formal dining room at the other. Malcolm remained by the stairs as Lucia wandered through the flowing rooms, her eyes agog at the utter grandeur of the place.

"What do you think?" he asked when she finally returned to his side.

"I think it's an awful lot to have to clean."

"And to heat," Malcolm confirmed with a tentative smile. "I pay a housekeeper to clean it for me." He cupped his hands over her shoulders and turned her fully toward him. "Tell me the truth, Lucia," he whispered. "Do you feel like you're out of your element?"

"Yes," she admitted frankly. "Mal, I was just about getting used to the idea that I could be rich, and now I see that I'm not rich at all."

"For God's sake, Lucia, you're the richest woman I've ever met," Malcolm countered, his voice quiet but adamant. "You're rich in all the things that count—intelligence, decency, kindness. I'd give anything to be half as rich as you are."

"But you are," Lucia insisted. "You're intelligent and decent and kind."

"I'm not evil? You don't condemn me for having all this money?"

"No, Malcolm," she said with a small laugh, lowering her eyes bashfully to his chest. "No, you're not evil. And I don't condemn you."

"But you feel overwhelmed by me," he muttered.

"No," she said, then paused to reflect. That was the truth, she decided. "Maybe I feel overwhelmed by all this wealth, Mal, but, no, not by you. I think I can separate the man from his money."

"I wish you hadn't phrased it quite that way," Malcolm complained. Realizing what she'd said, Lucia gave in to an embarrassed laugh. Malcolm laughed as well, but his laughter waned as he slid his palms over her shoulders and down her arms. He captured her hands in his and kissed her brow. "There's more, if you're ready," he murmured.

She glimpsed the stairway, which continued its arching ascent to another floor, and her heartbeat raced. "Another story?" she asked unnecessarily.

"You asked me what floor I live on," he reminded her. "You're about to see."

They climbed the stairs without speaking. Lucia's pulse continued to accelerate. She knew where Malcolm was taking her, and with each step she felt her confusion recede further from her mind. Yes, she *did* feel somewhat out of place at his parents' lavish party, and even in his luxurious house. But not with him. With Malcolm the man, she felt more in her element than she'd ever felt with anyone before. She *could* separate who he was from what he owned. She knew that even in his tuxedo, in his sumptuous home, he was Mal, a man who cared enough about her to keep her from being rash, to rescue her when she felt queasy, to be sensitive to her misgivings about money and to avoid intimidating her with his affluence. He was Mal, a man who had made the effort to see her soul and had discovered the beauty within her.

They reached his bedroom. Lucia roamed around the spacious room, admiring the simplicity of its solid, practical furnishings and its basic good taste. Her gaze alighted on the bed, and her breath caught in her throat.

"Are you in your element now?" Malcolm asked with a sly smile as he closed the door.

"Don't be so fresh," she reproached him, though her clear brown eyes were sparkling.

He opened his arms and she crossed to him. Their lips met in a deep kiss. "I've missed you, Lucia," he whispered when the kiss ended.

"It's only been a couple of days since we last saw each other," she remarked.

"I was afraid it might be forever," he confessed, bending to kiss her throat and then her exposed shoulders. "Lucia, if you knew how many times I lifted the phone to call you..."

"Why didn't you?" she asked airily.

"I didn't want to pressure you," he explained. "I wanted to give you the time to think things through about us. But I nearly went insane waiting." His hands ran across her chest, stroking her breasts through the slippery silk. "I love this dress," he said. "I love it so much I've got to remove it." He slid the straps from her shoulders and drew the dress down, catching her half-slip and panties along the way and stripping her naked in one efficient motion.

A shiver of longing rippled through her as he knelt to remove her sandals. She groped for his jacket and shoved it from his shoulders. He shrugged out of it and tossed it aside, then kissed her knee. "I love your knees, too. I hate that guy who pawed your knees under the table, but I can't say that I blame him."

"Don't hate him," Lucia murmured, her voice thick and tremulous. "He's taking Evvie Hooper out now."

"Good for Evvie Hooper," Malcolm said, loosening his bow tie as he rose from the floor. "My best wishes to the two of them."

Lucia's fingers scrambled down the buttons of his shirt while Malcolm concentrated on his trousers. As soon as he was undressed, he eased Lucia onto the bed and settled into her welcoming arms. His lips ravaged hers, his tongue joining hers in a blazing reunion as his hands reclaimed her body. His fingers cupped her breasts and then closed over her nipples. She responded with a breathless cry of delight.

As Malcolm touched her, she touched him, relishing his height, his sheer bulk, his weight upon her slender body. She massaged his upper back and smiled at his delighted groan, then worked her hands down his spine to the taut muscles of his buttocks. He groaned again. "Oh, Loosh," he gasped raggedly. "It'll always be like this with us. You know that, don't you?"

"Yes," she breathed. "I know."

He pulled back from her, his hand resting on her hip and his eyes piercing her. "Is that why you came tonight?" he asked.

She considered his words, and her response. "No," she assured him. "I came tonight . . . I came tonight because I cared enough to find out the truth about you."

He smiled—a sweet, satisfied smile. "This is the truth about me, too," he murmured, guiding her hand to him. "But only when I'm with you."

She caressed his swollen flesh and he shuddered. If anything could surpass what Malcolm's lovemaking did to her, she thought, it was what she could do to him. But no, she silently argued, nothing could surpass what he did to her, what he was doing with his fingers against her, and his mouth, hot and hungry on her breast, and his legs wedging between hers, opening her to him.

She accepted his body as she accepted his soul, as decent and beautiful as anything she could imagine. His soul inhabited her as his body did, a simultaneous merging that filled her with a complete, subsuming love that left no room for doubt, for questions, for fear.

Their bodies moved together, driven by that love, striving for its ultimate expression. Lucia sensed the approach and hurled herself toward it, ringing her arms and legs about Malcolm and compelling him deeper, leading him to her soul and letting him unlock it. At his magical touch it exploded, releasing the beauty Malcolm had seen in her, the beauty that was his, his alone to see and celebrate.

At her exultant cry he surrendered, freeing his own soul as he captured hers. They clung to each other, reveling in their ecstasy, shielding each other against the awesome power of the love that bound them together.

"Lucia." Malcolm's voice emerged uneven as he wrestled with his breath. His lips found the pulse point in her neck and grazed it. Then his head dropped wearily to her shoulder.

She ran her fingers consolingly through his hair, brushing it back from his damp forehead. "I love you, Malcolm," she said.

"Even after seeing my house?" he asked.

She smiled and arranged his head on her arm so she could view his face. "It's not bad, considering how difficult it is to find reasonable housing in the city," she joked. "But it *is* awfully big for one person, don't you think?"

"I bought it when I married Polly," he told her. "I thought maybe we'd fill it up in time, but—" He stopped speaking and burst into laughter.

"What?" Lucia asked, sitting up against the pillow and scowling at his unexpected cheerfulness. She had thought he was on the verge of discussing something mournful—filling up his house with the children he might have had with his ex-wife. To hear him laughing, instead, took her aback. "What's so funny?"

"I forgot to tell you—Polly's gone."

"Gone?" Lucia's frown intensified. No matter how wretched his marriage had been, Malcolm oughtn't to be laughing over the woman's death.

"Gone to Caracas," he clarified, accurately reading Lucia's troubled expression. "My lawyer phoned me this morning to say that she met a Venezuelan oil baron two days ago and decided to marry him."

"Two days ago?"

"When Polly smells money, she moves fast." Malcolm snorted. "Anyway, she's gone, and I don't have to pay her another dime. Which should please you immensely," he added, feigning seriousness. "Now I won't have to take money from you to cover my alimony costs."

"I'm glad to hear it," Lucia deadpanned, nestling into the pillow as Malcolm drew himself up beside her. "Because I've decided that my money—at least a major portion of it—is going to go to my father."

Malcolm's smile waned. "The skunks?" he asked disapprovingly.

"It bothers you, doesn't it?" Lucia noted softly.

He sighed. "It's your money, Lucia. Maybe I've given you too much advice about it already, but...but juggling skunks? Do you honestly think you're doing him good by giving him money?"

She relented with a smile. "I hope I am," she claimed. "I'm not giving him money for skunks. I'm giving him money to get some help. He needs counseling; he needs to talk to someone who can straighten him out. He can't afford that kind of psychiatric help, Mal. But I can afford it for him."

Malcolm studied her intently. "What does he have to say about this?"

"I don't know," Lucia admitted. "He may turn down my offer. If he does, I guess I won't be surprised. But, Mal, I *want* to help him if he'll let me."

Malcolm continued to study her, his eyes glowing with a gentle amber light. "You amaze me, Lucia," he whispered. "You're the most incredible woman I've ever met."

She felt her cheeks darken. "There's nothing so amazing about helping my father, is there?" she said modestly. "You help your father with his art project. I want to help my father with what he needs. You were right, Mal. Money isn't evil if you do something good with it," she explained. "What's sometimes evil is how people think of money, and what they do to get it. But it really is just a tool, and if I can put it to good use, then I don't mind having it."

Malcolm's tender smile warmed her. He cupped his hand beneath her chin and drew her lips to his for a kiss. "If that's the way you feel about it," he murmured, "then maybe you wouldn't be too upset if you wound up having a lot more of it."

"If you're thinking of dragging me down to Atlantic City to win another jackpot, forget it," she protested. "Once was more than enough for me."

"That wasn't what I was thinking at all," Malcolm insisted earnestly. "I was thinking more along the lines of dragging you to a justice of the peace and marrying you."

"A justice of the peace, huh?" she mused.

"Do you want a big church wedding?" Malcolm asked. "I've had one of those, Loosh, and I don't recommend them."

"A justice of the peace is fine," Lucia said quickly. "If we had a big, flashy wedding, everyone would feel obliged to give us gifts. Money gifts."

"What an evil thought," Malcolm teased. "Speaking of evil thoughts..." He bowed to kiss her again, and as his mouth ignited hers with fiery passion, Lucia found herself totally in agreement with Malcolm's thoughts.

Only they weren't evil at all, she knew, as her arms circled him and pulled him close. No, they were good thoughts, very good thoughts indeed.

MALCOLM WOUND UP not dragging Lucia to a justice of the peace. Instead, he dragged a judge to his town house. The judge, Lucia learned, was an old friend of the Royce family. She was learning a great deal about what it meant to be a Royce—a friend of judges and politicians and patrons of the arts. She doubted she'd ever feel completely at home in such company, but then, she was marrying only one particular Royce, and she couldn't think of any better company than Malcolm.

After the brief civil ceremony, Malcolm and Lucia hosted a small party for their guests. Evvie was there, of course, with a remarkably altered, respectful Rick Lansing on her arm, and so was Malcolm's lawyer and good friend, Mike Lopez, who sized Lucia up in all of five seconds and announced with mock disappointment that he didn't expect to get any big billings out of Malcolm's second marriage.

Naturally, Malcolm's parents were present to witness the event. The more time Lucia spent with them, the less awed she was by them. Malcolm's mother tended to talk about esoteric artists until Lucia's eyes crossed, but she was a charming woman, and she accepted Lucia into the family with warmth and affection. And Malcolm's father never let slip the opportunity to ask Lucia how her mushroom research was progressing.

Lucia's sister and brother-in-law flew in from Chicago, and although Celia announced that she considered Lucia's choice of a wealthy husband a distinctly pragmatic move, Lucia firmly maintained that she'd chosen to marry Malcolm despite, and not because of, his money.

Her parents came to the wedding, too. In the two months since his skunk venture collapsed, Lucia's father had undergone some changes. At first, Lucia's telegram had upset him dreadfully, and he'd spent a week ranting about how a daughter who thought her own father was over the edge wasn't a daughter at all. Then he'd sunk into a severe depression. And then, miraculously, he'd written Lucia a letter saying he was willing to seek therapy if she would assist him in paying for it. He had met with his counselor only twice before Lucia saw him at the wedding, and there hadn't been any instant break-throughs. But when he took her aside to say good-bye before he and Lucia's mother were to head back to the airport, he said, "Lucia, I'm proud of you. And some-day I'm going to make you proud of me. I've got hopes, princess. You know that's the way I am. I've got hopes and dreams. But *this* time, baby, *this* time it's going to work out. You'll see."

"I know it will," Lucia had agreed, giving him a lov-ing hug. "I already am proud of you."

Who cared that she and Malcolm received plenty of unwanted money gifts, even from friends and relatives who didn't attend their small wedding? As far as she was concerned, her father had given her the most precious gift of all.

Once the last of the guests left and Malcolm's house-keeper organized her troops for cleaning duties, Malcolm took Lucia's hand and led her to the basement garage. "We don't leave on our honeymoon until tomorrow," Lucia reminded him playfully as he opened the passen-ger door of his gleaming white Jaguar for her.

"I know that," he confirmed, tugging his necktie loose. "But we're supposed to spend our honeymoon night somewhere special."

"Where?" Lucia asked.

"It's a surprise," he said mysteriously.

She didn't question him further until the car had emerged from the Lincoln Tunnel on the New Jersey side. "We're not going to Atlantic City, I hope," she muttered.

Malcolm laughed. "No, but we're going to Shangri-la. Our own Shangri-la."

She pounded his arm with her fist. "Tell me, Mal! Where?"

"It's a surprise," he repeated.

Stewing, she stared through the window and tried to figure out where he was taking her. Within a half hour, they had neared her old neighborhood. She'd moved out of her apartment the week before, discovering that a major advantage of having money was that one didn't have to fret about breaking a lease and losing a security deposit.

She remained silent as she recognized familiar landmarks and tried to place them. That fast-food place—she and Malcolm had had dinner there, she recalled. They'd sipped their vintage milk shakes there the day they'd looked at houses.

Malcolm turned the corner, steering into a sparsely populated area of woods and small houses set far apart from each other. Lucia's eyes grew wide as she twisted to face him. "The ranch house?" she guessed.

"Bingo."

"Mal—" She shook her head in bafflement. "What's going on? Did the owner rent it to you for the night?"

"No, but he sold it to me," Malcolm commented.

"*Sold* it?"

He glanced at her, his face registering concern. "I thought you liked that house."

"I did. I loved it, until you started lecturing me about all the things that might be wrong with it. Remember? The roof, the furnace—"

"It all checked out," Malcolm assured her. "I had it inspected. Even the rain gutters were in good shape."

"But it was overpriced."

"I chewed the owner down," said Malcolm. "I got a fair price."

"But you thought it was too small."

"We can expand," Malcolm pointed out. "Once we've got a reason to. It's really not a bad commute for me. Weren't you the one who told me that lots of people make that commute every day?" He chuckled. "Maybe I'll join a bridge group on the train."

"What about your town house?" she pressed him.

"I'll list it for sale," he replied. "I don't want to start our marriage off in a place I bought for Polly. She's living in her Venezuelan hacienda now. And you and I should start off fresh, don't you think? I'm not so interested in living the fancy life on Manhattan's fashionable East Side anymore, now that I've seen what wholesome down-to-earth living can be like with you. Not that I regret buying the town house," he swiftly added. "It turned out to be an excellent investment. The value of that place showed a phenomenal appreciation. But it's not for us." He drove onto the long driveway leading to the compact, tree-shrouded ranch house. Once he'd shut off the engine, he turned fully to Lucia. "You aren't angry, are you?" he asked apprehensively, examining her shocked expression. "From here on in, Loosh, we'll make all the big decisions together. But I wanted to surprise you.''

"I'm surprised," she admitted, her gaze drifting past Malcolm to the neat shingled house nestled into its private grove. A smile spread across her face. "And, no, Mal, I'm not angry. This is my kind of home. Just think—I can cultivate mushrooms on the front lawn, and string up a clothesline and hang socks from it.''

"If you don't watch it, you're going to wind up in the primordial soup," he reproached her before swinging out of the car. He jogged to her side and helped her out, then swooped her into his arms. "Come on, Dr. Bowen-Royce. We've got a wedding night to attend to.''

She curled her arms around his neck and planted a big kiss on his lips. "Treat me right, Mr. Royce, and you're going to see some phenomenal appreciation yourself," she promised as he carried her up the walk and into their house.

Harlequin American Romance

COMING NEXT MONTH

#141 THE STRAIGHT GAME by Rebecca Flanders

E. J. Wiley looked at the man across her desk—one Colby James.
He claimed to be an itinerant sailor and dockworker.
Honoraria Fitzgerald called him her long-lost son and heir to her
San Francisco fortune. E.J. didn't know who was right—she only
knew he was her fantasy.

#142 WINTER MAGIC by Margaret St. George

Even as Teddi watched the icy flakes falling from the warmth of
the ski lodge, her drying throat constricted her breathing. It had
been six years since she'd seen her family and friends—and
snow. But it wasn't until her eyes lit on the indomitable
Grant Sterling that she knew returning to Vail was her greatest
mistake.

#143 A FAMILY TO CHERISH by Cathy Gillen Thacker

More than anything Christy Shannon wanted this family.
Orphaned and now widowed, she couldn't understand why her
husband had run away and denied his relatives. Until she visited
the Texas ranch and met his brother, Jake. Jake opened his
home to Christy, but he swore she'd never uncover the shocking
incident that was the brothers' secret.

#144 A CLASS ABOVE by Carolyn Thornton

Squawking roadside chickens, rundown pickups and circling
buzzards. It wasn't exactly what she expected when she
accepted the challenge of this hitchhiking contest. For risk was
Tara Jefferson's middle name. But little did she know that when
she hitched a ride with pilot Marcus Landry he'd be taking her
on the adventure of a lifetime.

Can you keep a secret?

You can keep this one plus 4 free novels